"A Greek myth retelling by a writer with such a deep connection to the culture and landscape of Greece is a rare, beautiful thing. Here you will find the Greek gods as you have never encountered them before."
— Natalia Theodoridou, Nebula Award Finalist and World Fantasy Award winner

"There is a dark, merciless, and terrifying side to motherhood not every mother is forced to face, but every mother is aware that it lurks behind her ribs, waiting for that one moment that changes everything. Papadopoulou unflinchingly exposes this side of motherhood in Winter Harvest. The transformation of Demeter from a grain harvest goddess to the harbinger of death is brutal, devastating, and left me breathless. She holds nothing back. This is Demeter like you have never seen her before."

— Heather Ventura Vassallo, co-editor of *Musings of the Muses* and *Daughter of Sarpedon* and co-owner of Brigid's Gate Press

WINTER HARVEST

IOANNA PAPADOPOULOU

Winter Harvest

First published in Great Britain 2023 by Ghost Orchid Press

ISBN (paperback): 978-1-7392348-5-0

ISBN (e-book): 978-1-7392348-6-7

Cover illustration and design © Yorgos Cotronis

Book formatting by Claire Saag

To my husband,
I couldn't have done it without you.

PROLOGUE

I told myself that letting my little brother run his rough hands all over me was simply an act of initiation and a way for him to gesture power.

It wasn't me prostituting myself.

Similarly, I told myself that making sure my womb clutched onto his seed and turned it into my first-born child, my Kore, my Persephone, was an act of love. It was evidence of my need to become a mother and have someone to call my own.

It wasn't an attempt to hold leverage against him.

Sometimes, though, when I am alone and I fall into the, admittedly rare, mood of self-criticism, I wonder whether I am lying to myself. Am I just finding excuses? The same as all my family has done for all the evil we have committed against others? Even against each other?

I am, after all, from a family of kin slayers.

WINTER

I remember light when I was born. Fleeting and vanishing light. I was crawling my way out of Mother's body, slowly realising that this was the beginning of everything. Thoughts of my identity formed in my mind, and I could see that glorious light and wriggled faster to reach it. It was beautiful. It was powerful, and I was irresistibly drawn to it, so eager and willing to meet it and claim it as mine. But, as I reached the end of the birth canal and Mother's internal muscles helped release my head from her body, I was snatched away.

Two powerful hands grabbed my head and pulled me out of Mother, still wet from her fluids as a newborn. I never got to suckle on my mother's breast, to gain from her that powerful link of comfort and safety in life. I never got to feel her skin.

Instead, I was lifted high and faced my father, Kronos. Our eyes met, and I was dumbstruck by his grandness. He was strong. Beautiful, even. The first thing I saw was him, and I was amazed by all the wonders the world offered, by all the bright light that existed in this world I had just ventured into, so much bigger and more interesting than the womb I lived in before. I was made of his majesty. We stared at each other, and I never forgot it.

Then, just as I was getting accustomed to the light and was eager to start my life, to live under that glorious clarity of the world, Father opened his mouth and let me drop.

I am not sure if I screamed. It was cold as I fell into his mouth and landed on his wet, dark red tongue. He tipped his head backwards, forcing my small body to roll down his throat, through his oesophagus, ensuring I had no chance to escape this new, dark place. The oesophagus was tight, and I squeezed and choked in it until I reached its end and fell to a lightless pit in which I was sentenced to spend the rest of my life.

I lay down there for a moment, all alone. It was bigger than the womb I had been in before. So much bigger, and that extra space made it worse. I hated it because it made me feel smaller, weaker, and cold. I had little concept of the world, of feelings, and even less of my situation, but I knew it was all wrong. I began to cry, wailing because I was so afraid, so helpless, without any option to save myself from that misery. All I could do was cry.

That feeling of vulnerable loneliness didn't last. Not long after, I felt arms around me and a low but constant warmth of power that was like my own. "I have been so lonely," a sweet, girlish voice said. She didn't introduce herself, nor explain how she was there. She simply held me tightly in her embrace, keeping me safe. She never let me go.

The embrace lasted my entire childhood. I was lucky and blessed to be born second. Hestia, my eldest sister and first born to Kronos and Rhea, was there to offer shape to the dark. Her body was my bed, my food, my home. She placed me against her girlish flat chest, and I felt her divinity burn inside her. Pressing my head against her chest and listening to the core of her power helped me realize my own existence. Through my close examination of all she was, of the flicker of power and divinity that resided in her—even though Hestia's shrivelled without sun and nurture—I felt my own self and power, a spark that humans might call soul, but my kind called divinity.

I stayed in her hug for days, years, or maybe centuries, listening to her body and being grateful for its ability to give shape to the nothingness that surrounded us. Time did not exist within our pit of darkness. During our time together, I wished I could see her face. I wished I could learn her features, understand her form, and see how similar or different we were.

Soon, I learnt to see with my hands. Each time I felt she had a nose or eyes, I was scared. She was like Father, the one who stole the world and its light from me. The only face I had ever seen.

"You are like him," I said once when I first ran my hands over her face. "Why are you so much like him?"

Hestia kissed my forehead and caressed my hair. "Father?" she asked. I was surprised she wasn't angry at my words. Her voice and body changed then, as if by having this discussion, Hestia was forced to take a new self. Her chest slightly rose with breasts and her figure grew fuller and curvier. She took my hands in hers and guided them over her face and then down her whole body. She repeated this act, allowing my hands to familiarize to her new shape and memorize all her details.

Then she lifted my hands and placed them on my face. She guided them over my body. I also possessed a nose, lips and all the features she did. The image of Father's face flashed in my mind. I was also like him. "Are we monsters?"

Hestia chuckled in the darkness, and I went back to her body, hugging it tightly, in need of the comfort it gave me. "No, sweet sister," she said. "Not yet, at least."

I didn't like her words, nor the realization I wore a face so like Father's. Why couldn't I have been born without his features?

"But we will one day become monsters?" I asked. I trembled in her embrace and pressed my head against her chest, above her growing breasts, feeling both of our divinities link in recognition of our similarity. That was the most intimate experience a being like us could have with another, to let them feel all they were.

Hestia kissed my hair again. She was the world in that never-ending darkness. She and I, alone but united in our bond, stronger like that. "It's not noses and lips that make a monster. Just because you have a mouth doesn't mean you will choose to use it as Father does."

I nodded, even though I didn't understand. Hestia sensed my confusion and kissed my cheek as proof of her point. "I used my lips to kiss you and give you love. See?"

I lifted my head and kissed her in return. "Me too."

Hestia and I spent a long time hugging each other, and we would have never separated if not for the first of the four bangs. Each one would mark an extra step of separation between us.

Whatever fell into our darkness was loud and fought against its demise. The walls of Father's stomach clenched until the new arrival dropped into the stomach and lost any chance of escape through the oesophagus.

The noise disrupted the entire world. It was the second time in my existence I had experienced fear. I clung onto Hestia, trying to keep her close to me but, for the first time in our shared life, she didn't hug me back. Instead, she stood. Her body changed more with that act. Her divinity changed and leapt outside of her body. This time not for me to share intimacy with her, but searching for something. Someone.

Someone who wasn't me.

The jealousy of that moment was my first dark thought. I hated with such passion whatever had stolen Hestia from me. My sister tried to walk away, but I held her hand tightly, terrified I would never find her again in that never-ending darkness.

Eventually, she gave up trying to separate from me. She linked her fingers with mine and pulled me up with her. "Let's go together, Demeter."

I followed blindly as she searched. Her divinity returned, and she sent it out again, each time in a different direction until she must have found what she was looking for.

"Hello," I heard her say.

There was a baby's cry in response to her words. Another of Father's children. One more eaten. Still holding me with one hand, she lifted the baby with the other.

"Demeter," she said and guided my hand over the naked babe. I shivered as I felt its body. It was covered in fluids, like I had been when I was born. It was a terrible feeling, but Hestia held my hand on the baby's body, leading my fingertips over its face. Like me and Hestia, like Father, the baby had the same features. "This is our sister, Hera." I am not sure if Hestia chose our names, or we did and told her in that first hug she gave us.

I didn't know how to respond, so I did what I always did when I felt lost. I leaned closer to Hestia, sucking in the comfort she gave me. To my dismay though, I found my space over her chest partly taken. I was face to face with Hera, as she also was pressed against Hestia's chest, finding home in her as I had once done. More jealousy and a touch of hatred filled me as I faced this new sibling. I didn't want to share Hestia with Hera. I didn't want to share the only thing I had in that darkness. "Wrap your arm over her, Demeter, to keep her warm."

I obeyed Hestia, more in fear of losing her love and being left all alone in the darkness, than because I truly wanted to comfort this new baby. I hated the feeling of the slimy gooey fluids over my arms, but I was loyal to my eldest sister.

Hera wasn't easy. She cried and fought us for all her infancy. Despite the tantrums and never-ending unrest, Hestia never complained. However, I felt her struggle. The crying stole our peace. The stress and hardship changed Hestia even more.

By the time Hera was a young girl, Hestia had the body of a full woman and her power was significantly spent compared to what it had been when I entered the stomach. It was as if the support she offered both me and Hera had been something she could never replenish inside her. Each flicker of power, each caress, each moment of warmth took its toll on my eldest sister. She kept us alive with a dire cost to her own self. I didn't know how to explain that or why it happened. I am very sorry that it happened to Hestia. I wish it didn't. Perhaps life would have been different if she had loved us less and herself more. Perhaps the world would have been better if she had done that.

Hera didn't bond with me and Hestia quickly, and never as strongly as Hestia and I had in our first era of life. Our little sister never held onto us as tightly as we did, but it would be unfair to say she didn't love us. She simply, for reasons I didn't understand, did not need us. I think even if she had fallen in that darkness alone, Hera would have survived. If she had fallen first, I wonder whether she would have helped the second child the way Hestia had helped me?

But we did love each other. It just was a harder love than the one I felt for Hestia. Hera never completely let go of us, even if she never held us as close. She guarded her divinity, allowing us to feel only small parts of it, as if she never managed to trust us fully. "It feels nice to let our powers meet together," I tried to convince her.

"No." Hera always refused. "What if it never comes back to me?"

"It will always come to you," I promised, even though I didn't actually know if that was the case. Mine had always come back to me.

Hera tried. I had to give her that. She tried to let go and trust us as completely as we did each other. Small bursts of her power reached us, and I let my own divinity, the essence of all I was, had been and could be, out as well. Yet, the moment my power touched hers, Hera shook in our arms, as if she was in extreme pain and panic. "No. No. No."

"Shhh," Hestia and I said in unison, withdrawing our own selves away from her to ease her pain and destress. Hera swallowed back her power. She tried many times to bond with us deeper, but the result was always the same.

Always the same fear of losing herself in us made her give up.

Perhaps for this reason, she left Hestia's hug quickly, preferring to only hold our hands and maintain a distance, but too afraid of the darkness to completely let go.

For reasons unknown to me, Hera matured faster than I did, even though I was older. I often speculated about it. Perhaps it was because she was a loner, or because she was more self-sufficient than me.

She was a grown woman when our world shook again. It happened the same way as it did before. The stomach clenched, and there was a loud bang of something—someone, as I now knew—arriving to change our dark world once again. Hestia turned her head towards the sound and, as with Hera, I felt her send her divinity outside of her body, in search of the new arrival.

I leaned towards Hera. "We will follow Hestia," I warned her and kissed her forehead, one of the rare times I showed her direct physical affection.

We followed Hestia in the darkness, each of us holding one of her hands, until we reached where the new child had fallen.

"Hello." We heard a voice in the darkness, different from ours.

"Hello, little brother," Hestia greeted. "Will you guide us to you? Keep talking."

The little boy did, and soon our small family string of holding hands reached him. Hestia passed me Hera's hand to free one of her own and we all lowered on the spot as she searched in the darkness for the little boy. "Hades," she said, and I felt the new body added into our embrace.

"You are so old already," I said when Hestia passed me the young boy to feel him, to meet him through touch. "Did Father not eat you as you were born?"

The question blurted out of my mouth. I was mad with jealousy of all the light he could have seen. Mad with envy and bitterness that he had that chance and not me. My hands were rough and hard with his face as I felt his features, so like mine, Father's and our sisters'. I must have hurt him with my careless touch, but he didn't complain. I respected that strength in him, which made me hate him even more.

"No," Hades answered. "I just got stuck in his throat. I went the wrong way and he choked, so he had to bring me back into his mouth and swallow me again."

"That's nasty," Hera said next to me. "Can I have him?"

I passed the young boy to her. Hera, to my surprise, took him in her lap and made cooing sounds. I had never expected her to be motherly, or anything like Hestia. But then, she had never liked being our baby, always so eager to grow up. I was shocked to see she possessed a tender side.

"Hi Hades, I am Hera," she introduced herself. "The middle one is Demeter and the first one to hold you was Hestia."

"Hello," the little boy greeted us again.

Hades, like Hera, didn't depend on us much. He never strayed away, and we all held each other's hands, in a circle now instead of the tight embrace we had before. We were too many. Unlike Hera, Hades was quiet, which might be why she tired of him eventually, but he was also more willing to let us see him, more open with his divinity. Unlike mine and Hestia's, his was cool but never cold. He liked to let his power out slowly, feeling Hestia's and mine.

Hades was the second most important person in my childhood. The connection I shared with him further illuminated further aspects of my own self. By exploring him I saw traits of myself, new similarities that I didn't share with either of our sisters. I also possessed something cool, a less boiling aspect of power. Mine was mixed, confused perhaps, but so clearly like his own coolness.

Despite that, I didn't love him as I did Hestia. I didn't take his distance from us as personally as I had with Hera either. I was beginning to suspect that perhaps all three of my siblings—even Hestia—kept something just for themselves.

It was only me who offered everything out without inhibition. This realization changed me, my first real and painful change. I couldn't believe my siblings never mentioned the pain of growing. My body stretched and my chest ached as it grew larger. My joints hurt and I grew stiff more easily than before. It was horrible, but I kept my complaints to myself. I didn't want to be thought of as weaker than Hera, who was younger than me, and I wanted to be steady like Hestia.

As I changed, I also withdrew from my siblings, finding their touch painful in many ways. As we all grew, each in our rhythms, our relationship became complicated and mixed with more difficult emotions. Hades grew fast. He was a large man before I managed to reach my full adulthood, and I started to fret that something was wrong with me. Something was different with me, and everyone was growing faster. Something was wrong, and because we were swathed in darkness, it wasn't visible to them, but I felt it.

How could they all be so far ahead of me? Hades and Hera were younger. I should have been more advanced than them.

"Relax, Demeter," Hades whispered whenever my worries got the better of me, causing my divinity to flicker and spike. He placed his hand over mine and squeezed it, letting his coolness seep into my skin. That act always mediated my power, restoring a fragile balance inside me. But it never lasted long during those terrible days of my growth spurt.

I wanted to stand up and walk. I wanted to stray off on my own, but without any light, I would have no way of finding my way back. Even Hera, the most independent of us, had never let go of our family. How could I do such a thing?

Why did I want it? How could I want to be separated from my family, to let them go when they were all I had in the darkness? How was that in any way logical or healthy?

Something was wrong with me. The pain returned in my joints and my mind spun.

"Relax, Demeter," Hades said, and I surrendered to his coolness. His hand changed as I held him. I felt his fingers grow larger than mine. His smell changed. He got hairier. All in the space of that one touch as he let his power guide me, taking responsibility for me. I hated him as I grew grateful for his support. In that one touch, which steadied and restored my insides, he had surpassed me.

I was last.

It was perhaps because of that bitter thought that, when we again heard something crashing into the dark stomach, I stood up first. I didn't want to be last anymore. By that time, I knew the sound meant a new sibling had arrived, eaten by Father, like us. I was determined this new baby wouldn't get ahead of me too.

"Demeter, don't pull so hard," Hestia scolded me as I led our family string towards where I felt the bubbling new-born power. "Demeter!" I felt her power mix with Hades's and Hera's. I ceased my pulling and waited for the over-whelming flow of their powers to end.

"I am sorry," Hades whispered in my ear, and the pain slowly faded.

We continued onwards, this time me and Hestia together leading the way. That new baby felt different than Hades and Hera. Its power came as a slap to us and then withdrew. We were only able to chase it whenever it made its position clear.

I was impatient and sent my power searching for it.

"Demeter, no!"

Hestia's warning was too late. My divinity had spread and found the babe. I was shocked at how unstable the baby's power was. It clutched onto mine.

"Come on. Let's hurry," Hestia urged and pulled us to-wards the new arrival.

This time, I didn't want to reach that greedy creature, whose power had clung onto me so tightly I felt I was suf-focating. I wanted to let go of Hades's hand and free myself from having to meet this new sibling. But it didn't let go of me. It clawed at my power, demanding my attention. That demand made my body hurt as I grew further. Hestia pulled us ahead and I was too weak and too scared to resist.

My whole body shivered when we reached the baby. It reached for me like a beast and tried to nearly merge with me, overpower me. It was a little boy, but nothing like Hades had been. He was wilder as he leapt at me, and I felt him bite my chest and suck at my power. I tried to push him away, but the boy dug his teeth deeper.

"Take it off me!" I cried.

"You need to calm down. He latched onto you, and he needs you now to grow," Hestia said. "Hold him and show him he is safe. Then he will calm down."

I didn't want to do as she asked. I didn't want that monster, which in my mind was so much more like Father than any of us, eating me. I didn't want anyone else eating me and reducing me to a shell of who I was. Myself was all I had in that darkness; the only guide left.

"No," I protested, and grabbed the boy with both hands and threw him away.

His cries were raging and his anger so harsh. Hestia let go of Hera's hand and my little sister cried at her loss.

"I am going to find him and return. Stay together and make noise," she instructed. Her voice faded as she walked further away from us.

I wanted to let go of them because I didn't want that hungry beast to come back to me. I wanted to cut myself away from them. I tried to untangle my fingers from Hades's grip, but his hand froze against mine, nearly merging our cold flesh. "Hestia said to stay together."

"No. I don't want to stay like that anymore," I said and tried to break off, but my flesh was not mine anymore. My power spiked, and Hades's own divinity attacked me. This was the first battle I had. The first time I felt that divinity could be a weapon and not simply an extension of one's self, meant for bonding and expressing closeness.

As I realized that my siblings had the power to hurt me, I felt my own ability to reciprocate the pain. Something wild, something which could both freeze and burn—but which I didn't know how to control—existed within my chest. It banged against my body from the inside and demanded my whole body to change in response to it. It wanted to destroy my skin, give it scales. It wanted to change my face, to change my hair, turn them into hunger omnipresent.

It scared me that such monstrosity resided in me. It scared me that within my core, I had the capacity for such hunger, such desperate desire to consume all.

His face, always at the edges of my mind, flashed at the centre. His eyes, whose look I still didn't know how to describe, started right at mine. The only light I had ever seen. The only part of the world I knew was Father's eyes and their ugly, ugly glee. I had always feared that because I had a nose and a mouth just like him, I was a monster. But until I could see my eyes, to see if they had the same mad-with-fear look, I could never be sure.

That coldness inside me banged against my chest, demanding me to change. I didn't want to. I let Hades win the battle, surrendered to his control, and he pacified my divinity, which calmed that rage which lived in me. The banging eased. The monster in me withdrew, but its presence had become too well known. I could never again ignore it.

I stayed still and cold under Hades's power. I was lost to the world. Whatever they said to me, or to each other, I never heard. I was only gazing at Father's eyes through my memories. I was again living through the moment when he held my right leg, which often ached, and inspected me. Then he opened his mouth and let me fall. I lived through that moment again and again. Each time it restarted, I noticed something new. I noticed the cold of the wind and the burning of the sun. I smelt Father's terrible breath, and I heard a cry somewhere behind me. I fixated on that one haunting memory, the only one I had of the world outside, like a wound that pained but was also pleasurable to poke. I scratched at it, never letting it fade. I would never again push it to the corner of my consciousness. I promised myself it would always be at the centre, the memory that my own father had eaten me.

The realization that my own siblings could fight me, change from my comfort to my pain was a shock. The realization that I could turn into their pain and none of them knew—understood at all—that I hid a monster in me was a form of self-discovery I wasn't ready to face.

I don't know how long it was until Hestia returned with the crying boy.

"Meet Poseidon," she said and handed the boy to Hera, who passed it to Hades and then he to me. By the time Poseidon reached my arms, he had grown into a child. He held onto me with despair, similar but less urgent to that he'd exhibited as a babe. He grabbed my long hair, not pulling it, but holding it tightly in his fist. "He is afraid to lose you again," Hestia explained. "Give him time."

I did as she asked. My ice merged hand with Hades took a very long time to separate and when it did, Poseidon sat in between us. I was sad about it. I missed the cooling and balancing help Hades's presence offered me. Our youngest brother was a loud child who turned into a loud and difficult teenager. He held me tightly, never losing that hunger, but managing to control it in some ways.

That made our relationship bearable. But he was always the sibling I loved the least.

I never let my divinity mingle with his again. He tried very often. He showed me all of him, that pulse of power that came and went in and out of his body, always expecting me to reciprocate. I never did.

This caused him to be more vocal. "Demeter," he constantly proclaimed. "I will get you out of this darkness. I will grow strong and big, and my power will tear Father's stomach. I will set you free. You will see how grand my power is."

The subtext of his words was a plea. Would I love him more if he managed to offer me the world? Would I let my power caress his and give him some of the peace he thought I had to offer?

"Hmm," I replied. "You need to grow first. And grow right."

"I will," he promised.

"Demeter, Demeter. Always Demeter. Don't you want to save the rest of us?" Hera mocked Poseidon.

He never replied to her comments. He only held me tighter, squeezing my hand as if we shared a secret that the others didn't know of. I am not sure why he thought that. I didn't understand why he loved me so much more than the rest, when I was the one that showed him the least affection.

There was a fourth bang. It shook the stomach and we all trembled as it crashed. It was different from the previous times. It was heavier, and the stomach didn't take well to this new incomer. The walls clenched and acid was expelled in large quantities.

"Stay together," Hestia ordered.

I felt her presence vanish, as it did when I had thrown Poseidon away. I didn't try to escape this time. Poseidon held me tightly. His power clung over my skin, begging for entrance. Begging for some attention and comfort. I didn't want to let him in, but I felt pity for the poor child, and I leaned my body closer to his, letting my lips touch his forehead and offer him a kiss.

These scraps of love flickered happiness in him. He wrapped his arm over me, letting go of Hades momentarily, and placed his head against me. It reminded me of what I used to do with Hestia, back when she was my whole world. When her body was my home, my comfort and all I ever wanted. I didn't want to become that for Poseidon, but I knew I couldn't throw him away as I did when he was a baby. Instead, I let him hug me, climb onto my lap and latch onto me, but my hands never reciprocated that love. That one forehead kiss was all I could give him.

"He is with me," I said to Hades and Hera. "He is scared."

"I am not scared," Poseidon reacted but didn't let me go. "Not at all."

"Hold my hand then, Demeter. To make sure we don't get lost."

I did as Hades asked. His coolness had changed, matured since the last time I held him. His skin was different. I had forgotten how much bigger his hand was to mine. Our fingers interlocked, and his coolness travelled over my skin like thousands of cold kisses. I couldn't resist smiling at his comforting touch. I had missed him, and I didn't even realize how much.

I let some of my divinity go to him, my own soft coolness reciprocating the act.

Poseidon dug his nails in me as I did that. He was probably filled with jealousy over my bond with Hades, but I didn't care that much for him. I didn't care at all for him, really. So I completely ignored his reaction, until he realized that it was futile and gave up.

Hestia returned alone. "It was just a stone," she told us, and sat down next to Hera. The moment she was back, Poseidon moved back to his seat between me and Hades, ending our brief reunion. His attempts to gain my attention never stopped. Instead, he grew more persistent and I could feel, each time I rejected him, how his bitterness increased. It was reflected in the way his body grew. His insecurity was sickening and nearly made me feel guilt. I had failed to be to him what Hestia was to me. I didn't like that thought. Did Hestia feel for me as I did for Poseidon? Did she resent me and the others deep down for the way we clung onto her, always demanding from her?

It hadn't gone unnoticed that Hestia had grown weaker than when I met her. After my experience with Poseidon, I wasn't surprised. She had been depleted, given us pieces of her power to raise us, leaving her less than she was born with.

"But why a stone?" Hera asked. "Why would he eat a stone?"

Hestia didn't have an answer. None of us did, and the silence of that lack of knowledge increased my insecurities. It was evidence of how little we knew of the world and our parents. All I knew of our father was his hunger, his greed, that overcame his fatherly instincts and sucked us all into that terrible darkness. But I was struck by the thought that he had to be something more than just hunger. He rarely ate other food, which we then ate in his stomach, allowing us to sustain ourselves.

That stone meant something. But I couldn't figure out what. It weighed on my mind, and I think it was the same for the others. Maybe we were all shocked with our own lack of knowledge, but no one spoke of it.

Sometime after the stone, we found a piece of fabric had also fallen alongside it. I puzzled over it. Why would the stone and the fabric go together? I had no answer to my question, only a realization of how little I understood the world.

The world was ending. That was my first thought when the entire stomach shook and gurgled. I held in my hand some food that had come into the stomach. We were all ready to eat it when the shaking began.

"What's happening?" I asked, terrified. "Hestia, what's happening?"

Even after all these years, I went to her in my moments of fear. My power trembled. I felt the same from all my siblings. The stomach clenched, suffocating us inside it, pushing our bodies together.

"I don't know, Demeter," Hestia said. "Hold onto each other." She offered the only piece of advice she was able to give. A phrase she had raised us with. Staying together was our only weapon in that dark pit we had been thrown in to grow and rot. Out of sight. Out of mind.

The stomach kept clenching, suffocating us but also pushing us upward. Our bodies were tightly pressed against each other until we reached the top of the stomach, at the opening to the oesophagus, where we had all fallen through once. My face ached as it was pressed against the stomach walls, as acid was released and fell around me. I felt it damage me and I used my power to fix the wounds, but it kept coming, and I knew that there was no way to evade it for long.

"The only way is up!" Hera said. "We need to go up."

We didn't know what we would encounter. I had longed for freedom all my life. I had longed for light, fixated on the one moment of life between Mother's womb and Father's stomach, but the stone and the realization I knew nothing about that world made me equally fear the way out. Facing Father was a terrible thought. I didn't want to see his eyes again, face that hunger.

I didn't want to be eaten for a second time. This time he could chew me instead of simply swallowing me.

"Poseidon first," Hestia ordered, and I felt Hades pulling Poseidon away from me. He tried to stay close, pulling my hand with his, but I let him go and Hades was too strong and managed to break us.

Hestia spoke again. "Hades, go with him, make sure he finds his way out. Hera, follow them."

My two younger siblings did as they were ordered, and it was only me and Hestia left in the darkness of the stomach. I reached her and touched her. If the tightening ended now, we would fall down together, and life would be as it originally was.

"You go up," I told her. I still didn't know if I preferred the familiar darkness of the stomach over the unknown light.

"No," she said. "I will be last. You go first and then pull me up."

I didn't want to obey her. Yet, the one time I hadn't done exactly as she asked was with Poseidon, and it had ended up turning into a nightmare relationship for me. I never wondered how Hestia knew so much. I never wondered how she gained such wisdom. Had she perhaps lived in the world above more than us? Had she not been eaten as she was born? These questions rang through my mind as I obeyed her words. I climbed the small pass. It was dark like the stomach, but tight. A tube which I was nearly too big to crawl through.

"Grab my leg," I told Hestia. She did as I asked, and a few moments later, the oesophagus clenched even more, pushing us upwards as it choked us further. I felt her right behind me as we both travelled up.

The light was sudden as we reached the tongue, and then we both rolled out of the mouth. My head hit against Father's teeth. They scratched my body as he spat me out. I was covered in his saliva, his acids, his stomach fluids. I was cold again. I was as cold as I had been when I was first born.

I crashed against a bush. The branches broke my skin, and I was shocked at the feeling of physical pain, so different than any unpleasantness I had experienced in the stomach.

Father's stomach was filled with darkness, void of nearly all sensation, and my body had never experienced the pain of the world outside. His stomach had shielded me from that, even though I knew it wasn't planned by him. I let out shrieks of pain and discomfort as I untangled myself from the branches. My escape from the wooden arms caused further scrapes, but then I was on the cold ground. I dared to look around to see the world. Father's large form was bent in two far away, surrounded by a bright, glorious blue.

It was beautiful. My whole being shook in admiration of the colour. It validated my desire for light, that there was something worth finding outside of the stomach. How could anything ugly and bad exist under such a magnificent colour, which engulfed in that moment my entire self and remade it? I inhaled deeply, and the cold air shook my lungs, but I didn't want to give it up. It was glorious. It was a feeling of pleasure for which nothing in my life had ever prepared me. Even the stinging pain as my eyes adjusted to the light was wonderful, because it was so new and different from anything else I had experienced before. I couldn't believe that such a feeling existed.

I looked below, and put my hand over the earth, feeling its strength. Gathering a fistful of the soil, I brought it to my nose. I was overwhelmed by the smell. I rubbed the soil over my face, letting it drip over my naked body. I held one of the branches that had broken my skin before and examined the way it felt in my fingers. Their edges were fragile, but their roots and core were strong. I smelled the leaves that had grown over them, and my nostrils were hungry for more.

I stood up and walked away from my landing site. I was desperate to find more. I didn't understand what more meant. I think it was everything. More smells, more textures, more colours. Perhaps even more pain. Even the stinging of my flesh as my divinity healed it contained some pleasure. I was desperate for it all.

I walked to so many places. I didn't stop for anything. I couldn't stop. I wanted it all. I wanted to see and feel everything within my reach and explore all the experiences that were beyond it. I let my power out, so harshly that I was shocked to see it interact with the world. I was shocked to feel that everything in the world contained a power, a feeling of self on their own, and it mingled with me. Only, it did so differently from my siblings. I saw hunger in the world, clear and unashamed hunger but, I think, most of the things I encountered didn't possess greed.

I managed to reach a large pool of water eventually, changing the scenery from the forest I had landed in and its green hues. The water was another interesting colour. I approached and examined it closely, surprised it was see-through, as I could see the life residing in its body, but all together, it somehow absorbed the colours around it and showed its own blend of them.

"Oh my, you are determined." A young male voice spoke behind me, and I jumped up scared.

I screamed and let all my power out. It was the face of a monster, a face that had so many similarities with Father's that the memory of him eating me resurfaced. I had just managed to see and feel the world. I couldn't lose it all again. I couldn't return to that darkness when I now understood all I was missing. I wasn't going to. Never.

He was speaking, but I couldn't hear anything beyond my screams. He dashed at me and put his hand over my mouth. The monster inside me leapt out, and I fought him off. He met my clash, but he was so much stronger than me in brute strength that I was overpowered quickly. His hand remained pressed against my mouth, clasping it shut, and our eyes fixed against each other.

"I will remove my hand and you will not scream again."

Despite his phrasing it as a statement, I still nodded my agreement. Strength wouldn't save me. If I was to escape his eating, I needed to act differently. He pulled his hand away and, as I promised, I remained silent.

"My name is Zeus," he introduced himself. The name meant nothing to me. "And you must be Demeter, right?"

"How do you know my name?"

"The rest of our siblings told me."

Our siblings. I had been so overwhelmed and hungry for the world that I hadn't thought of them once. Before I was able to ponder over their fate or my own lack of thought for them, the possessive adjective he used made me ask other questions. How could he be one of my siblings when he wasn't eaten by Father? How could he be my family when he hadn't experienced the same darkness, nor faced Father's hungry eyes as he let his body drop in his mouth. I didn't know how to describe my feelings to him. My confusion. I just stayed silent, staring back at him.

I didn't see it in his eyes. I didn't hear it in his voice. Rather, I felt it. I recognized it is perhaps the better phrase, because I had it in me too. I had felt it in all my siblings. Kinship. We were made of the same thing. That realization scared me more than it comforted me. I knew where we came from. I remembered my old fear that we were all monsters.

I remembered Hestia's cryptic words when I expressed that specific fear to her. We weren't monsters in the darkness of Father's stomach. Yet.

That last sound had poisoned all the comfort her words had offered me. I wondered about Zeus, this new brother I had gained, who had never felt the darkness and the loneliness, that complete absence of nearly everything. Had he become a monster as he grew up?

"You weren't eaten?" I finally asked, to break the silence.

He shook his head. "No. Mother saved me. She gave Father a stone to eat."

"That explains the stone," I said, remembering how puzzled we had been when it crashed in the stomach. "Mother?" I asked and felt something trigger in my own stomach. I had so rarely thought of her.

"Rhea," Zeus said her name with such comfort, such ease that I wanted to slap his face and scream of how unfair that was. "But she didn't raise me. She hid me in a cave in Crete." His words were odd, even to a creature like me who knew so little. Why did he feel the need to tell me he wasn't raised by Rhea? What did he hope to achieve by telling me? To prove he had suffered too?

"And why did you come find me?"

"To take you to the rest of us. So, we can fight and take back what is rightfully ours. Kronos needs to pay for what he did to Uranus. Gaia asks for that. He needs to pay for what he did to us, his own children. Rhea wants that."

The idea of fighting was a foreign concept to me. But my short time in the world outside of the stomach had been enough to learn its meaning. The world was filled with stories of fights and wars, passed down from the times before my birth. Nobody forgot such terrible things; the world was marked by them forever. It was why I knew that war and fighting were terrible.

"Fight? Alone, against Father?"

I couldn't imagine a point to that fight. How could there be any chance of victory against such an enemy? He was bigger and stronger than all of us.

"I have gathered allies," Zeus answered. "Father has made many enemies."

What a horrible idea! We would join in hatred of one entity. Even I understood that such allyship was weak, and likely to turn into a different war once the common enemy was defeated.

"Come with me, Demeter. When all six of us are united, then I will tell you all my plans." He offered me his hand. I didn't want to take it. I didn't trust him and feared him, but I wanted to see my siblings. I wanted to see their faces, which my fingers knew but my eyes didn't.

"OK," I finally agreed and held Zeus's hand. He placed his arm around my waist and, to my discomfort, took a moment to squeeze my breast. He let out a laugh at my displeasure, as if it was funny.

I didn't have enough time to register his action, though. Gasped in wonder when Zeus's divinity overpowered me and took me in a few powerful jumps towards Crete, to the cave he had grown up in. I was dizzy and ill when we landed. I fell on my knees, holding my head as I tried to get the world to stop spinning. My eyes couldn't focus on any object and my stomach swirled, making me feel terrible nausea.

"Demeter," I heard voices call my name.

A long cloth was wrapped around me, the first time I was dressed, and I felt the comforting coolness of Hades as well as the nurturing warmth of Hestia. I closed my eyes and relaxed in their presence, retreating into the familiar darkness I had longed to escape from. Hestia wrapped her arms around me, and I rested my head against her chest. I kept my eyes shut, choosing to be in the dark, enjoying, after years of separation, the feeling of her, the way she could be, even now in our older age, my home. My comfort. My Hestia.

That beautiful feeling didn't last long. Before I knew it, Poseidon's greed took over. I felt him claw at me with his power before his body reached mine. He clung to me, wrapped his arms over me, not with comfort and tenderness like Hestia or calmness like Hades, but with that terrible hunger which had always overpowered our relationship.

"You are OK," he whispered against my ear. He had grown hair on his face since I last saw him. It pricked my skin, and I opened my eyes in annoyance.

I still hadn't seen the siblings I grew up with. I still hadn't seen their faces. I hazily knew my own face. As I opened my eyes, still in the embrace of my siblings, I found myself looking at Zeus. He had retreated from us, and there was a strange look in his eyes. Something was trying to be hidden, to mask itself, but I had caught a glimpse of it. I contemplated whether it was envy of the bond the five of us shared because we had grown up together? Was it anger that he wasn't the centre of attention? Or was it pity for the clinginess?

I looked around, waiting to see the faces I had touched all my life. Through Poseidon's unruly black hair, I saw

Hades standing with Hera next to him. He was a tall, lean creature, with wavy black hair that reached his shoulders. Hera also had black hair that ended in curls above her breast. She was beautiful. I was shocked at how beautiful my little sister was. She wore a red dress that ended just above her ankles, while Hades was bare chested, with a cloth wrapped around his waist.

I turned to my left and saw Hestia. Her face was older than the rest of us. She was wearing a yellow dress identical to that of Hera, but her hair wasn't black like Poseidon's, Hera's and Hades's. It was a lighter brown colour, very similar to Zeus. Her eyes were brown with a tint of yellow. I wondered why it was only her face that was so much older, so much more tired than all the others.

"It is nice to finally see your face, Demeter," Hera said.

I turned back to my little sister. "Me too. You are beautiful."

She blushed at my compliment, but not out of humility. I think she had already learnt how beautiful she was. She lifted her head high and her lips moved into a smile that betrayed a word I had learnt in the world outside of Father's stomach. Pride. Hera was proud of her beauty.

"Poseidon, get off me," I ordered my youngest brother—second youngest since Zeus was the youngest, I reminded myself—and pushed him with more strength than I should have away from me. He lingered on me, so desperate to touch me, but still obeyed. He moved just a little bit away from me, and I finally faced him as well.

Young, with thick, curly black hair and striking blue eyes, Poseidon was a handsome youth. His male beauty was equal to Hera's female one. His body was well sculpted, also being bare chested and wearing nothing but a cloth over his waist that reached his knees, just like Hades. His eyes stared into me, and I was so surprised to see such desperate need for me in them. He loved me, I realized. I had always assumed that whatever he felt for me was a form of hunger, casting Father's gaze on him, but I had been wrong all this time. However much I hated his dependence on me, Poseidon's look was a desperate form of love, one he was unable to resist, and I had never earned but still received.

I turned back to Zeus. That something hidden was there, and he masked it again the moment he realized my eyes were on him. But I had found the word to describe it.

It was a look of confusion.

I was given an orange dress to wear, different in colour to Hestia and Hera's but identical other than that. I sat down amid my siblings as Zeus stood in front of us in the cave. He had lit a fire which gave us playful shadows that danced on the dark stone.

"We will wage war," he declared. "We will defeat Kronos and his allies and take our place in the world. You were imprisoned in his stomach, and I was exiled in this cave until adulthood, until I was strong enough to free you and now lead you as we forge this new era of life, this new world."

He spoke with passion, moving his hands emphatically and sometimes screaming words instead of speaking. I had never seen anything like it.

"Why should you lead us?" Poseidon asked, voicing the question I was thinking.

"Because I am the one who knows this world," Zeus answered, a bit too quickly. "I am the one who has already gathered allies and," his eyes narrowed momentarily as he chose his next words, "I am the strongest of all of you."

His words stung, making me clench my fists. We had never compared our powers. They had never been on a scale before. We had only been different regarding our powers and divinities, manifestations of who we were. How could one compare the comfort of Hestia's warmth to the calm coolness of Hades? How could anyone compare Poseidon's waves of power, that went in and out in rhythm with Hera's narrow but concentrated power? How could they compare themselves to me, who was both warm and cool, a mixture of two different forces?

"We are all unique."

He ignored my words. "It isn't your fault. It is Kronos's fault. He kept you away from all stimuli, and that maltreatment, that negligence, influenced you. Some of your potential, we can restore, but none of you will ever reach the height of who you could have been. And you all have Hestia to thank you haven't withered more," he said, and we all turned to her.

"What do you mean?" Hades asked.

Zeus blushed and turned to Hestia, who remained quiet and looked at her hands. "He just means that because I nurtured all of you with my strength, you were protected from further harm."

"Not just that," Zeus interrupted Hestia. "She has withered in power to keep you all healthy as you are. That is why she looks so old, and her power is so mild."

Hestia's power was considered mild?! What she offered us, that feeling of comfort and safety, that feeling of home, surely was the most glorious, the most important power of all. I didn't say anything, just stared at her. She avoided our gazes, staring down at her hands in what I suspected was shame. "Tell us of the allies, Zeus."

Our youngest brother hesitated. Hestia didn't want that conversation, and I felt a deep sense of loyalty which dictated I support that decision. It contrasted with my curiosity, but my loyalty and love to her proved stronger. "Yes, tell us, little brother."

He winced at the term, uncomfortable, perhaps, with his youth "I have spoken to our grandmother, Gaia, who resents Kronos because he imprisoned her other children. If we free them from Tartarus, they will join our side."

The tension from the revelation of Hestia's position was still evident and there were still many questions to be asked, but not one of us had the courage to speak.

"When do we leave, then?" Hades asked, choosing as well to shield Hestia from further questioning.

Zeus spoke of details, commanded us to his strategy, and it was only at night, as I stared at the sky—old Uranos's power—that I wondered: When did we consent to him? When did any of us choose to follow him to war? I had followed him to this cave with suspicion, intent on finding out more. I never promised to be his soldier—his ally, as he would have preferred to call me. But I had somehow become that.

I watched him walk out of the cave and jump into the sky, disappearing from view, and we all lacked because of our different upbringing. Had Zeus embarrassed Hestia to distract us? I remembered his confused look from earlier, and I reconsidered its meaning. Confusion could mean many things. Even I, with the few experiences I had of the world in that brief time after my landing, had come to understand that. He could have been confused because he didn't have enough information about us, who each of us were. He could have been confused because he didn't understand our actions, if he had never felt love before and that was a lack he suffered from.

Or, the thought formed slowly and fearfully in my head, he could have been confused that we, his own kin, felt love for each other when he didn't feel it for anyone? He could have been confused not at the act—which he understood—but as to why we acted upon it? The thought itself was confusing and complicated, dependent on many unknown variables. I didn't know enough to explain my suspicion, even to my own self. It could be completely baseless, my own prejudice and envy against Zeus manifesting itself into a thought, clinging onto any reason I could find to cast him as a villain. My words failed to capture the meaning that lurked underneath my thought. The moment I thought I understood it, I was wrong, and it evaded me again.

I turned my eyes to my sleeping siblings. Would they understand? If I tried to explain to them, would they think the same?

Unable to decide what to do, I walked outside of the cave, and stood under the dark, starry night sky, contemplating the situation. I was about to walk back inside the cave and wake my siblings, now that we were alone, away from Zeus, when Hera came out. She stretched her body, showing her curves underneath the fabric of her dress. The moonlight suited her and made her look even lovelier.

She noticed me sitting on a rock and skipped, like the little girl she never was, towards me. She sat on my lap, something she had avoided doing for many years, preferring her independence, and wrapped her arms around me.

"Aren't you tired?" I asked her.

She shook her head and smiled. There was something hidden in her smile, something that gave me an ominous feeling. Her eyes were glittering, her face was glowing, and her power was, for the first time perhaps, outward looking.

"I am too excited," she confessed.

"Why?" Beautiful and eager to grow up Hera couldn't be so excited at the prospect of war. She couldn't be excited at the prospect of blood, pain, scars, and death.

She giggled, a sound so unlike her, and leaned closer, bringing her face towards my ear. "I am to be married," she confessed, then moved away and put her finger over her lips, which were stretched over a wide smile she couldn't resist. "To Zeus. He asked me before he left. He said that he will make me his queen, his one and only!"

Hera married to Zeus, tied to him forever. Our parents were siblings, so I knew this wouldn't be a reason to change her mind.

"Are you sure?" I asked her. "We barely know him."

Her eyes sharpened as if she was seeing me differently. I saw her pride cloud them. I saw how she didn't hear my love and concern.

"Are you jealous?" she asked, and jumped out of my hug. "Did you want him for yourself?"

"No," I assured her. "I don't. I just want you to be happy."

Her face calmed, but her power started to retreat again, shielding herself from me as she did when we were in the stomach. Her old words rang in my mind. What if her power never came back? What if she lost it?

That fear had expanded to include Zeus and the happy life she envisioned with him. I wanted to tell her that it was a mistake, but I had no reasons to support it. I wanted to help her, because I loved her, even if not the way I loved Hestia. But I knew, naïve and unwise as I was, that whatever I said would never be enough to convince Hera that her future with Zeus wouldn't be beautiful. I knew if I showed her any truth that shattered her perfect future, she would turn her hate towards me.

So, I stayed quiet and did the second-best thing I could think of. I opened my arms, inviting her back to my hug, and she sat again on my lap.

"I want you to be happy," I repeated. "I want you to have a grand and beautiful wedding, dressed in the finest silks, and have the entire world to celebrate with you." Her eyes glowed again, and she let her power reach me in appreciation of what I narrated to her. "So, promise me you will marry him after the battle, not before."

Her eyes flashed with suspicion. She studied me as her enemy, but the beautiful image of the wedding I described had impressed in her mind enough for her to nod.

"To have the wedding you deserve."

She nodded. "The grandest wedding of all."

"Yes!"

I kissed her forehead and hugged her tightly. I had secured her time to rethink her choice, to meet Zeus a bit better. I hoped it would be enough to help her see him clearer. I hoped it would be enough for all of us to do the same.

"I am going to sleep," I told her. "Tomorrow will be a hard day."

Zeus landed back in front of the cave, and Hera left my hug immediately. She placed her hands at her side and slowly walked towards him. I stood up and watched as she approached him. I watched her pure and blind adoration, the way she opened to him in ways she had never done to us. She surrendered her entire self and power to him. When had he earned that? How did he earn it from Hera, the most guarded of my siblings?

I watched him and saw how his mouth spoke constantly, saying thousands of words to swallow Hera, but his eyes stayed the same. His face didn't glow, and he didn't surrender to my little sister as she had done to him. He spoke to her and then leaned down to whisper something in her ear. She giggled and shivered under his touch, but his eyes were directed straight at me, and he smiled, letting a small part of his divinity reach me, inviting me to surrender to him the same way.

I rejected him and walked inside the cave.

I lay between Hades and Hestia. Poseidon, by instinct, came closer to me, and I closed my eyes, trying to sleep. Some time later, Hera lay next to us, while Zeus stood guard at the cave entrance.

Was he standing guard to protect us? Or to keep us in the cave? Away from the world, the same one he had gained his power from. Was his gaze a new darkness we had to live inside?

I suddenly missed Father's stomach and its darkness. It had robbed us of so much but, unlike Zeus's gaze, it had allowed us a sense of privacy, a freedom that I thought Zeus would never tolerate. I realized the predicament he was slowly putting us in. He had undervalued Hestia and entrapped Hera with visions of glory. We could never unite against him. We could never deny his supremacy without turning on Hera, without feeling doubt over Hestia's decisions.

His look of confusion flashed in my mind again. What was it he didn't understand? What didn't I understand?

The next day, we followed Zeus away from the cave. I had wanted to speak to Hestia about my fears, but each time I tried to isolate her, Zeus interrupted us and called for our attention. I tried to speak to Hades and even Poseidon privately, but Zeus had asked them to run next to him, forcing a distance between them and us, the females.

"We will stand united, Brothers!" he told them. "We will protect what is ours." His eyes darted back to me and our sisters. Our brothers might have been uncomfortable with the separation, I sensed they were, but they didn't argue with it.

Somehow, Zeus had convinced all of us never to argue with him. How could I be the only one who wasn't convinced? What if everyone thought as I did and none of us dared to voice our thoughts? We surely couldn't end up trapped in silence because we never got the time to speak.

Hera had already announced to everyone that once they won, she would be Zeus's wife. My plan to delay their wedding worked, and I judged from his reaction that my youngest brother had wanted it to take place sooner. Despite his annoyance, he was smart and didn't do anything to insult or hurt Hera. However, I believed we all felt trapped by that development. We all felt divided between our love for one sister and our fear for a stranger taking over as our leader.

Our journey was long, and Zeus led us through places which defied all logic of life on the way to Tartarus. We reached a cave in the Peloponnese, at the southernmost edge of the middle leg that described its geography. It was called the Cape Tainaron. The cave mouth stood by the sea, which was described by a different but equally powerful blue to the sky I admired. Darker. It was the closest thing I found on Earth that reminded me of the stomach.

I enjoyed the soft sounds of earth and water as they merged with each other. I stared at the sun, letting its warmth and power caress me. We had to follow Zeus into the cave, walking down to the core of the earth, where the strongest darkness ruled and where our father had imprisoned his brothers out of fear that they would rise against him.

My moment of comfort and inner peace under the sun ended quickly. Poseidon came by my side and held my hand in his.

"Are you scared?" he asked.

I wondered if he asked about Zeus or the journey to Tartarus.

"Of what?" I asked. "The journey? Or something else?"

He didn't seem to understand my insinuation. "I am afraid of going back to the dark," he admitted. "But don't tell anyone."

He had spent the least amount of time in the stomach, and perhaps for that reason he had never reached the settled state I had gained. I nodded and, in a moment of rare kindness and affection towards my unruly, hungry, greedy but also loving brother, I went on my toes and kissed his forehead.

"It will be ok. This time we are not eaten, we go by our choice, and we go to free others. We are not prisoners, but saviours."

He sighed, and before I had the chance to react, he moved closer to me and planted a kiss on my lips. My eyes snapped open. I took a step back and faced his fully red face. He tried to move closer to me again, but I moved away.

"We need to go," Zeus called and saved me from the awkward moment. I dashed towards him, escaping Poseidon and his affections, knowing I didn't reciprocate them and would need to find a way to deny them.

I grabbed Hestia's arm for protection, and we began our descent towards Tartarus.

The darkness was complete. Our only guide was our power and each other as we moved deeper and lower into the earth. It felt different than Father's stomach. Its power signature was different.

"This is our grandmother, Gaia," Zeus explained when I inquired about the feeling. "She is powerful but not like us. She is," he paused searching for a word to describe her. "Much more abstract than us."

"And she is our ally?"

"Yes," Zeus confirmed. "Since we are going down here to save her children. Therefore, the journey is easy. She has stopped all her deadly vibrations so the way in and out remains clear of trouble."

It would be a lie to say I understood what he meant. I am not sure I understood enough to even have further questions. This was another sharp reminder of how little I knew of the world and the rest of its inhabitants. During our journey, Zeus had told us of our lineage, of the Titans and the grudges that had existed. The alliances that couldn't be broken. His tales always ended with, "But Father now has too many enemies, and I have gathered within them many allies. Even Helios has agreed to remain silent until the fight begins. Once he sees how strong I am, I am sure he will be at our side."

The darkness of Tartarus was heavier even than the one in Father's stomach. It was so heavy and so cold that I felt the monster in me rise, as if in recognition of the darkness, coldness and emptiness that ruled it.

"Uncles!" Zeus called, and there was a loud roar that made the entire world shake. I held onto Hestia tighter, terrified of the sound, its echo, and the power that pulsed all over me. "My name is Zeus, and I am the son of Kronos and Rhea. I have come to free you!"

More grumbling and roaring sounds were heard in the darkness. They eventually died down and a new, sinister laughter began.

"Kronos during his last visit boasted he ate all his children. Are you made of his shit, Zeus? Did you come out of him from the other side?"

Zeus remained quiet. The dark voice echoed, and only when it was completely silent did he speak again. "I escaped that fate thanks to my mother, Rhea. And then I freed my siblings. Poseidon, Hades, Hera, Demeter and Hestia. We are all standing here together. We have come to free you and rage war on Kronos and any who stand with him. End his reign of terror."

This time, his words weren't met with laughter but pensive silence. I wondered if my siblings felt the same need to break it as I did. I leaned against the closest wall of the Earth. The moment I did, the power of Gaia jolted something in me. Something pierced through my skin, travelling deep into my existence, where the dark monstrous me existed. In darkness again, where no one could see me, I felt it stir. I felt my skin wanting to change, to lose its softness and be filled with scales and other protective battle garments. I felt my hair rise and fill with poison. It crept under my skin, and I held my mouth shut as I pushed it down. It didn't fight me as hard as the first time it made itself known, but neither did it go back as deep in me. It stayed closer to the surface, more aware of everything around my body.

"Free us, then," the voice finally said, and my dark self settled under my skin, like a layer hiding from everyone but me. And Gaia. I felt our connection and knew she had seen me in a way no one else had.

I didn't pay much attention as Zeus freed Gaia's imprisoned children. In the darkness, I only slightly noticed his hands grab the barriers of their prison and lift it off. My brothers were called to help, and I saw their power unite with Zeus, subservient to his will and guided by him as they lifted more of the binds. Sensing their struggle, Hera and Hestia went to their aid, joining in the effort to release the prisoners.

I stayed still, barely noticing what was happening. All my thoughts revolved around what I felt crawl in me, pushing against my skin but never breaking it. Was it toying with me? Was it failing to take over?

"Demeter!" Zeus called, and I was snapped out of my thoughts. "Come and help!"

My feet obeyed. I felt my body walk towards the binds. My hands held them and some of my power went under Zeus's command. But not all of me. So much of me stayed focused and concentrated on the monster that pulsed under my skin.

Eventually we managed to lift it all, break it apart and make enough space for the prisoners to get out. I sensed they were large beasts. The world trembled as they exited their pit. Even when I felt their massive presence, I couldn't break away from my deep desire to dig into me. I loathed that monstrous irritating parasite in me and yet I couldn't leave it alone. I couldn't stop trying to catch it, trap it and examine it. I even thought to pierce my skin myself to find it. But I knew it was nothing physical. It was, as Zeus had described Gaia, abstract. And it was inside me.

The walk out of Tartarus and back to the cape was harder. The presence of these large giants around us made the journey more dangerous as they squeezed out of their mother's body. It struck me as odd that they were trapped back inside the place they had begun their life, mirroring somewhat our imprisonment in Kronos's body. The earth shook with each of their steps, and I pitied Gaia for having to birth such monsters a second time.

When we reached the light, I started running towards it. I passed Zeus and all the others, so eager to be away from the darkness and to see my body. Had it changed? Was I still the same me that had entered such terrible darkness? Once outside, I searched all of myself and was filled with a mixture of pleasure and disappointment that I remained the same. Why would I want to change? Could I really think this hidden and darker self was the real me? That the maiden called Demeter was simply the shell of something more real? I feared this other presence taking over, but also, I was unhappy it hadn't.

What was wrong with me?

My ponderings were cut short as the whole cape shook. The sea trembled and huge waves rose. I turned and came face to face with the creatures I had helped free. They were monsters. Terrifying, ugly monsters that I immediately regretted setting free into the world. Even Father looked less terrible than them.

They fell into two categories. The first were three ugly beasts with a hundred hands each and fifty heads. The second was another trio of large beasts, slightly smaller in size than the first set, with a huge head and a single eye in the middle.

The monsters stretched their bodies and took deep breaths. It felt as if they sucked all life around them through their nostrils. Zeus was tiny in comparison, but stood in front of them. The rest of my siblings were hidden from my view behind these large creatures. I imagined Hera hated their ugliness.

"These are the Hecatoncheires." Zeus introduced the creatures with the fifty heads and a hundred hands each. "Cottus, Briareus, and Gyges." He turned to the three one-eyed monsters. "And these are the Cyclopes. Brontes, Steropes and Arges."

We didn't have time to introduce ourselves and meet our new allies. A large rock flew towards us, and we all dashed away to avoid it. The earth shook as the rock landed, and I knew it was a signal of disaster. We turned towards the direction the rock had flown from. The sun and its reflection over the sea's waters made it hard to see, but I didn't need to squint. Our new allies announced our attacker.

"Kronos!" All of them roared our Father's name and ran into the sea, causing the water to rise and drown the world as they clashed with their brother. They grabbed large chunks of earth and threw them at Kronos in response to his assault.

The war had begun. I had to fight in it, I told myself. I had to move my feet and leap into it with all I had because it was about my survival. Could I ever allow myself to return to Father's stomach? Live in that complete darkness?

I decided that I could but didn't want to. With that in mind, I gathered all my strength, concentrated it on my feet, and made my first jump into the air, exactly as Zeus had done when I first met him. This time though, I was in control and that made all the difference.

We were changing the world. Literally. All of Greece shook and boiled as we grabbed large chunks of earth and threw them at each other. New islands were created, and others were completely lost to the world. I watched how all my siblings grew to become much more like Father. I did too.

Some of them took to war better than others. Poseidon, keen to become a hero, let his power scream out, making waves, thrashing all our older relatives. He grew harsher and wilder day by day. I often paused in between my own battles and watched how his hair grew longer and frizzier and how his eyes shone with something so like what I had seen as an infant in Father's eyes.

I had mixed feelings. On one hand, I loved the exhilaration of it, when I didn't think of who I was attacking and who all my loved ones were becoming. On the other hand, I hated what I learnt.

Pain. Blood. I had never been wounded before. I had never been hit or tortured and during the war, this was all I had.

A large tree was swung towards me by a faceless monster whose name I didn't know. Their names didn't matter. I ducked the hit and dashed towards my enemy, punching, and hitting with all my power.

Cries were heard from the tree, distracting me. This small lapse of my attention made my hands move slower, giving my enemy the chance to throw me off. I didn't let the crying distract me a second time. I went at the Titan with all my might, ripping out their limbs, leaving a still alive but immobile creature, terribly destroyed by my anger and power.

I went back to the tree where the crying came from. I removed branches from it until, somewhere at the top of it, I saw a group of nymphs huddling together and crying. They were the weakest and lowest in our hierarchy of power. Barely immortal and essentially without any skills but beauty and servitude.

"Hey." As I stepped closer, they screamed and hugged each other tightly. "What are you hiding there?"

They only cried and shook their bodies. "You shouldn't be here. It is dangerous," I said.

One of the nymphs, probably a favoured daughter of an important Titan, shot me a sharp look. "Nowhere is safe anymore. We lived in our forest, not bothering anyone, and then our entire world was flung like a toy towards the sky."

"Nowhere is safe anymore," another of the nymphs repeated amidst her wails and clutched her friends or sisters tighter. I could never tell nymphs apart easily, especially ones that originated from the same place.

I didn't have an answer to their pain. What could I say? Where could I suggest for them to go? Would there even be any point asking them to leave Greece? Our war extended beyond its geographical boundaries. I took another look at them. I heard another cry, different from their female high-pitched sounds, and approached again. They pushed me away, yelling and crying, trying to shield whatever they hid, but I forced my way through.

Inside an opening of the tree was another young nymph, who still looked like a child. Our eyes met and I froze. Her eyes widened and lowered, and I was terrified because I recognized her look. The way her pupils dilated and her body trembled was familiar. It was something I had felt, seen reflected in my father's eyes, on my own infant face. They were terrified of me. They thought I was the monster coming to eat them. To take their life, their freedom, their dignity away and imprison them in a complete and total darkness.

My face spasmed, and the dark part of me pushed, as if it wanted to come out but not to fight or kill or demand dominion. This time it wasn't rage that pushed it but a mixture of guilt and acceptance. I had become the monster of my childhood nightmares. I brought my hands to my face, feeling rather than seeing. My hands had been my first eyes. Through them I had learnt my family and myself, away from light. As with the first time I had done it, a short tremor built inside me. A head. Nose. Eyes. Lips. Chin, Cheeks.

I had it all. All the features of Father, and the same question sprang in me. Am I a monster?

Hestia's words came as a response. Not yet.

But did that still apply to me? If I made people cringe in fear as those nymphs did, had I not become the monster? Had I not become the same hungry creature that devoured the world to satisfy my needs?

Then my eyes travelled down to the young nymph's breast, and I saw a baby, sucking on her still girlish tits. She was so young and already a mother. My mother hadn't loved me, not really, because she didn't know me. Hestia loved me, but I wasn't hers the way that babe belonged to the Nymph.

"I am sorry," I blurted out and ran away. I didn't engage in any more fighting. I simply evaded anything thrown at me and ran as far as I could. My siblings called my name, demanding I return, but I had enough. I couldn't take it.

It was only when I landed on a skerry that I stopped fleeing the war. My eyes darted up to find that perfect blue sky, the most magnificent and powerful colour I had ever seen. Instead, I came face to face with the God who had begun all that devastation, the same power that allowed the glorious blue I adored to exist. This same entity was the original creator of the sins which plagued our family and Greece. Ouranos. My grandfather.

He looked like Father; their relation was evident in his features. He was staring down onto the islet from the sky, where he lived. From where I was standing, his body was perfectly visible, made of flesh, clouds, and his wild divinity. I understood then what Zeus had said about Gaia as I stared at her once-upon-a-time husband. Ouranos wasn't simply multifaceted and big. He wasn't simply a being that encompassed the entire sky, but his existence flickered, as if it was constantly changing, never defined the way my body and my flesh were.

"Hey!" I yelled up. "Hey!"

He stared at me, and I was stunned by how sad he looked. Then my shock turned into fury. How dare that creature be sad? How dare he look at me with pity when he was the one who started it all?

"I am speaking to you!"

He blinked and then he squinted. Was I so small and insignificant to him that my presence was ignored?

"Hey, little girl," he greeted me. His voice wasn't like any other I had ever heard. It was everywhere. It encircled my body, which shook from its vibrations. It wasn't deafeningly loud but simply huge, as he was.

"Come down!" I demanded.

He shook his head. "I can't. I can never join Gaia again." His eyes moved towards the centre of the fight.

"This is all your fault!" I accused him.

He nodded, surprising me with his admittance of guilt. Annoying me with it because I hadn't expected it. I anticipated he would deny my claim, or threaten me, or say he was betrayed but all he did was nod and plead guilty to my accusation.

"You started this disease that plagues our lands. This familial nightmare. You started the fight between fathers and children. You forced mothers to choose between their children, between them and their spouses."

I turned to look at the battle. Everything looked so small from that distance. Every piece of land that flew seemed like a stone. All my siblings, uncles and relatives were tiny. Nearly all of Greece was electrified with colours of their clashing divinities. It was deadly and so many lives were lost. So many creatures were perhaps eradicated. And yet, the colours and the mad power had twisted themselves into beauty. Or maybe the power was beautiful and some of the beauty remained as the rest of it was twisted into war.

"You did all this," I repeated. "They throw entire forests, entire islands and all that lives on them. Cutting families apart or bringing species to extinction. This world is your fault."

I turned my gaze back up at my grandfather. His eyes were focused on the same sight as mine and he looked sad, remorseful. Tears rolled from his eyes and fell on me, soaking me in his grief. His divinity entered the pores of my skin and my dark self recoiled at the sudden explosion of emotions. I was suddenly choking. I covered my head with my arms, suddenly crying too.

"My pain is your fault," I accused him. "You took all the love my Father could have for me. You took my chance to grow up in light. This curse that plagues our blood started from your crotch."

His tears lessened and I dared look up at him again. His wet grief had soaked my dress. It made my hair heavier and turned the soil under my feet into mud. His body flickered and his face lost all focus, but another part of him was made visible. The place between his legs where his genitals once were was a terrible wound, chopped badly.

"My son did this," Ouranos said.

My father.

He punished his father like that, taking such a precious part of his nature away from him and still, despite all that, he still ate us. He still gave in to the same impulse and the same fears which lead to this battle. Would they eventually lead to one of us—or all of us—doing the same to Kronos? And would one of our children one day hate us the same way? Would the terrible circle of abuse and familial betrayal never stop?

I stared at his wound as it vanished and saw his face again. "It is still your fault."

He accepted my words without question again. He only looked sad, but what was the source of the sadness? Was it what had happened to the world because of him? Was it how his children turned out because of his actions?

Or was it for his pain that he was sad?

These questions made my own eyes itch, and I cried too. It wasn't sadness, though, that inspired those tears. It was rage for the situation I was in. All my doubts over Zeus flooded my mind again. All my bitterness for all that I had lost growing up in Father's stomach, for lacking a mother. My fear that I didn't know what was truly happening or why. That I was losing my freedom, which I had just received again, and I didn't even know when it happened and if I had consented to that transfer of power.

I ran away from the islet, from Ouranos and his questionable sadness. I didn't know what the root of his pain was, and whatever answer I could find enraged me, each for different reasons. My dark self, the monster inside me, roared, and I nearly let it out.

As I jumped and travelled back towards the battle, I felt my skin grow harder, my body fill with poison and my whole-body structure change, giving me a whole new self. But Ouranos's grief was still on me, and it was real. Whatever transformation was happening to me reverted, and by the time I landed in the heart of the battlefield, I was wearing again the self I was born in.

Zeus had reached Kronos. He was holding thunderbolts in his hands and threw them at his face. I stood and watched as all my siblings but me approached him, as the path towards him opened. A path with bricks made of our dead relatives. I didn't understand why it had to be that way. Why did I have to choose between the darkness of his stomach or the rage of his eyes? Why hadn't anyone asked me if I wanted any of this?

Unable to find an answer, I grabbed everything on my path as I joined the rest of Kronos's children and their allies to end my Father's reign and restart the order of the world without him and his allies in it.

I think he recognized me as I landed a blow against his knee. I think he knew which one of his children I was. But I never managed to ask, to make sure. That was the only time our eyes met, and then Zeus managed to give the final blow. He used all his divinity, all his power to cut our father to pieces.

His body broke into a myriad pieces, blood and divinity splashing around us as he was defeated.

At that point, as he fell and his time ended, I could see the pattern repeated and I looked away. I saw Rhea standing from afar and watching the death of her husband by the hand of the only child she had managed to save from his darkness.

My feet moved towards her, but I never reached her. I stood at the top of a volcano as she cried. One eye held tears of happiness and perhaps pride for her son, and the other eye held sorrow as she mourned the loss of her husband. Ouranos's eyes weren't visible from where I was standing.

Her husband was her brother, the one who had freed her and her siblings from the terror of her own father. Did she always suspect he would have to be vanquished by the hand of his child when he castrated their father? I looked below me at the earth, where Gaia was. Did she hate her son for separating her from her husband? Was that one extra reason she joined against him? Or did she cry for his destruction simultaneously with her joy that her other children were free?

Rhea had never tried to get in touch with us after Zeus freed us. I hated her suddenly as much as Father. Why hadn't she saved me? Why did she give birth to any other children after Hestia when she knew the fate which awaited all of us? She was irresponsible for sleeping with Kronos and taking the risk. She was irresponsible and cruel for letting us be born into this terrible and ugly world, to a father that would imprison us in his stomach.

I hated her for saving Zeus too, although that jealousy was harder to understand. Harder to explain. However, it revolved around a clear question in my mind. Did she love him more than the rest of us? More than me?

For that, I decided—although I did not manage to figure out what specifically that was—she wasn't my mother. I rejected her.

Time is different for us than it is for other species. It passes us differently. The time after Kronos's defeat felt like simple days to me, while for other species it was a much longer and more difficult transition. I watched Father cut into pieces and taken down to Tartarus alongside his allies. The Titans who sided with us—some admittedly towards the end of the battle—were spared that fate. But not without punishment for being Titans.

Zeus had already declared the world order was to change and we—the children of Kronos—would be its new rulers. We would take over much of the power and responsibility once held by Titans. For that reason, to show our supremacy, he started building a new palace, with large halls, beautiful gardens and full of food and indulgence on the highest point of Greece, on mountain Olympus. Which is why he declared our new name was the Olympians.

While he re organized the world, Hestia and I helped Hera prepare her wedding. During those early days of the new regime, my time was filled with flower arrangements, dresses, guest lists and decorations. Hera wanted everything, determined to grab some level of power as the wife and only love of the new King of the Gods. I often wanted to ask when we had decided Zeus was to be king. When did we accept his supremacy? But my questions stayed in my mind. We had just exited a terrible war which had changed my siblings. They all wanted peace. They wanted to be able to enjoy life, and I didn't want the responsibility of starting a new era of strife, a new war but this time between us.

And, I reminded myself, as I held needles in my mouth and sewed another dress for Hera to reject, this time I was going to be the one in power. This new regime would make me able to dictate my destiny. If I went against it, I took the risk of ending up in Tartarus myself, in darkness alongside those who once were my enemies. Alongside Father.

I looked up to see Hera enter the room. Her beauty seemed to have been spoiled with pride, not just over her exterior self, but over everything. It was as if she saw servants in all of us.

"Demeter," she called me. I took the needles out of my mouth and walked towards her.

"Yes, little sister," I greeted her.

"Zeus wants to talk to you."

"Why?" I asked, puzzled. He and I had never been alone since our first meeting.

Hera shrugged. "He just asked me to tell you."

I had no interest in spending any time with Hera's future husband. And I was afraid to spend any time alone with him. But I also had no reasonable excuse to refuse his call. "I will go find him, then."

"Can you bring some ambrosia on your way back?" Hera asked.

I nodded. "Of course."

As I exited the room, my eyes met with Hestia. She sent a wave of her divinity to signify comfort and reassurance. It was an unspoken language between us that I was glad still existed under the light of the sun.

It took me a while to find Zeus. He was sitting alone on top of a rock, staring down at Greece, his new kingdom.

"Demeter." He spoke my name when I sat next to him.

"Hello," I greeted.

He put his arm around my waist. "Isn't our new world beautiful?"

It was. The view of Greece, a terrain filled with mountains, islands and the dark blue sea was a sight to behold. "Yes."

His hand squeezed my side, grabbing my flesh with eagerness and the hunger that was so like Kronos's. "You never want to spend time with me, Demeter. Why is that?" His hand moved higher on my side, resting just below my breast.

"I don't have a reason," I answered. "You don't try to spend time with me either, little brother."

I had noticed how consistently he hated being called a little brother. He hated that he was the youngest, and I felt a niggling desire to never let an opportunity pass to mention it.

"I wanted to discuss the future. I have done that with every other of our siblings. Unfortunately, since you and I never seem to spend any time together, this conversation had to be the last one."

I wondered if that meant there was little left. "So, what do you want to talk about?"

"As you know, much of the power that rested in the Titans and older Gods will be transferred to us. Our brothers and I have split the major powers in three. I will take the sky, taking over much of Ouranos. Poseidon will take the sea, taking over much from Oceanus, and Hades will rule the Underworld, taking over from Erebus and his lineage. Now, for you and our sisters, the major question is marriage."

"Marriage?" I was shocked at that. Why was our main question about marriage? "Are we not to be Goddesses in our own right?"

He laughed at my words. "Yes, of course you are. But matches are also to be discussed. I will marry Hera, and she will become the Goddess of matrimony and women as my Queen."

I wasn't sure what kind of power lay in those words. It was an immaterial one compared to the power given by the sea, the dead or the sky.

"OK," I said, just to fill the silence.

"Hestia asked to remain a virgin. Her power is much spent in raising all of you, and I have granted her wish. She will be the Goddess of the hearth."

That was another immaterial power, lacking the brutal, physical manifestations that our brothers controlled.

"That suits her," I said. Her body had been my home for all my childhood and girlhood. Her body had been my entire world, and its warmth had become the centre of our family identity in Father's stomach. She suited that role.

"So that leaves you, dear sister. Both Hades and Poseidon expressed their desire to marry you, make you either the Queen of the Underworld or the sea. So, the choice is yours. Who do you pick?"

I remembered Poseidon's kiss and the shock which filled me. Why were these my options? My dark self, my hidden monster came to the forefront of my mind, unable to resist making its face known.

"Neither," I answered.

"We need descendants, sister. We need powerful descendants to ensure our power is solidified. It would be hard for you to stay a virgin too."

"I don't want to stay a virgin," I said. His eyebrows rose in surprise. I realized I didn't want to deny myself motherhood. I didn't want to be alone, watching other families. I simply did not want to marry any of my brothers. Or perhaps anyone. The memory of Rhea came back to my mind, and her mixed sorrow and pride. I didn't want to have to love anyone but myself and the ones that came from me.

"Oh," he said, and I was proud to see him lose his words and composure. The conversation wasn't going as he expected. "Well, that is different."

"We fought for something different," I said. "To make a different world. I will have a child but no husband."

"Don't you want a protector? Who will take care of you?"

The answer came out of my mouth without hesitation. "Me. I will take care of myself." Then, he travelled again closer to me. His hands over my body and his face approached mine.

"But you need an alliance that will keep men from raping you. Males often find it hard to resist, and you are far too beautiful for your own good."

How I hated him when he said that! How I wanted to tell him that I could avoid that fate all on my own, but I didn't. I wanted to show him how I had a dark self. To show him the monster I could become, the one I feared becoming but was not able to banish away.

I wanted to say that the fault lay with the hungry eyes, not the body they lusted for. I wanted to scream that this new world we were to build should change the laws and stop this incessant need to devour each other, in all the ways our predecessors had done.

Instead, I closed my eyes and allowed his hands to travel over me. I allowed my mouth to open. I tried to convince myself it was my choice. I hadn't refused his touch and didn't tell him how I hated the way he hurt me. I tried to convince myself that I was strong and right for doing this, that there was no other choice. He was gentle because I didn't fight him. He moved above me in quick moves, making animal sounds and muttered words about himself as he glowed in his divinity. The monster in me—or perhaps all of me—snatched some of his divinity and pulled towards my womb, trapping it there and mingling it with mine.

When he finished, he lay on top of me, polluting my skin with kisses and grabbing me hard. His power reached to me and tried to force me to obey it, in that nonverbal way that only creatures like us could. He wanted absolute devotion, but I didn't give it to him. I would never give it to anyone.

"Gaia's power is untaken." I moved from under his body and started putting on my dress again.

"Our brothers and I will share it."

"I will take some of it, too," I declared. I didn't want to ask for it. My eyes ran over the world of Greece, bursting with life and wildness.

"I am not sure if that is fitting for you."

"It is," I insisted.

We stared at each other in silence. The entirety of Greece lay beneath our feet. Our bodies still held the evidence of what we had done, the deplorable and ugly transaction that occurred between us. I was determined to get my share and I wouldn't take an immaterial and abstract power like Hera and Hestia. I wanted something that I could hold, that I could change, no matter how small Zeus made it seem. I was not to be a Goddess of sisters or mothers, or of fidelity or whatever else Zeus considered apt and fitting for females.

"And if I don't?" he asked me. "If I don't give you any of that power?"

I wasn't prepared for that question, but the monster in me was. I let it out and felt it slightly changing my look, lifting my eyebrows, and making my eyes change into something different and scarier. I saw it reflected in Zeus's eyes, the way he tensed and hid his male genitals from my view, as if he was afraid I would eat them.

"I will tell Hera you raped me. I will convince her to cancel the wedding. I am sure Poseidon and Hades will want to defend my honour. Poseidon will lash out in jealous rage. If you don't give me what I want, I will start a new war."

He started laughing but I remained silent.

"Don't underestimate how much they love me," I told him. "Even Hera," I added although I had no way of knowing whether my little sister would be on my side. "We grew up together. That is a bond which still holds strong. Do you honestly think that what you have with them is equal to our entire childhood?"

He continued laughing but the quieter and stiller I remained, the more fake his laughter turned.

"You wouldn't lie like that. You think you are tough, Demeter. You think you are different from Hestia and Hera, but you are not. You wouldn't have the guts."

I shrugged. "Maybe you are right. Maybe not. But is it so terrible for you to give me something of Gaia's power that you would risk it?"

His laughter died, and all that was left on his face was an ugly smirk. He resembled Father so much at that moment. He was in love with power already. My doubts and discomfort about him rang true as he approached me, still naked and pushing his divinity threateningly towards me.

"You will have agriculture," he declared. "Making flowers and trees grow pretty, making seeds turn into plants for me to smell and trees to bear fruits for me to eat. You will have the laborious work of harvest, hard and tiring."

I smiled at him. He was so arrogant. He missed completely that he indirectly made me the Goddess of Food, one of the most vital elements of life.

"Yes," I agreed. I felt the powers shift into me. Once they were completely transferred to me, I added. "I will sleep with whoever I want and will be free to do whatever I want, and you will keep Poseidon and everyone else away from me."

His face contorted. "Why would I do that? Because you lay immobile beneath me?"

I shook my head. "Because I am the mother of your child. One of the first children of two Olympians." I placed my hand over my abdomen. "And because you don't want the mother of your child to be disrespected. That would look bad on you." We were different creatures, and conception was a matter of choice rather than chance for us.

I didn't wait for him to speak again. I turned my back and started walking away, not simply the sister of Zeus anymore or the daughter of Kronos. I walked away from that mountain top as the Goddess of the Harvest, a Goddess of nature, and finally free to control my destiny.

I stood by Hera at her wedding. My belly was slightly swollen, and I felt Zeus's eyes focused on it, trying to find out if it was a trick or a real babe lived in me. I walked behind Hera, kissed her cheek and wished her well in life. It was the first time I betrayed one of my siblings. I knew I ought to tell her what kind of creature Zeus was. I knew if I insisted enough, she would listen to me. But I didn't, because I felt the life which lived inside me. That baby which bound Zeus to me, ensuring some protection from our link, was also my own bondage to him. If I went against him, I would put my own baby at risk.

And that spark of light that lived inside me was too precious to ever risk.

I promised my unborn child that I would never leave it alone. My eyes and my hug would always be close, always open, and eager for its needs. I caressed and felt its divinity rise in me, revealing itself to be a daughter, my Kore, and I knew as my power and her own mingled and met each other that she would give me the happiness my life so far lacked.

Joy awaited our future life.

SPRING

The years of Kore's childhood went by too quickly for my liking. Zeus had by that point birthed more children, but my Kore was possibly the first child conceived by two Olympians, and that showed in the glow of her body and face, with both the power of the sky and the soil. She was beautiful in that fusion. My brother was an absent father, and I was left to make most decisions over our daughter without any intervention. I brushed her hair each day and night, teaching her the names of all the plants and flowers, and all the secrets of the world. I shared with my girl the gifts of giving and taking life, instructing her how to help a plant grow to be beautiful and how for it to be harmful, and the importance of balance.

"Your daughter seems to have taken mostly after you, Demeter," Hera said as I watched my girl play with other youths on Olympus. We stood on the high wall that looked over the small garden I had built for Kore to play with her friends. Unlike the rest of Olympus, it was an enclosed space, surrounded by walls and trees, ensuring privacy for Kore and her friends, but also giving me multiple spaces to sit and keep an eye on my child.

My little sister meant the words as an insult, but I had no interest in playing her games. Our relationship had never been the same since her marriage, and whatever love we shared never recovered after she learnt I had slept with her husband before their marriage.

I robbed her of all the power she wanted to have as his wife and mother of his descendants. But her anger towards me quickly spread towards all women, the ones she was supposed to protect, because Zeus slept and had children with any female who caught his eye.

"It is a shame that her beauty is spoiled by the dirt that cover her clothes. It isn't becoming of one of the daughters of the King of the Olympians to look like that." Her eyes slanted towards me, and I could feel her silent judgement. Hera had much contempt for my power and position, constantly proclaiming herself the Queen of heavens, looking down to the soil where my power resided.

"Thank you, sweet sister," I said. "I am glad my daughter has taken after me. She shows a true gift for my divinity. She has become my precious little helper." I smiled widely at my sweet girl as she waved at me, and I raised my hand back at her. "Your daughters are beautiful too," I said, knowing full well that Hera had given birth to many children, but very few of them had shown significant power. My one child was stronger than most of hers.

Hera didn't respond. Her eyes turned again to Kore. I watched my sister try to hide her bitterness and was saddened by the state she lived in. I pitied Hera, but I couldn't bring myself to console my sister, embrace her, kiss her head and act as a loving elder sister ought to. Perhaps it was because I hadn't warned of the golden cage she was walking into and left her to her fate. Perhaps because I blamed her for choosing this life. Or, because I felt guilt for being one of the first people who made it visible.

"I will be off," Hera said.

I nodded.

After a few hours of watching Kore work and play, I walked away from the wall passage. Olympus was a unique place, changed by the presence of all the Gods as much as it shaped our natures. The tallest mountain in Greece, amidst its many peaks most of the Gods lived, temporarily or permanently. The most important characteristic they all shared in Olympus was Zeus's favour, which also dictated how much of their time they could spend on the mountain. It was why I went travelling with Kore amidst the humans. To avoid the politics.

I walked through the long open passages that linked the marble-white buildings. Each of the passages had narrow gardens that I tended and changed with each visit. It was in these places that I experimented with new plant creations. I did like these small gardens that linked all the residences of the Gods. I liked how at any moment I could look up and the vast horizon of the world was available for me to gaze upon. Zeus had claimed the design was to show how welcoming his rule was. I knew better. It was so he had as few barriers as possible to seeing all his subjects, so there was no place for anyone to hide.

I placed my hand on the soil, letting my divinity shine through, easy and simple as breathing was for humans, and my fingers tingled as the soil responded to my touch and life sprang out of it. I smiled.

"Shall I water, sweet sister?"

I smelt the stink of fish before I felt the long scratchy beard against my neck. "Yes, please," I said. "Only freshwater. It will not take your sea salt."

My young brother placed his hand on the soil and water leaked out, wetting it.

I carefully evaded Poseidon and stood a few feet away. "Thanks."

He watched the flower grow fast, powered by both mine and his divinity. I followed his gaze, noticing his monstrous nature—if all his children were anything to go by—leak into the flower, giving it an odd look, like a dog, in the way the petals bloomed through the stem. "What we can do together!"

I remained quiet. I hated when Poseidon came to Olympus. His jealousy towards Zeus kept him away most of the time, preferring his water palace in the bottom of the sea, filled with his shark-like wives and other beautiful but cruel females who considered his brute violence manly. I tried not to judge them.

I didn't say anything, looking around and realizing to my discomfort that there were no other passers-by.

"I saw your Kore," he said, and my eyes were on his face sharply, the hair on my body rising and my divinity ready to burst out of control at the mere idea that Poseidon looked onto my child, knowing full well that he could only look at her through the lens of hungry lust.

"You will never get close to my daughter, do you hear me?"

Poseidon let out a boastful laugh. Loud. Rude. And ugly. "Don't worry for your little petal, sweet sister. You know who I want. You have always known."

I closed my eyes in annoyance, trying to keep my behaviour under control. "Mmm," I only said. "I need to go."

He grabbed my arm as I turned around. My body stiffened and my divinity clashed with his. It was weird and dangerous. We were so similar, born of the same parents and both raised inside Kronos's dark stomach. Unlike my siblings, I didn't shy away from the memories of our imprisonment. It was an important reminder that Gods fell and no one—not Zeus, not Kronos, not Ouranos—was invincible. In the darkness of our father's stomach, I remembered a different life with my siblings. I remembered them as children, crying and afraid, desperate for love.

In that darkness, we had loved each other more. They all changed, corrupted by the world, when Zeus took them out and forced himself as our leader. In that darkness, I remembered, we were equal. It was for these dark memories that I forgave Poseidon's lust. For the little boy-God he once was, swallowed soon after me, who always said he would save us all one day. He never managed to get over the fact that Zeus was the grand saviour instead of him. It was also my guilt for the constant rejection I offered him from when he was a babe and didn't know any better.

Our powers clashed. Nature and Sea, two grand forces we were given, both of us forced to have them incomplete, as Zeus didn't know how to trust any of his family. But we were both strong.

"Do you remember how you used to say you would save us inside Father's stomach?" I asked.

As I expected, his power dwindled as the memories of our dark childhood returned. "I don't like talking about that time."

I smiled and let my power lower. "I am leaving," I told him. "I suggest you go back to your waters. You will be happier there, little brother."

I didn't wait for him to answer and walked away quickly. I knew he wouldn't follow me. For all his faults, Zeus wouldn't have rapes and fights take place on Olympus. It was meant to be a pure space. Even he never did his horrendous chases here, only below the mountain tops where he turned into goats, bulls and mosquitos and created his own series of demigods. Poseidon wouldn't dare to go against him.

I returned to the balcony where I had left Kore and found her running around the fields with her nymph friends. I didn't approve of these friendships. They were a bunch of silly girls, too interested in clothes, husbands and lovemaking, but Kore wanted them, and I couldn't deny her such a simple joy. I lifted my hand and waved from the balcony.

"Your mother, Kore!"

My daughter stopped running and followed her friend's gaze to see me on the balcony. She lifted her own hand and waved at me. She gathered with her nymph friends around her. I watched their shoulders tremble as they giggled, hugged each other, and kissed each other's faces. I was patient as I waited for Kore and her friends to finish their girlish ritual and my daughter made her way to me. She climbed the stairs in a few quick strides and jumped to sit on the large stone that surrounded the balcony. My small guiding light was as tall as me and burst with life and divinity. I was always stricken by how bright she glowed and how beautiful her nature was. I often thought she had taken nothing from Zeus, just from me. She was just mine and that was how I liked it.

"How was your game?" I asked and offered my hand to her.

She took it obediently and we walked holding hands as she narrated stories from her games that I barely listened to. I picked up a bunch of grapes as we walked and fed some of them to her.

"We will be leaving Olympus soon," I told her. I had decided it was time for us to leave for a while, until Poseidon was back to his water palace and I wouldn't need to worry about his constant attempts to corner me or—as I always feared—his attention turning to Kore.

"But we just came back?" Kore complained. "Do I need to come with you?"

My eyes turned sharp, and she cowered at my look. "You and I are always together. Never apart."

She lowered her eyes, and I saw her mouth turn into a pout. "I am not a child, Mother. I am old enough to stay here, under my father's protection."

I wanted to tell her she ought not to have any trust in her father. She ought not to believe that he loved her at all and never depend on him. Zeus had kept his distance from me, and that naturally included keeping a distance from Kore. We had never discussed it. It was never something that we verbally agreed on. He simply stayed away, and I never asked for him to be involved. On the contrary, I liked to walk and roam around humans, taking care of the plants and ensuring there was enough food and life for every creature. I had taught my art to Kore, who helped me, keeping her away from Olympus for large spans of time. And keeping myself away from Zeus and the rest of my siblings too.

"It is not up for debate, Kore."

I saw her tantrum coming and I sent my divinity onto her. I didn't like doing that. I didn't like forcing my will on her, and it pained me more than she understood to have to be this firm and this strict. She didn't fight me, never did. She simply lowered her head and once she was calm enough, I went closer to her and pulled her in my arms.

"Don't be mad at me," I begged, and she relaxed in my arms. "I can't live without you. You are my whole life, my happiness, my joy. I can't bear a moment without you, but I need to go down and ensure everything is going well. It will be fun," I told her, and I could feel how she surrendered to my will without believing me.

"Yes, Mother," she said, and I kissed her forehead again. "Can I ask if any of my friends could come with us?"

I didn't have any inclination to have a nymph by my side, babbling and showering me with compliments, but I heard the way Kore's voice hitched at the desire to be with some of her peers. The ones she considered her peers at least.

"If their parents agree, of course."

My approval cheered her and she stood up immediately. "Thank you so much, Mother." She kissed my cheeks and hugged me tightly. "I will go tell them immediately!"

Before I had the chance to say anything, to try to stop her from leaving me again, my daughter had run away from me.

I was unsure whether I wanted to run after her to grab her attention, but I decided it was best to return to our rooms and pack our few belongings.

The door of our rooms opened and I smiled, knowing my girl had returned to me and we could spend more time together, without the interruption of others.

"Kore," I said, but it wasn't her who entered.

"I am afraid not," Hestia replied. "I saw Kore running down the hall. She told me you are leaving again?"

I nodded and waited for Hestia's disapproval to grow. It came to me as a soft caress, full of lament and unhappiness. "Why so soon?"

I closed my eyes, tired of having the same conversation with her each time I decided to leave Olympus. "I have too much work."

Hestia's eyes softened. "Your work ethic is admirable, sweet sister. But we have many children now. Give some of your power and responsibilities to others. Share it, and you will find more freedom to enjoy your time here, with us."

She kissed my head, and I felt her warm power reach me, caressing my face with her hands. I shook my head, refusing that prospect as I always did. "Because it's mine," I said, answering her follow up question with the same words I used each time.

"And Kore, why does she have to be denied the chance to live among her family?"

"I am her family," I said, and I knew the words were a mistake the moment they came out of my mouth. "She sees you. We come as often as we can."

Hestia didn't respond to my words. She kissed my hair again, and I gave in to the warmth of her comfort. But I couldn't relax in her embrace like I did as a child.

"I am afraid I will lose her," I admitted to Hestia. "That I will turn my back for one moment and when I look again, she will have changed into someone else." I wrapped my arms around her. "I am afraid that if I share my power, I will lose my place, my life."

"We are never returning to that darkness, Demeter. Neither you nor Kore will ever be trapped in darkness."

I knew her words were true. Zeus wouldn't eat his children as our father had done, and I doubted he would do anything to me. If I was obedient, I was safe. So long as I didn't go against him, which I didn't do if Kore was by my side, he was safe from the discord that I could sow, and I was safe from his petty rage.

I suddenly wanted to admit to Hestia the existence of my monstrous self that hid inside me. I wanted to confide my fears that I was the child that was the most like Kronos, the one that hid inside a terribly chaotic and destructive self. But how could I? I couldn't even face the monster myself. I couldn't even voice the words in my thoughts. How could I tell Hestia and face her look? Would I see shock? Would it be fear? Understanding?

Would she hate me?

Only Kore kept my monster calm. It was only her presence that made me safe for the world. It was only her, my guiding light, my sweet girl, that was the way to fight against my dark self.

"Mother." Kore sang my name as she approached with three young Nymphs behind her. I imagined they were the ones she had managed to convince to go strolling among the humans to keep her company. "You know Acaste, of course."

I did know the Oceanid. I nodded as a greeting and then Kore made space for the other two nymphs to appear next to her.

"And these are Diopatre and Othreis."

I examined the two young girls, who both lowered their heads out of respect for me. I crossed my arms. "Nice to meet you," I said to break the silence. "Kore, are these the friends you want to bring along to our travels?"

She nodded.

"And their parents have given their permission?"

All three nodded, and I waited for the two new friends to introduce themselves and their parentage. Diopatre spoke first.

"I am the daughter of Sperkheios and Deino." I was surprised it was another water nymph, the daughter of a river God and an Oceanid. "They have both said that it would be an honour to accompany you, the Goddess of Harvest and one of the original Olympians, in your travels. And, of course, keep company to Kore, your beautiful daughter."

I wondered if my daughter didn't discern the barely disguised attempt at flattery. The young nymph, a naiad if I remembered correctly, was sent to win favours for her parents in hopes that I could help give a good marriage to Diopatre, as well as take her off their hands for a bit. How could Kore stomach their friendship when it lacked all honesty?

Yet I couldn't really hate the girl's eagerness to come with me. She had probably barely been in the real world, away from the gazes of her parents and potential suitors. And I did pity her, because I knew the most likely fate that awaited her was to be one more courtesan-wife to Poseidon, bearing either monster-like sons that a human hero would slay, or daughter nymphs which Zeus would try to sleep with, and Hera would hurt in turn. It was sad, and I understood the young nymph's desire for something else. I nodded my head slowly, accepting her companionship.

My eyes moved to Othreis. "And you are also another daughter of Sperkheios, right?" I asked, and she nodded. "And your mother?"

"She was a human," Othreis said. "But I have borne two sons to Olympians," she added in haste, wanting to raise her status.

I remembered her story then. "By Zeus and Apollo?" I asked, and she nodded. "And then you left your child by Zeus exposed in the wild to die, for fear of our Queen?"

She seemed surprised that I brought that fact up. "They are both grown now," she said. "Men with families of their own. My son Meliteus founded a city as well, in Phthia."

"But you still abandoned him? And his half-brother raised him?"

She had no choice but to nod. I examined the girl in detail and slowly let my power reach her. She lowered her face and demeanour more, showing just how afraid she was of me. She looked like a teenager and yet she had two grown children. She trembled like a fish even though she was an Oread nymph, affiliated with the mountains.

"OK," I said finally, too tired to express more judgement over her.

I turned to Kore and motioned for her to follow me.

"I don't like you spending time with this last one," I said in a whisper as we walked away. "Are you sure you want her to come with us?"

Kore nodded profusely. "She is so scared, Mother," she said. "You don't know how afraid nymphs are, how powerless."

"I do know. As I know of many Nymphs that didn't abandon their children to die so they could save themselves."

"And how many of these nymphs, Mother, suffered more at the expense of Hera's jealousy?"

She had a point. My sister's rages and cruelty towards the females she ought to protect was known in all of Greece. Even Zeus avoided her when she was angry.

"OK, she can come." My daughter had a kind heart and I shared in her kindness. She was the most beautiful and wonderful part of me. I kissed her forehead and then cupped her face. "We will leave tomorrow at dawn. Let them know that if they are not ready to descend with us, they are not coming."

Kore nodded eagerly, and I watched her run back to her friends, so eager to leave my side again. I watched them giggle and hug each other, so full of youthfulness that I felt kind towards them. It was going to be fine for them to tag along. What did I have to worry about, other than girlish giggles and stories of love? I had survived worse.

During my stays on Olympus, I avoided meeting Zeus as much as possible. This time I had seen him from afar and only talked with him once in Hestia's company. But I knew it was impossible to escape his gaze. He could find anyone he wanted on Olympus, his castle, the seat of his power and glory. Although it wasn't my role to be the gardener of Olympus, I had been one of the people who made sure there was always plenty of fruit on the trees and beautiful flowers with lovely smells. I didn't do it to maintain the perfect image of harmony and power that Zeus wanted for Olympus, but I knew my tasks always aided this goal, and I couldn't let my work go to waste just to spite him.

He appeared out of nowhere in front of me as I was walking around the gardens, smiling softly at the pretty flowers I had hand grown and which had flourished in my absence. His smug face was the same as always, although he now bore a beard to appear older.

"Hello, little brother," I greeted him, enjoying his discomfort at the reminder of our age difference.

"I heard you are leaving again, Demeter," he told me. "It feels like you barely got here."

I knew he didn't care about me leaving, and I resented him for pretending he did, speaking as if he wanted me to stay in the company of our siblings. He was only here to provoke or taunt me, to act in a mean way to pass his time and exert power, to remind me, as he sometimes did, that I was under his power and control.

"I will be back soon," I answered, refusing to take the bait of the argument I was certain he was trying to pick. Another thing to add to his ever-growing list of petty incidents and grudges without real cause.

"Taking my daughter with you again?"

His words surprised me as it was so rare that he claimed Kore. My tongue twisted in my mouth because I hated even uttering my daughter's name in Zeus's hearing. My mouth filled with a warm liquid which tasted like poison, and I felt my monster stir under my skin in preparation for battle. I stayed silent and waited for him to get to the point. I was prepared for him to make a fake plea for me to stay by his side, to side with him on another argument he had with one of our siblings or one of his children, or another relative. Or I wondered whether he wanted me to give extra attention to a particular kingdom because a daughter (or more) of the city-state king was to bear another of his countless children.

"I think Kore should stay here."

I wasn't prepared for that. I froze. The poison in my mouth grew bitter, and I moved it between my teeth, ready to spit it on his face and bite him, like a snake. This was the first time Zeus had expressed any desire to keep Kore by his side. I knew he interacted with her every so often, but their relationship had always been guarded, always in the presence of many others. I feared this development. It had nothing to do with paternal desire or care for our child. He wanted something from her. My mind flashed with images of how he had touched me, how he had used me, and of Father's hungry eyes. I would never allow anyone to look at Kore that way.

"No," I simply said and walked away.

His surprise at my defiance faded quickly and he chased after me. I felt his power spike at me, in annoyance at my disobedience. "She is too old to be running after you, risking her safety amid the humans." He grabbed my elbow, forcing me to look at him again. I nearly spit the poison that kept erupting from inside my mouth on his face, wondering how it would change him if someone actively tried to hurt him.

I knew exactly what kind of danger he meant. It was that exact fear that made me tremble at the idea of leaving her in his care. "Then keep an eye on her, as a father ought to. If both of our gazes are on her, protecting her, then there will be no harm."

I pulled myself free of his hold, swallowed the poison in my mouth, feeling its deadly nature return inside me, where it had been made, and started walking away again.

"Demeter!" he growled. His voice was loud, erasing every other sound. The entirety of Olympus, maybe even

Greece, heard it. I stopped walking but kept my back to him, not fully giving in to his power. "Kore is to stay."

"No," I repeated, and resumed walking again, actively defying him for the first time since we met. I didn't think about how this could affect me. I didn't imagine what reason he could have for wanting to keep my daughter close to him. I knew it had nothing to do with wanting to bond or her safety. There was something else he planned. Was it a slight against me? Was it a way of ridiculing me, showing me his superiority? I imagined he had never forgotten how I looked at him when we slept together.

Or was it part of a secret plan to depose me? I had heard that he had a new son, strong and bursting with divinity, named Dionysus. I had heard the gossip that spoke of his hefty power, of how he was perhaps stronger than some of the oldest Olympians. It would also tip the power balance towards him to have more of his progeny in the Dodecatheon, rather than his siblings, all of whom, in one way or another, hated him. Was he planning to replace me? Would he exchange my power for Kore perhaps, knowing that I would never oppose my child? Was the plan to keep her by his side and turn her against me?

The potential loss of the place I had in the world scared me. It was a prospect I had never imagined or planned a way around. I had fought against the Titans, lived in the darkness of my father's stomach to have this little sliver of power and freedom. I felt my monstrous and wild self inside me stir again, whispering plans of revenge should my brother try to depose me. My body hurt as my rage grew. My flesh itched as it wanted to change, and I was unable to stop this time. I only managed to divert the change: not a monster but a gecko serpent, one of my favoured animals.

I relaxed in the new form I took, different and closer to the darker side I had, and made my way around Olympus until I reached the stables, where my chariot awaited. I ought to turn back to a human-like form and say my good-byes to my siblings, make an appearance and show Zeus he hadn't affected me. If he was planning to depose one of Cronos's children, I should make myself known, but I was too tired to interact with him again.

Next to my chariot my beautiful and muscular three-winged serpents rested. Two were gold and shone like small suns as they reflected Helios's light. The third was a mixture of brown and green scales, flecked with touches of gold, giving it a rather strange and alien appearance but not less impressive. They lifted their heads in recognition of my presence and then went back to their lazy doze. I stayed in the company of their natural element, a reptile, and mingled my gecko body with their large serpent forms, absorbing the sun as they did and returning to a sense of peace as I felt their life forces travel all over their bodies. With them, as with many animals and, for the most part, humans, it was simple. None of the complexities of the politics of Olympus reached me, and I allowed myself to rest with them.

I turned back to my normal female form as Helios took his chariot into the sky, starting a new day in Greece. I went to pick up our few belongings quickly and returned to my chariot. I leaned against one of my serpents, tapping my feet nervously as I waited for my daughter to appear, so that we could escape Olympus together. Only, the thought of escape rang hollow. There was no escape. There was no way for us to escape Zeus's gaze, unless we went to the farthest edges of the world, where unknown dangers existed, and the lands were ruled by other Gods.

"Hello." A timid voice spoke and snapped me out of my thoughts. I turned to see Othreis kneeling in front of me.

"Hello," I greeted her. "Stand up, Othreis. We will be on a journey together. You can't be kneeling each time you face me. We won't get anything done."

The nymph stood and approached the chariot. Her eyes, so small and girl-like, gazed over my winged serpents, admiring them.

"You can touch them," I gave her my permission. She lifted her hand, but her cowardice was stronger than her curiosity. She stared right into the eyes of my serpents, mesmerized, but her hand stayed still, until eventually she brought it down. I wondered if she had always been like that. Or did her liaison—or was it rape?—by Zeus, abandoning her child in terror of Hera, kill whatever spirit or vigour she might have possessed?

"They are beautiful, Goddess."

I looked at my winged serpents. Their scales glistened under Helios's light and their bodies were lean and strong. "Yes, they are. I am surprised. Many nymphs don't like them."

She shook her head. "I am an Oread. When I was a child in the mountains, I used to find snakes and other reptiles under rocks. I used to be friends with them."

"Do you wish to return to the mountains?" I asked, suddenly struck that I didn't know why she stayed on Olympus.

"One day," she said. "When I can, I will return. But the other Oreads are stronger than me, harsher in many ways, like the rocky mountains that define our nature. They need time to forgive my meekness."

I was surprised by her honesty and, perhaps due to my own prejudice, I ignored her trauma, her loss of all her family because of Zeus's attention. "Well, we will need to travel to some mountains, although I don't think we will get to Mount Othrys in Malis."

She didn't answer. She only kept gazing at my serpents, amazed at their beauty and looking suddenly so sad and so much older. These emotions didn't fit her flesh and petite form. It was unnatural to see such sorrow, such deep regret, in a face that was so young. How much had she lived beyond her years? How many obstacles had this young nymph been forced to face that she now wore this look in their wake?

"Mother!" Kore's voice rang out. Othreis's face immediately changed to a brighter and friendlier look, absorbing some of the youth and rejuvenation my sweet girl had embedded in her divinity. Kore ran to the chariot, nuzzling the serpents and then coming to me. "Good morning." She smiled widely at Othreis.

Right behind her, the other two nymphs followed. I waited until they both bowed, and I told them, as I did with Othreis, that they shouldn't bow each time they see me and urged them to get onto the chariot. Thankfully, they obeyed quickly, and I took my seat at the front of the vehicle, with Kore behind me and the three nymphs squeezed together at the back. I turned to my serpents and whistled softly to them. They were my guides, and I only needed to give them the destination.

They began flapping their wings, lifting up into the sky. The nymphs squealed as we went airborne, feeling the cold air and the sweet burning heat of Helios's eyes. I turned to face Olympus behind me. A majestic place, still under construction. Eventually, each of the Twelve Olympian Gods would have a palace of their own at a different peak of the mountain. Each would reflect the majesty of its owner, filled with staff, demigods and followers of our choosing. I didn't care so much for it. I didn't like being in a fixed place, easy to find. I didn't like Olympus's apparent perfection either. I preferred the subtle faults of the human world. There was something wrong in the way Olympus looked. Everything had been smoothed over, disguising any evidence that cruelty existed within it.

And it did. I knew it because I had seen it. It was all a façade, and I was thankful to escape it, even if it was just for a short time.

Zeus's eyes were on us as we flew. Where he was standing, he was the all-seeing God of the Sky, and he saw our departure. His power came at me in spikes, filled with his annoyance at my disobedience, and I repelled it as I turned my back. I was still afraid of whatever he might do in revenge, of him trying to take my power or diminish my importance, but I decided it would be a fight for when I returned to Olympus.

"Look down there," Othreis said in a cheery voice. "That's where I was born."

"It's beautiful," Acaste said. "I was born in the water. There," she pointed to a spot in the sea. "All of my sisters and brothers as well."

I was pleased with the nymphs that accompanied us. It was a surprising sentiment, as I hadn't expected them to be anything but a burden. Instead, all three of them took to my notes and guidance and assisted in small ways as I inspected and ensured the land was fertile, food would be enough for all life forms—as long as there were no overindulgences—and visited my temples to collect the offerings made in my name.

"Mother?" Kore asked as I worked on ensuring the roots of a tree were healthy. "Acaste said that many of her sisters live nearby. Can we go visit them?"

I stood up and hung my scythe in my belt. "I have too much work, Kore. We can go once I am finished."

Kore opened her mouth to protest, but the barest twist of my raised eyebrow silenced all her objections.

"Once I am finished, I promise we will go. It won't take me long."

She nodded, and I watched her walk away from me. Her shoulders were lowered, and her step was slow. She knew what she was doing and so did I. But I was the parent, the one responsible for keeping her safe, and I knew she should never be too far away from me. She was still not able to navigate the dangers of the world.

I returned to my work, examining the roots of the nearby trees, testing the quality of the fruit. I ensured there were no infestations of insects that might harm the future food, that there was no imbalance to report to other deities. It was long and tiring work, as Zeus had said it would be when he bestowed it upon me—a punishment for him—but it was mine, and I didn't mind it one bit. I rather enjoyed it and the purpose it gave me.

I often stopped and lowered my form as human farmers, fruit gatherers or hunters came close. I shrank my divinity, the soft glow on my skin vanished, and I made my appearance smaller, hunched and unthreatening. I stood far from them, letting them come to me if they wished to be kind to an old woman. The hunters often did. I was always surprised by that.

They often walked close to me, judging me as a poor and destitute old woman, and they left without a word or any sign of acknowledgement of the bread or food they slipped towards me. This encounter was different though. I made myself small, hunched by a tree, and waited for the hunter-like form to approach and then leave. Instead, the hunter walked towards me, and I soon realized that it was a woman, dressed like a man, and what I had assumed was a killed animal she carried at her back, was a babe wrapped in animal fur.

"Are you ok, old woman? Are you lost?"

I shook my head. I liked interacting with humans. It was a humbling experience, especially when they didn't know I was the Goddess who made sure they had food. I liked it when they were kind. I wished I could perhaps be kind the way some of those humans were, without gain.

"Yes, thank you," I said, and my eyes went to the babe at her back again. "Aren't you worried that your baby will come to harm when you go hunting?"

She surprised me as she laughed. "He is a strong man, my son," she said.

I looked again at the bundled red and pink flesh she carried. His breath wheezed as he inhaled, and I immediately knew his struggles. "Are you going to the town nearby? To see a doctor for your son?"

Her eyes narrowed in surprise and then caution. I didn't blame her. How did I know of her son's condition?

"I am a healer," I offered in haste, and her eyes relaxed. I should let her go, I thought. I shouldn't interfere. Healing wasn't my realm of divinity, and it would be unwise to meddle in someone else's business. I would be angry if another God or Goddess tried to affect the soil. "His breathing, right?" I asked, despite knowing better.

She nodded. "He had a terrible cough and now his breathing always sounds ragged."

"May I?" I asked, and she immediately passed the boy to me. I let him relax in my arms, softly sending him pangs of my power and blessing his little body. I sat on the ground and touched different parts of the baby's body, feeling his internal organs.

The mother watched me with a hitched breath, terrified and anxious for my verdict. I heard the breathing of the little boy ease as my power cleared his lungs from any infection and he took deep breaths.

"That's amazing! Just like that, you took his pain away!" she exclaimed.

I carefully wrapped him with the furs again and handed him back to his mother.

"What is your name, great healer? I will tell every mother in my village and any other I visit of your skills!"

I shook my head and stood. "I am just passing by here. They won't find me."

She seemed to not want to believe me, but she didn't protest. She started frantically searching in her pockets for something until she offered me a copper coin. I looked at it and her eyes lowered, and I felt shame emanating from her. "I don't have any more to offer as a thank you."

I looked at the copper and placed my hand over hers and let the coin touch my skin. I didn't need it. It meant nothing to me, but it would ensure food for this woman and her child. I didn't even know how much or how little it was. Yet, I took it. This useless metal, I took from her.

When I was certain the humans of this region would be well fed, making sure all their trees were healthy, their soil fertile and vibrant and their seeds blessed with my divinity so they could take root and grow strong, I started walking towards where my chariot, Kore and her friends ought to be.

Instead, I found the place deserted. Neither my chariot, nor my daughter were anywhere to be found. My anger didn't spike. I remained calm and sat and waited for my daughter to bring the chariot down. She had done it before, taken it to fly in the sky, and I didn't imagine she was anywhere far.

I started getting worried as the day passed and there was no sign of her. I was beginning to make plans to ask for Hellios's help when I heard my winged Serpent's frantic flying. I looked up and was momentarily blinded by the setting sun, but I recognized my chariot as it dashed towards and then crashed on the ground.

"Calm down," I told my flying serpents, but they hissed and twitched, telling me in their own language that something terrible had happened. There was an emergency, and we had to go. I climbed onto the carriage and before my second foot had even left the ground, they started flying again. They flapped their wings harshly, flying faster than ever before, forcing their bodies to their limit. But they didn't stop, they didn't complain. They only fought against their own stamina and their own pain to make haste. I didn't say anything. I didn't want to distract them as I realized how hard they fought to keep going.

We reached a shore that I recognized but whose name I couldn't remember. I saw the three nymphs that accompanied Kore as well as some other Oceanids – Acaste's sisters I presumed—gathered together. My eyes searched frantically for my child. My sight blurred as I hunted every corner, every hiding spot, but she was nowhere to be found. I sent my divinity searching all over the earth; all the soil of the world screamed for Kore, but there was no answer to be found.

SUMMER

I jumped to the ground, not having the patience to let my chariot land, and stormed towards the Nymphs. They hugged each other in terror, crying and wailing. I should have approached slower. I should have spoken more kindly to them; these weak, powerless creatures had so little influence over the world that whatever had happened wasn't their fault, or anything they could have prevented.

However, my sight had blurred due to my terror for the terrible absence of my daughter, the void I felt inside me and all over the world, because I had searched for her and she wasn't anywhere to be found. I had no patience to be calm, to coax the truth from between their tears.

"What happened?" I sent my power towards them, choking them and taking over them as they screamed even louder from the pain. I didn't bother thinking that the more I hurt them, the harder it would be for the words to form. I didn't contemplate the damage I could do to these girls, daughters in their own rights to parents who might suffer from their pain as I did for Kore. "Where is my daughter?!"

My voice rang loud, and the world shook from my panic and rage. Their weakness and pitiful state enraged me instead of inspiring pity. I spoke as I had never done to any other creature before. As the Goddess of food, an Olympian that ruled the world and had defeated the old regime of Titans. The daughter who had fought against her own father and won, resulting in his demise. I felt my monster scream, pushing against my skin, and I let some of it out. I think they saw it. Both my divinity and my physical form must have been altered because of its influence, because their eyes widened. Whatever I was at that moment inspired terror in their little minds, so soft and fragile, so weak.

I loathed their weakness, blamed them for it. I wanted to punish them for it, for being unable to rise beyond their tiny nature.

"We were playing a game," one said. "We turned around for a moment and she was gone. We thought she was hiding. That it was part of the game, but we can't find her."

Acaste and her sisters started crying loudly again.

"Stop this!" I ordered, and their wails ceased.

"Kore wanted to come here. She said it would be ok to take your chariot and return before sunset, but we couldn't find her and didn't know what to do. I asked the Serpents to come and find you," Othreis said. Her form was small like a mouse, her voice came out squeaking and I raised my hand to slap her.

She didn't try to defend herself. She awaited the violence, and I didn't stop. I didn't think how cruel it was to force my power on her simply because I could. To vent my anger and frustration on her body. I didn't consider then how I used her in the same spirit as my male relatives had, to satisfy my own urges.

I hit her face hard, scratching her skin as she fell on the ground. Despite the force and the pain my gesture caused, Othreis managed to keep her mouth shut and no whimpering noise escaped.

"You morons, you imbecilic little parasites, no good to the world at all but to breed monsters and demigods. You lost my child! The daughter of two Olympians."

"We are sorry," they all said in a chorus, and I hit some of them again in punishment for daring to speak.

The world moved in circles around me. I tried to catch onto any part of it to make it steady. I had to keep my mind. I had to stay logical. She couldn't have disappeared. She was somewhere I hadn't searched yet. These thoughts pierced my anger, allowing me to focus on what truly mattered. Finding Kore. If she was found, if she was next to me again, all would be well again.

"Where was she standing when she vanished?"

Othreis walked ahead of the other nymphs, and I followed her. She pointed to a patch of flowers, a mixture of narcissuses and chrysanthemums. I knelt by their side and caressed their petals. My daughter's divinity was all over them, so clearly engraved in each petal that I knew she had given birth to those flowers and brought them out of the ground as I had taught her to do.

I placed my hand over them, caressing them slowly and feeling Kore. Her light, carefree nature was smoothed all over the leaves. The soft breeze of life which characterized her was evident as I touched their stems, but when I tried to follow the trail of her power, it was gone. Or rather, it went back inside the flowers, as if they were all that was left of my child. I searched for her in them, fearing she might have turned into a flower in an attempt to win her game, but she wasn't inside these plants. There was only her memory over them, her scent and feeling. I left the flowers and expanded my search, trying to find a link, a track to follow that would lead me to her.

There was nothing. No other part of Earth bore any traces of her but these flowers.

I closed my eyes. I was trapped again in the darkness of Father's stomach. Alone, in that complete and utter lack of stimuli I had been raised in. I didn't care for anything. Every feeling washed over me, slipped out of me, as if I was wearing emotions as clothes and I just undressed from all of them, leaving them in a pile somewhere I could never reach again. All my joy, all my love for my work, my pride, everything was gone.

My daughter wasn't with me anymore and without her, the world had no light. No joy. No life.

Othreis let out a gasp, which prompted me to open my eyes. I saw those flowers, which a moment ago were colourful and vibrant, withering. The last remnant of my child dying as my despair for her loss grew. Their petals fell and their stems dehydrated. They grew soft and wrinkly, their skin loosening as their insides died. Eventually they grew black and mouldy. They died so quickly that the changes were visible to everyone. I looked at my feet and saw the grass I stood on was the same. I sensed Othreis walk away, retreating from the black mould while the other nymphs were frozen in terror.

My monster was all over my skin, as if I was wearing it. It was so close to taking over. I was so eager to stop trying to fight and let everything go. Without Kore nothing mattered. No fight had any value. Why would I care if I became a monster? Why would I care for anything that happened to me without her in my life?

It was only the hope, the persistent and undying wish that whatever happened, I would find my daughter again. That this wasn't my end. I hadn't yet exhausted every avenue to finding her. For Kore, I needed to remain as much myself as possible, so she could recognize me when we were reunited. I closed my eyes again, tears rolling down my face. They were burning hot and full of poison, full of death.

I pushed my monster down, regaining some control over myself. When I opened my eyes, my sight was darkened, and I wondered if I had dreamt my escape from Father's stomach and my life thereafter. The darkness didn't last long. Light pierced through, the blackness breaking into pieces until I was able to see the world again. I followed the darkness as it flowed down and realized it was my own tears which had blinded me. The dark drops fell on the soil, killing all life.

"Run," I told the nymphs. My voice came from the soil to them, vibrating all over their weak, soft and pretty bodies. "You said my daughter disappeared. You only looked away for a moment and she was gone. If you are standing there when I turn my head, I will crush you."

I heard sounds of running, water splashing and seconds later, when I turned my head, I was all alone. They were gone, and I stood alone and in pain at the shore, with a dark mould surrounding me. I was thankful for their quick disappearance. That none of them were courageous enough to stay and try to comfort me, to assist me. There would be no going back for me then. Because of their fear, they had saved me from turning into my worst self. It was impossible to kill an immortal being, even a nymph, but I could bestow other horrible fates on them, twisting their nature in ways unimaginable to them. I would have done it then.

I lifted my gaze to the sky. I saw Ouranos there, still in his dismembered state, lurking amid the clouds. He spied on me, and we stared at each other like we had done at that skelly when we first met. He wept, and the storm of his tears hit my body. He let all his pain out, all his sorrow, regrets, and anger, but none of these feelings poured inside me. They splashed off me because my own pain, despair and sorrow was a shield against them. Realizing that I wasn't going to pay him any attention, he stopped, but didn't disappear. He stayed lurking in his cloud form and watched me.

I turned towards Olympus. "Zeus!"

There was the sound of thunder and I knew I had his attention.

"Help me!" I screamed. "Help me find our child!"

I waited for another clap of thunder. Another sound of recognition, a nod that I just had to wait, and he would unite with me for our daughter. That even though he didn't care for me, there was some feeling of love for Kore. That even though he might not even love our child, he would play the part of the grieving father. I waited and waited for that sound, the day passed and then the night until I finally knew without a doubt that he wasn't going to help me.

"Curse you!" I yelled at him. "Curse you!" I howled, using all of Greece's soil as my mouth. I screamed again and again as more poisonous tears ran down my face and the soil under my feet grew cold and sorrowful, unable to bear anything that resembled joy or life.

"I will find her myself!" I yelled. "Alone. Myself. She is mine and only mine, after all."

Whether my brother heard me or not, he never gave a sign. I stamped my foot on the ground and turned around, leaving the place my child was lost. By that point, there was no plant alive left there. All were dead, reflecting my despair and hate for the world without Kore.

I walked all over Greece, not bothering to hide my presence from anyone. Uncaring of the trail I left behind me of rotted food and barren crops and trees. It was a clear line which showed where I had searched for Kore and where I hadn't found her. My pain grew as I covered more and more ground and none of my siblings or other relatives came to find me. I had left such a clear trail for them to follow. As my despair grew, I let go of all my responsibilities. All my divinity offered the world was sucked away, and even places I never visited started to suffer.

By the time my search led me to the kingdom of Arcadia, there was a famine, and death prevailed. I heard prayers to me, screams from humans who begged for their small gardens to grow the barest of food, for crops to offer enough to survive. I answered none. Instead, the more I watched the faces of humans crying and begging, dying and pleading with me, the more I relaxed. The sight of their agony and despair calmed my inner darkness. My monster didn't need me to change anymore because I had made the entire world its reflection.

I walked among their villages and cities, searching in all their faces for traces of my daughter, for clues as to where she was. In a tiny Arcadian settlement, I faced a daring young man. His body was dark, his skin clung over his bones. Hermes would come soon to collect his soul. I the few houses were filled with faces like these, but that male body, a ghost of youth and so close to death, drew me and I approached him. He opened his eyes with difficulty and looked at me. The effort was too much, and my divinity burnt so harshly in my grief that his body seemed to shrink more, and he covered his face with his bony hands.

"I am sorry, for whatever we have done, I am sorry, Great Goddess."

I studied his body and face. I absent-mindedly listened to his cries and then he opened his arms and showed me a blue babe, dead for days. It was a horrific sight, and the old me, the one that was mother to Kore, would have felt something for him. In my current state of grief and anger, I only watched in satisfaction.

"Why? What sin did I commit that deserved this pain?"

I didn't answer. I simply walked on to the next town where I was greeted with the same sight of death and feminine. The same question was posed to me again, and I walked away from it each time, until, when I was asked it for the hundredth time, I turned to the small humans who clung to life and observed them with a touch of emotion I hadn't found the courage to feel for a long time.

"You did nothing. I am simply sad. I lost my daughter and without her, I have no life left in me."

After that, words travelled from human settlement to human settlement. The prayers directed to me changed. They were no longer pleas for mercy, but prayers for me to remain strong, offering me their support and comfort. They prayed to other Gods for my daughter to be found, for them to help me in my quest, for them to console me in my hour of need. That act warmed my heart slightly. The homogenous support and love from the human species eased my despair and made me hate life less. It wasn't enough for me to return to work, to ensure there was life and food, but it did please me. It comforted me, and I hadn't realized how much I needed that relief. So, my pain, although widespread and harsh, ceased to be as poisonous. By standing by my side, aiding me in their tiny way, the human species escaped extinction.

I roamed amid the forest, and when I reached the next Arcadian town, I saw the dead had been cleared from the streets. Whoever survived had gotten enough energy from the little food available to do it. The prayers for me and Kore never stopped. All of humanity, perhaps out of love or perhaps out of fear, was begging for my daughter to be found. I often looked up at the sky and wondered how long it would be until Hermes brought me a message from Zeus, telling me that I had a duty to attend to. Each day I looked at the sky and there was nothing coming for me. Neither help nor reprimand.

Whenever I thought of my siblings and how they shunned me at the time I needed their support the most, my bitterness grew and a plague hit the crops, filled with disease and insects. Then my pain eased as the prayers and pleadings intensified, not just to me but to my family. All of Greece begged them to support me, and still not one of them, not even Hestia, came down to find me. I avoided thinking of my family to eschew death.

I eventually stopped visiting the human settlements in Arcadia. I was certain if my daughter was among them, a human voice would have told me. They were that desperate for my sorrow to end and for the old order of life to resume. I turned my focus to the wild, hoping that perhaps my daughter was somewhere in the mountains or forests. Walking through them was painful, and a part of me felt intense sadness at their sight. Death prevailed in them. They were cemeteries of natural beauty, littered with animal corpses. My sorrow had turned the forests dark and lifeless, ghosts of their old selves. The animals were dying as the humans had. Some even turned to cannibalism in their desperate hunger, poisoning themselves by eating things they shouldn't. Madness ruled all the Greek forests.

I was standing in front of an old tree, older than me, watching how the bark had turned black when the smell of fish reached my nostrils. It was such an ill-fitting stench in this place. I didn't need to turn to know that my younger brother had come to find me. I turned to see Poseidon materialising from a stream which cut through the dead trees.

"Zeus is angry with you," he said.

"And he sent you to tell me?" I knew Zeus wasn't enough of a fool to think that of all our siblings, Poseidon would be the one to convince me to stop. "I would have thought Hestia or even Hades would have been the better choices."

His face twitched, unhappy with my immediate rejection of his presence and the belittlement of our relationship. He looked again like that greedy, needy little boy that tried to clutch onto my breasts, bite my nipples and devour me, just to keep me close.

"Nobody sent me. I came to see how you are." His face lowered as he spoke, and I felt how his divinity twisted because of the conflict between his injured pride and his desire or love for me.

A wave of guilt passed through me. I had been lamenting that none of my family came to help, and the first one who did, I rejected. Did I deserve to be alone when I treated others attention with such disdain?

"I am shit," I answered truthfully, and I was glad his face grew more uncomfortable thanks to my crude words. "I lost my daughter."

"And the whole world knows it. Everything on land is dying."

"Your seas are safe from me then. Why do you care?"

His eyes twitched, as we both knew that what I had done to the soil did affect his water forests, even if not to the extent that nature above ground did.

"I don't like it when you are so unhappy. You know that I feel you always. Since I was a babe, I always felt you constantly. I know you, Demeter."

The small part of me which felt guilt vanished with his words. With Poseidon, Zeus and all their progenies it was always about themselves. How they felt. How they related to everything. I closed my eyes and tried to calm my mind, to calm the monster that was inside me.

"You don't," I muttered. "There is so much about me you don't know."

He ran his hand through his dark hair, as if he wanted to tame its unruly nature with that one act, and came closer to me. "But I do. You and I are different from the rest. We feel more than them. Look how your sadness has made the world mourn. How you feel spreads out. Your love makes life, and your sorrow brings death. I am the same with my seas."

I studied his face and wondered if he was bluffing. I had never spoken to anyone of the dark side of me. I couldn't think how he would have known of it. I was sure he must be bluffing.

"You are expressive. That's not what I am," I finally said, trying to see if he would say anything further to my dark self.

Poseidon nodded, but he had stopped listening. He walked onto the soil, leaving the stream, and came towards me. He opened his arms, and I took a step back. Zeus's words from aeons past rang in my mind. Who would protect me from the savagery of men but my connection with another powerful male? I had stayed safe all those years because I was the mother of his child. But our Kore was gone, and Zeus's gaze wasn't on me.

"Let me make you feel better," he said. "I can give you another child."

My eyes widened at his approach. "I don't want a monster," I snapped. "I want my daughter. My one and only daughter!"

"I will give you a better daughter," Poseidon said. "A stronger daughter. One that will not be a soft petal, but strong and wilful. One that will pierce the world like a river, forcing it to change to her own will. Or a son, strong and beautiful."

I didn't wait for him to say anything more. I didn't need to. I saw how my words didn't reach him. My emotions, which he claimed he was attuned to, didn't reach him. Or if they did, he didn't care. None of them cared about me. All the men in my life had wanted to control me, to take from me. My father ate me. Zeus expected me to sleep with him for power, and now Poseidon wanted to take what he deemed his right to have from me.

I immediately started through the forest, hoping to escape him. But whatever madness had possessed him, he was unwilling to give it up. He was always a step behind me. Always too close for me to hide. My power flickered, and the monster in me wanted out.

The familiar feeling of my skin pulsing was on me. I felt as if my body grew scales, my hair was just beneath the point of becoming poisonous, and my face grew. I was changing at the worst possible moment. I momentarily thought that I could give in to the darkness in me. I could let it take over and perhaps whatever I became once that happened would repulse Poseidon enough to let me go.

I decided this was the best course of action, the safest way for me to escape. Any animal I turned into, he would match it to continue his pursuit, but a monster, a repulsive expression of the darkest aspects of my nature and divinity, that could be my only way of escaping this fate.

I willed my monster to do it, to fulfil the threat it had posed in my life all this time. But even though my skin pulsed stronger than ever, even though I felt so much change happening under my humanoid form, it never pierced the exterior. I couldn't let it out. I wanted to, but I couldn't. I had fought against it so hard all my life, and now that I needed to be able to give in, I realized even that release wasn't easy.

I was running and my body was changing, again and again and again. I became so many animals, so many forms for seconds until I exited the forest. I hadn't chosen a direction. I didn't know where I was going, so when the trees stopped surrounding me and I realized I had exited the forest, I panicked. It was going to be even harder to hide or escape Poseidon without the trees. I was bare for his eyes, and I contemplated turning back, but he was too close. I turned my gaze ahead to the valley I had reached, filled with mares. I searched for places to hide, people who might be able to help me, and recognized immediately the shepherd, Onkios, a son of Apollo, the pretty son of Zeus and a human.

This was my best chance of escape. These animals had a stronger divinity, blessed as they were by Apollo and his son. I could hide amid them. I could suppress myself enough to pass as one of them.

Poseidon's power was crashing out of the forest, scavenging the wooded area for me with his waves of divinity. He would reach me soon. I transformed into a mare and walked as calmly as I could amid the animals. I lowered my head and bit a piece of grass as Poseidon's power washed over me and the other animals. I imitated their presence, hiding everything of myself.

He exited the forest just as I lowered my head and examined the field of animals. His eyes scanned the area and to my horror, I saw him turn into a stallion. He was a beautiful horse, dark with long shiny hair, and he walked amidst the mares. Onkios didn't even realize there were two extra animals in his herd. He was lying on the grass, gazing at the sun, because he felt safe in the protection his father's name gave him and his animals. My daughter had felt safe the same way. He was a fool if he believed Apollo would do anything to protect him, should real danger ever come. The best he could hope for was that his father would defend him in petty arguments.

I still had a chance to escape, if only I was able to avoid Poseidon's detection. I kept my head low but felt, as cautiously as I could, his presence. He walked amid the animals, smelling them, and even mounting one or two, spreading his seed or taking his chance in case they were me. I moved around as slowly as I could until, without realizing how, he was behind me, and before I had a chance to change or to raise an alarm, he climbed on me.

He mounted me in that form, and I trembled under him. He was heavy and even in the form of a horse, he stank of fish. My bovine nostrils flared, and I tried to escape him. I tried to walk away. At that moment, as his power tried to subdue me, I turned to my monster and asked it to help me.

I begged that part of myself to take over, to cause whatever havoc it desired, so long as it could help me escape that moment. The pulsing strengthened again but it was too slow, too late. Poseidon's power burst in me and whatever transformation was about to happen to me ceased. The moment had passed, and even though I gave up fighting and rekindled all my stress and fury, there was no further change. As if this horrible part of me knew that we had lost this fight and I should keep it hidden still. I felt Poseidon try to coax me to take our humanoid forms, but I refused and stayed still, watching the green leaves until he released me.

At least in the forms we had, the deed didn't last long. It was only the second time I had ever been in an erotic union, and I wondered which one was worse. The transactional act with Zeus or the violent one with Poseidon. One was the rape I did to myself, converting my body into an object, and the other was the same, only that another converted it to an immaterial thing. I decided this second experience was worse.

Physically, it didn't hurt, but Poseidon hurt me in a way no one else ever had. Not even Father, when he robbed the world from me. Not even Rhea, who birthed me knowing I was going to be eaten. I had never managed to forgive them, and I found that in my list of the unforgivable, Poseidon's name was etched alongside our parents. I didn't even hate Zeus as much as him at that moment. I regretted every moment of kindness I ever offered him. I regretted every caress I had bestowed upon him during our time in the stomach, every kind word I said. I regretted not shredding him to pieces when he was a babe. I had allowed him to grow into this monster. I had allowed him to hurt me and so many other females and males he decided existed for his pleasure.

His hungry gaze, which I had felt even before we exited the stomach, was my mistake.

He changed into the form of a man and walked naked in front of me and amid the rest of the animals.

Onkios still had no idea what was happening.

Poseidon grinned widely, traces of pleasure lingering in his eyes. His power flickered and surfed towards me, like a wave meeting the shoreline. My rejection was harsher than any other time. Lost was any form of pity I held for him, for the harm I had inflicted when I grabbed him as a babe. Lost was any part of me that cared, even just that little bit because of our shared experience. I only felt disgust, and an anger harsher and wilder than any I had ever felt before. Even my panic at realizing that Kore was lost didn't make my divinity boil with anger and hate as he had done.

He tried to coax me again to turn into a humanoid form. Instead, I let myself grow cold, emulating Hades as much as I could, and I felt him retreat from me quickly. His face changed. First to confusion, then to shock and finally to anger, but it was nothing compared to mine, which was bubbling under the cold exterior I forced upon him. The complete disregard I had for him I knew further wounded his pride. I didn't hold anything back. I let all the harsher and uglier parts of me out, no longer caring to maintain a positive appearance for anyone.

Leave me! Never enough! I hate you! These were the sentiments I sent towards him, and he felt them all. I pushed them towards his being again and again and I cloaked all of them with darkness and the memories of the void of Father's stomach.

And he understood and fled.

Once he was lost, I looked around me and saw that all the vegetation, every single plant, was not simply dying. It was dark, black as night, making the world a rotten and wasted space, worse than I had done before. The mares yelled and some fainted as they ate the black plants. There was poison all over us, and they soon died from it. The alarm they raised and possibly the rotting smell which took over the field, roused Onkios from his sleep and he yelped as he faced the dead vegetation and his sick animals.

"Don't eat," he screamed to his animals. "Nothing," he begged. He looked up at the sky. "Father! Apollo! Something is wrong."

Only once I faced the darkness that spread from me, did I let the horse form fade. I let my body take the form of a human and stood amid the fainting and dying mares. Onkios noticed me, but whatever insult or other words he had for me died in his throat as I turned to face him. I don't know how I looked then, but I must have been monstrous and raging, as the man cowered and stayed silent, avoiding my gaze. He moved to hide behind the animals he was supposed to protect, as if these could have been enough of a shield if I wished to hurt him.

I turned inward then, for the first time seeking the darkness, and I found it ready and eager to meet me. It was different than when I tried to release myself to it, it was the exact opposite because I went to its world, in the darkest and deepest parts of my mind where it had been waiting for me all this time, where it had been trying to get me to come so I could see it for what it truly was.

Finally, it whispered. You accept who you truly are.

Do whatever you want. I am done with this pretence.

I felt that dark self join with me and didn't fight it. Instead, inspired and empowered by my invitation to merge with it, it was cool and kind. It slowly enveloped my body, and I closed my eyes, letting the feeling wash away the rest of my emotions. It wasn't an exterior change as I had always feared it would be. Whatever form I took from now on, the monster and I existed together. Monster, maiden, crone, lizard. It didn't matter. The monster and I were in it together.

The darkness in me nudged me to walk away before Apollo, or someone else who might demand answers for what I had done, arrived. I didn't fear giving them, but the monster realized that in this new state of who I was, I needed to be careful because I didn't know who I had become. At that moment, even my love for Kore, the purest part of me which had been the source of my sorrow, was overshadowed by the pain and rage I felt for what had happened to me.

I walked away, following the air and a beautiful smell which I wanted to both destroy and possess. I walked slowly until I found myself in a small patch of trees on a rocky river I immediately recognized as Ladon, named after its protector deity, one of the myriad sons of Oceanus and Tethys and father of a couple river nymphs. They were all lucky I didn't see them, if they were near the riverbank. I slowly took off my dress and let it fall. I walked over the cloth and into the river. I did that in a way that seemed like I didn't possess my own body, but as a ritual I had to perform.

The water was cold, but I didn't feel any discomfort. Instead, as I walked into it, my mind returned to the memory of my childhood, the darkness which was pleasantly familiar. The thought struck me: How could that void, which had robbed me of life itself, which I always claimed had traumatized me as I was growing up, be a familiar comfort? Even if the cost of that lack of pain was a lack of joy, a lack of life itself.

I lifted water with my palm and let it fall over my hair. It trickled slowly down my body, and I let its healing and cleansing powers move over me but, despite the river's strength, it was only a superficial and surface cleansing. I don't think I ever expected for it to wash my anger away, my humiliation or my pain, but I had thought that it would calm these emotions.

Instead, I washed something else off me. I cleansed myself of something completely different, and what was left by the time I finished was a pure feeling that merged all my darkest pain. Wrath. It didn't consume. It didn't explode in me in an exclamatory way. It just settled all over me, and that was my new being.

I had lost my child. I had been assaulted by my own brother, and in my pain, which was clear as day and all of humanity could attest to its scale, not a single one of my siblings came to aid me, or at least comfort me. Childless, family-less and scared.

I walked out of Ladon, leaving my old clothes behind at the opposite shore. I walked completely naked in the forest, as I had done when I escaped the stomach, but this time there was no trail of destruction coming from me. Even that feeling of affecting nature had left me. I left everything as it was, and I would continue to. There was no work for me to do nor undo. It was just going to take its course. I had washed my godhood role away. I didn't know or think then for how long I would do that. It could be a day. It could be a century. It could be forever. It simply didn't have anything to do with me for the time being.

I walked aimlessly around the arcadian forest I was in, until by nightfall I reached a small house standing amid the trees on its own. I examined it before I entered, and only when I was closer to the gate, I noticed an old blind woman sitting on the front porch, with a small fire lantern next to her. I approached, and without saying a word or alluding to my presence, I entered her house. I wore a dark dress I found amongst her things, old fashioned and old like her, and then, just as uncaring as I was when I entered, I walked out.

Those dark clothes weren't enough, though. They represented that I was not the young goddess who once wore an orange dress, and made flowers and trees, but I needed more to show to everyone who I was. Even after all that had happened to me, even after all the washing I had done, I still needed to appear to the world, for everyone to know me in the form I currently occupied, unknown as it was to me. Changing myself was a process of finding the words, the sentiments that could describe me, and clothes weren't enough for that.

I started walking towards the closest mountain I could see. I entered the Phigalia region, so I knew the mountain I headed towards was Elaeum. Not that geography mattered. All that was mattered was to find somewhere to hide where there would be no life. Somewhere that would be like the Stomach: dark, void and empty of all but me.

Momentarily, I contemplated going to the Underworld, to my brother Hades, but I couldn't bear his presence, even as a thought. If I was to return to the comfortable absence of everything from my old life, I didn't want to return to the clingy family that used to define it. I wanted it to be my darkness only. My space, where I could cease to think, to feel, to be anything other than me, in the most abstract way.

Abstract. Zeus's old description of the older Gods came to me, and I tensed all over from the thought.

No.

No, I agreed with myself and kept walking. My thoughts themselves had to cease.

I walked up the mountain, ignoring all the problems I saw, ignoring all the faults I could fix until, not far from the bottom of the mountain, I saw a dark cave opening. Its shadows enticed me, as if the lack of light that reigned inside that part of Gaia's body was calling me. As if the Moirai themselves had decided earth had carved a hole inside itself for my sake, knowing that one day I would come looking for it. I entered, certain that it was the one and only place left for me in the world.

I went deep into the cave, and soon I was so far underground that there was no sound or light. I lay on the cold ground, unable to sleep as humans did, but empty and free from everything in that darkness. Even the initial sensations of coolness, stone and dampness left me quickly. I felt all of me, every inch of my skin, every nook of my body, and I was more aware from my physical form than ever before.

Time ceased to exist. There were no days, no nights, just the tingling feeling of me, and that soon lost much of its presence, as I moved less and less.

But that soft feeling of absent floating, of being free of all sensation wasn't allowed to me for long. Damned life reached me again.

It was a kick inside my stomach. A fluttering bundle of life inside me which stirred my entire body awake. Life. Damned, damned life.

I jolted awake, moving without thinking, and breaking the spell of the emptiness which had settled over me. The discomfort of gaining back sensation was immense. I felt all my pain, my anguish, my yearning for Kore and my bitterness for being led to this place and being left to tend for myself. I tried to convince myself I had imagined it. That, among all the misfortunes which had fallen onto me, this couldn't also be what the Moirai had in store for me.

I placed my hand on my stomach and felt the two presences in there, fighting with each other and demanding of me. Just like their hateful, pathetic father, these two babes clung and sucked my power. The act happening inside me reminded me of Poseidon's arrival at Father's stomach. The way he lunged at me, bit my nipple, and tried to suck. The way I had flung him away before Hestia brought him back, and the way that even as a toddler, he was always on me. His grabby hands all over me, taking any chance he could to be closer to me and have me all to himself. All my effort to not feel, to not exist, was gone because I was stuck with these two monsters inside me.

Monsters, beasts and cruel. Whatever they looked like, they could only be a combination of these three options.

"Just like your father," I muttered as they drained me to nurture themselves. "Always more, more, more!"

I gave them nothing. I held everything back, and the beasts fought me. They begged me, screaming in their own nonverbal power that I was their mother, and they were starving. They wanted to be strong, to have power, to be born and command the world. I denied them everything. I refused to be responsible for the creation of another set of Poseidons, who would never be happy with what they had. I refused to assist in the creation of another pair of jealous, petty, greedy and ungrateful mongrels that would rape and take anything they wanted, disregarding others' needs and feelings.

I sent down into my body all my darkest feelings, my most poisonous essence, and they took it, while also complaining it wasn't right.

"That's all you get," I told my growing belly. "My hate, my anger, my pain and my disgust for your father."

Soon, I realized that one of the two babes in my belly was hoarding whatever flicker of positivity I could give it, starving the other of any spark of life, letting it absorb only hatred and anger, only mindless emotions. Not that I willingly gave them any.

Whatever flicker of emotion that wasn't about how much I despised them and wished them dead, the sneaky one stole from me. Grabbing whenever a memory of Kore passed through my mind, and I felt the slightest touch of positive emotion. The hateful, greedy monster, just like its father, was determined to get what it wanted. Destroying and desecrating everything in the process of the acquisition of life.

I started fighting the sneaky child, completely ignoring the other one, who kept absorbing and growing only with the scraps and throwaways of the other. I tried to destroy it, to make it born a mortal so it could be killed. I wanted it dead, and I tried to do so before it was born, but that terrible child was determined to save itself. Instead of letting me kill it, poison it and expel it from my body, it fought me.

It tried so hard to live that I had to focus all my attention and all my power to it, so I could change its nature permanently, to make it a stillborn human that would never harm others, but the moment my divinity touched the sneaky child's, the horrible, hateful mongrel, I paused.

The force I felt from that terrible child was the exact replica of the darkness I had been fighting all my life. Pulsing with the cold, never ending rage and nothing else to stop it. It had its father's tenacity for greed, for complete lack of care for others, but the darkness was mine. And that stunned me. I hated them both, wanted them dead, but the surprise gave it, and as a result its weaker sibling too, enough time to grow bigger.

How could that monster-child resemble me? How could any part of me be in it? I refused them. They weren't mine. They weren't made of me. I denied them and yet those hateful mongrels had managed to share similarities with me.

"Out," I screamed and started hitting my overgrown belly. "Out!" I punched myself and used all my force to expel them from me. They weren't ready, not fully and they resisted, but there was nothing they could do or be, or even express in their way, to deny me my freedom from them. I pushed and pushed, forcing my genitals to open wide.

The stupid and starved one came out first. I knew it was going to be a monster the moment it reached the edges of my body. I felt its misshapen form as it tried to get out of me. There were too many legs, no hands. The spine was wrong, a box-like feeling rather than a linear entity. I let out a scream and I was greeted with the sound of neighing.

The monster was struck in between my legs, only half its body out.

"Get out!" I commanded, but the beast was stuck. "Out! Out!"

This was nothing like the birth of my Kore. That had been so much simpler, and my baby had been as eager as me to come out into the world and meet me. But this terrible creature was so stupid, so weak and so incapable that it couldn't even be born without assistance.

Amid the pain, I thought it was good. The beast would surely be born mortal and die, ridding me of its presence. With one deep push of my power, I bent as much as I could and moved my legs high, like the way a frog does when they swim or jump. I put my two feet either side of the large horse head sticking out.

The foal cried, neighing as my legs pressed against its head, partly crushing its soft bones. Its body tore mine as I forced it out. I ripped the umbilical cord and threw the monster away. Its body hit one of the walls and its neighing sounds increased, as it desperately cried out of fear and out of despair for the dark world it had entered.

"Now you," I said, and turned my attention to the sneaky child which had managed to gain even more time by sacrificing its sibling. "You are worse than that horse mongrel. Lying and deceitful."

I used all my strength to force the second baby out. I imagined that it would tear me apart as well. It would have a terrible face and terrible body, another equine like monster, maybe identical to its twin. I pushed it out, even pressing my belly with my hands to make it leave, like humans did with pimples. I squeezed with my hands and pushed with my inner hip muscles while that terrible child fought.

"Out," I demanded, and the child, having no other choice, succumbed to my power.

That second birth was easier. I didn't feel an enlarged head or any odd number of extremities. Instead, once it was out of my body, I heard a baby's crying, just like Kore's. I looked between my legs and saw a girl, looking perfect, in a pool of my blood and body fluids. I watched it with fear, much more so than its horse twin.

I grabbed the second umbilical cord and bit it off, severing completely my body's connection with the bitch daughter of Poseidon. I lay back on the cold stone and waited as my body healed, in that quick and time defying way that characterized Gods. My hair was full of sweat from the pregnancy and labour, and my clothes were soaked with dirt.

I closed her eyes, trying again to force all feelings from my body, and to return to that void of my childhood, my original plan when I entered the cave. But my body still hurt from the birth, and no matter how much I tried to empty myself, I found it impossible.

I found that even the darkness, which I had given in to and was so used to fighting against was different. It wasn't smaller or less dangerous, but it was missing something. Instead of that pulsing darkness, that monster I feared I would become was transformed into a different kind. This one didn't fight against my flesh, didn't force dominion over me. It stayed still and waited for me to make the first move.

I delved inside myself again, letting go all preconceptions of the brief meeting I had with its previous incarnation. I was in a mental space as dark as I remembered Father's stomach to be. Only that it was my own and within that space I was face to face with the monster. I studied its face, visible and still completely part of the complete and utter dark. It was a terrible mix of beast and man. It had the head of a horse but instead of hair, snakes, lizards and insects were attached to its head. The rest of its body was fairly humanoid, and with its two hands, it held two animals. Its left squeezed the life out of a dolphin, but never enough to kill it. The marine mammal was squirming in the monster's hand, trying to escape. The right hand held a dove, with much less animosity, and the creature didn't try to leave. It sat comfortably and by choice in the open palm.

"Are you the monster that lives inside me?" I asked.

"I am Demeter," it answered.

The answer shocked me, and I felt a threatening fear at the utterance of the words. "No, I am Demeter."

"You are one Demeter. I am another."

"There cannot be more than one of me. I am me."

The monstrous Demeter laughed at my answer. "You still don't accept who we are. Let me show you," she urged and stood up. I did the same and remained still as it approached me.

"I am me," I insisted. "The one and only Demeter."

"You are the Demeter who lost her daughter, who was raped by that sea beast," she said and squeezed the dolphin hard in her hand. It squealed in pain. She paused, examining my black clothes. "This isn't enough, and you know it. You need to take into the rage and darkness, let it change you, not simply wear a black dress. You are not enough to get our daughter back."

"Kore can be found?" I asked, but the other Demeter didn't respond.

"Don't you want to be the Demeter who will not be denied? Or do you want to stay the you who is trampled over, who doesn't have sex for joy and desire but for duty or by force? Are you happy in the pathetic way you have settled yourself to?"

I lowered my head and pondered over the words, the insults she called me. I lifted my hand and waited for something to happen as I accepted whatever damning change was about to occur. I felt the wet presence of the dolphin in my hand. I lifted my eyes and saw the other Demeter watching me. The dolphin was trying to escape, it was trying to leave my grasp and be freed from my rage. I watched it and saw all the sea in its existence. It was Poseidon and his violence. It was Poseidon and his desire for more, more, always more from me. It was also me, always struggling to be in balance.

"Not balance," the other Demeter corrected my thoughts. "This is balance," she said and showed me the dove which chose to stay.

I looked at the struggling dolphin again. It was me, yes. But not struggling for balance. She was right. I was striving to be liked, approved, and accepted. I was striving for Zeus to give me the power I was owed; that was mine by birthright and because I was strong enough to wield it. It had always been mine. I did not need to debase myself to sleep with him to claim it.

I squeezed the dolphin suddenly, adding to its pain. And I squeezed and hurt both the old me and Poseidon and his seas.

The sound of neighing and crying broke my mental world into pieces. The dark Demeter faded as I was back in the cave, no longer holding the dolphin. But I knew I needed to change. I needed to become, first in appearance and then in spirit, that other Demeter—strong, methodical and without any guilt or pity—so I could, one day, get my daughter back. I visualized the monstrous Demeter and gave up any desire for beauty. I didn't want for Zeus or Poseidon, or anyone, to look at me and call me pretty. I didn't want anyone to look at me and think that I was worth capturing.

I wanted them to watch me and imagine that I was the wildest and most dangerous force in the world. I was the darkest version of myself. I was not the Goddess of Harvest and Food, but rather the Goddess of Starvation and Famine.

My face hurt as I made the first change, transforming my features into that of a horse. I got a muzzle, with a large mouth, large teeth and wide-open nostrils. I smelled through them the foal I had given birth, as it struggled to stand on its legs and failed. The pathetic mongrel.

I smelt the cunt who crapped herself as I enveloped her with my power, my hatred for her and all she reminded me of.

My skin changed, gaining a soft furring. Finally, my hair rose up, coming to life as a myriad of reptiles. They stood up and I could see through them as well as through my horse eyes. The two children kept crying, screaming all over the world, both with their mouths and their untrained power, that I was a monster and they were terrified of me.

"Die, live, whatever," I whispered to them. "I am done with both of you."

I turned my back and walked deeper into the cave, but no matter how far I went, no matter how deep and dark my world and I were, I felt the vibration of their crying and fear.

I was able to hear it. And I hated them even more for still living, for not accepting that the world would be better off with them dead and that I wasn't their mother.

Eventually, I must have reached far and deep enough, as the crying of that terrible girl ended, the twin who fought the hardest to draw life and power from me. At that spot, I sat, marking, with my power, a throne to sit on. The stone walls of the cave gave in to me and allowed me to transform matter itself as they expanded and formed my seat.

I closed my eyes, ignoring everything and everyone from the world outside. In that silence, I rested. I had no plan as to how my new self would bring me back my one and only true child, my Kore, my daughter. I only knew that I couldn't go back to my aimless roaming in the world. I couldn't go back to hunting for her as I had before.

I needed help. The word stung in my mind. Hadn't I changed into this hybrid form to become independent? I tried to find that dark Demeter again, to meet with her in that mental dark space, but she was gone. Or rather, she was me.

There were no more multiple Demeters. I was all of them.

Help, I thought again. I need help. But the word stung me again as I thought it.

No, I corrected myself. I need clues to resume my search. I needed witnesses that would tell me the truth, not someone that would grace me with their help.

I wasn't going to exit the cave and kiss the hands of others, asking and coaxing for their attention and help. I would not scream for Zeus's aid. If I needed his attention, I would go and get it. If someone knew of what happened to my child, I would walk up to them and force the truth out of their mouths.

That wasn't help. That wasn't dependence. That was taking what I was owed.

That was rewriting my story, returning to the moment when Zeus tried to marry me off, to make me the Goddess of something abstract, and I didn't simply refuse but stated that it wouldn't happen. That was me shaking my head when he made sexual advances towards me, pushing him away and still becoming the Goddess I was born to be.

Even the strongest God couldn't turn back time. I couldn't return to that moment and rewrite it, changing my past. And even if I could, I didn't know if I would risk Kore for it. My daughter was somewhere, waiting for me to save her. I was changing for her.

No. I was changing for me, so I could have her back. I couldn't exist for someone else, not even for Kore.

My thoughts moved in circles in the darkness of the deep cave. I thought of the same sequence again and again, sculpting my inner self to mirror the self I truly was. Again, and again. Circle upon circle of thought, I carved myself in the image of the one that would get her child back, no matter the cost. No matter the pain.

My mind was so occupied with my transformation that I didn't even realize someone was close until I heard the sound of two goat-footed steps. They clacked with the stone of the cave, and my serpent hair felt the vibration of the in-comer against my stone throne. I opened my eyes and waited for whoever was coming to appear.

I stayed as still and as silent as I could, hiding my presence and withdrawing my power completely to avoid detection.

The incomer brought light, and soon I was faced with a familiar face. Brown wild hair, a growing baldness and two ugly and misshapen horns protruded from the dark-skinned head of Pan. His bottom half, dark brown goat hind legs and an ugly hairy cock hanging in between them, walked slowly towards me. His signature flute was hanging from his belt, and he paused when he saw me.

He surely wouldn't be able to recognize me. There was nothing left of the Goddess of the Harvest he had once known. I wasn't surprised by his presence. He was known to wander in Arcadia, one of his favourite hunting grounds for nymphs and other unsuspecting females.

Another rapist, I thought. Another man without any respect for those he claims as beautiful. Another male that thinks that something—or someone—is beautiful for their pleasure and not for their own.

"A horse, mad and wild, ran out of this cave and I was told to come investigate it," he said, as if I had asked why he was in my cave. "Who are you?"

I raised my eyebrows at his question. Should I reveal myself?

"You should leave, Pan," I ordered him.

My voice betrayed my identity. The shepherd God clapped his hands over his mouth and stepped back.

"Goddess of Harvest, of life in the soil! Of agriculture," he said, falling to his knees. "Please come out. Please exit this dark cave and return to the world. We are dying in your absence."

I stayed silent and crossed my legs as I watched him from my throne. "Why? Am I missed?"

Pan lifted his head. "Missed, Goddess Demeter? The entire flora and fauna of Greece is begging for your return. There is no prayer uttered from any lips that isn't about you."

The news pleased me. They all realized how much work I put in. How I was instrumental to the survival of everyone and everything!

"Even sea life?" I asked, wanting to learn if my little brother felt my rage too.

Whether he knew or not, Pan nodded. "All the Gods, even Zeus himself, are searching for you."

I shrugged. "They didn't come to help me when I needed them. Why should I go to them now?"

Pan stammered sounds, trying to find an answer. His gibberish sounds ceased and then, in a moment of rare diplomacy for the goat God, he said, "I cannot speak for your siblings and the other Olympians. I am just a lowly God of the mountains, but my Father told me that they all want you back. He said they miss you dearly. We all miss your caring and nurturing nature."

"Caring? Nurturing?" I mocked his words. "Come and take a closer look at me."

The mountain God brought his torch closer to my throne. The snakes on my head hissed at him, and he let out a sharp yelp of terror.

"What happened to you? Your beauty. Your softness. Gone."

"Do you think I should exit my cave still?" I asked. "Do you think my siblings and the other Gods would want me?"

Pan didn't have an answer. He walked backwards, and before he was five steps away from me, he started running. My snake hair hissed and echoed in the cave as he sprinted away.

"Run, run!" I mocked him, and the sound of his goat feet echoed as he escaped from me.

Not even me. The sight of me.

I wondered who would come next. Pan was a known blabbermouth and loyal to his father. I imagined him running out of the cave screaming for Hermes, who would fly to him as quickly as possible. And once he narrated to his father the sighting of me, my new state, the messenger God would rush to his own father and tell Zeus.

Would he come himself? To scold me and force me back? Would I be ready to resist his power? I had prepared myself for the battle of wills, but was I truly ready? Had I armed myself enough to face the King of the Olympians?

If he sent Hestia, could I refuse her? Could I be cruel to her, who had been my home and centre of life during the darkness of our childhood? She never wanted to return to that darkness, and my choices would have forced her to.

Maybe he would send Athena, his favourite child, the one that was only his, to convince me?

Maybe Artemis, his daughter that was close to nature like me.

The possibilities were endless. And one among them was that he would send all the Gods and Goddess, all the demi-gods, all the human heroes and the nymphs and the animals to find Kore. If he did that, I thought, if Kore walked into the cave to get me, I would stop it all. I would come out and life would be back as it once was.

My snakes hissed at the thought. No, I would come out, but wouldn't stop it all. I would still need to punish those who took her, those who knew of her disappearance, or of her whereabouts and didn't run to tell me. I would need to find and punish them, even if that meant turning on my siblings.

To make sure that no one, not even Zeus, ever dared to steal my daughter from me again.

The names of the possible visitors I could have played different scenarios. I tried to predict each one. I tried to imagine which one Zeus would choose, and the more I tried to think like him, the more I realized my dream of Kore coming to find me was unrealistic. My youngest brother would be angry with me, vengeful and petty, just as he always was.

He would be fuming with rage that a female had bested him like that. He would be swamped in prayers and demands from all humans to bring me back, no matter the cost.

He was a proud creature, though. He wouldn't give in to me so easily. For that same reason, I doubted he would come himself as well. It would be too much ridicule for his ego to cope with. He would fear that I could convince one of our siblings to come to my side, creating the rift between us that I had threatened him with when we began our reign. He would fear that sending one of his children, I might consider an offense and he wouldn't risk that either.

He needed to send me someone that wouldn't be swayed by me, would have old lineage and parentage and I would need to respect.

Aphrodite, the only Olympian that was a child of Ouranos, would be an option. She was technically an aunt to us. She would be furious at me. Nothing killed off her erotic cult as much as disease and starvation. She was notoriously easy to anger, notoriously prissy and hard to please. I doubted he would trust her as a diplomat of good will. No, he wouldn't send her.

Who was left?

A Titan? I rejected the option. He would fear they could side with me in an attempt to overthrow him. There were very old grudges with the Titans, and a very thin balance between them and the Olympians. He wouldn't risk that either.

I kept searching for the name that would make sense. The one that would be old, strong and undisputable for me to listen to, but not involved in any of our grudges.

"I can hear your thoughts from before entering the cave, Demeter," came a tired sounding voice.

Oh yes. Who else but the three hags? Yes, he was clever, my little brother. I had to admit that his choice was perfect.

"You look terrible," another female voice said.

"Move away so I can see her too," a third voice snapped. In the darkness, I heard the disgusting sound of their creaking bones as they moved.

"Oh, my, you are uglier than us," the third voice said, and they started laughing.

The three Moirai approached me. The darkness didn't affect them. They were above and beyond such issues. They sat on the rocks around me. Their work could never end; just like mine its absence had terrible repercussions. Theirs even more than mime. They took out their spinning and began their never-ending ritual of birth, life, and death.

"Zeus sent you, I presume?"

"Yes, your brother asked us to speak with you."

"Is that the word he chose?"

Clotho laughed at my direct question. "Oh, your brother thinks he can command us, when he must obey us. We don't do as he wants. We simply know what will happen."

"And did you know that I would lose my daughter?"

"Oh, yes," Lachesis said. "That part of your life was clear from the very moment your thread began spinning. Same as your daughter's. There is nothing that could ever have stopped it. It is a fixed moment in time, in the development of the entire world. Few Gods even have such strong and definite fates as this pain you feel now. So clearly and ironclad foretold."

"And you didn't tell me?" I asked them. "Is this also foretold?" I pointed at myself, my new state.

"Yes, Demeter. That is foretold, as it is that you will find your daughter again."

I closed my eyes and tried to think. Their words were always true. They never lied. But that didn't mean they had to tell the whole truth. That was why the Moirai were the perfect choice for Zeus to send. They were old and young, sometimes appearing like perfect young maidens, other times as old grey-haired hags, always unnatural in whatever form they possessed. They were too old to be maidens and far too energetic to be hags. They were endless.

Abstract. The word came back to my mind. Zeus had sent them knowing he couldn't control them but could depend on them not to interfere with me.

"Did Zeus know? Did you tell him?"

"You brother doesn't ask before he does things. He simply thinks he knows all. We told him he couldn't force you to stop. Your fate is not his to learn, but yours to live."

I didn't wonder whether they truly trusted what they said. At that moment I didn't care if the whole world knew even my darkest secret. "So, you are here to send me out into the world? To fix plants and give food and obey him?"

Clotho laughed again. "Oh, Demeter." The condescending kindness irked me. "You need to obey the course of your life, not your brother. But yes, we are here to tell you it is time to exit the cave."

"In a world without my daughter?" I said. "This world has no meaning for me."

"You have two more children, don't you? Would you exit for them?"

Of course, they knew, the hags. They probably knew it would happen before it even did. I clenched my teeth tight and held my hands into fists. "I only have one child. Only Kore. The other two are nothing."

Atropos, who had remained quiet for the entire conversation so far, snapped a line with her scissors. I waited for her to speak, to say something that would finalize the words of her sisters, but the last of the three Moirai remained quiet. Ready to cut the threat of life wherever Lachesis directed, but completely silent and uninterested in me.

"For Kore, then. Exit to find her," Lachesis said. "Do it for that reason, since you reject your other two."

I shook my head. The snakes on my head moved negatively on their own, stretching and rising all over. Other lizard-like creatures crawled among them, and I felt cockroaches even in between the battling bodies on my head and the nape of my neck.

"But I don't know where she is. I have searched everywhere on earth and couldn't find her. Nobody came to help me."

"The state you were in, nobody could," Clotho said. "Do you think anyone would dare to approach you as you spread death all over? You were like a madwoman. You were not in control, and everyone was afraid to help you."

I listened to her words carefully, contemplating if they were true. In my grief and anger, could I have pushed away any creature that wanted to help me? Had I lost valuable time because of that? If my child, entrapped somewhere beyond my reach, suffered longer than she needed because I was too consumed by my emotions, I wouldn't be able to become a kind entity ever again. I was destined to remain the creature I was now.

"You will never go back to who you were," Lachesis said, as if she was reading my thoughts, a power I knew she didn't possess. All they knew were the facts of life. Even common men had the chance to react to the facts of their own accord. "But staying as you are now will not help you and your daughter."

"I need to transform again?" I asked and felt ire rise. I had just settled into my new self.

"You are still a sorrowful, vengeful, angry being. Still spreading death without thought or plan. Some deserve it, some don't. You need to change to be dangerous, but not so threatening that no one dares approach you."

Lachesis showed a specific spot on her thread, and Atropos used her large scissors to cut where her sister pointed. Another life gone, just in the time it took for the third old woman to use her tools. I had watched them work before and was fascinated how much harder it was for Clotho to spin a thread of life, for Lachesis to measure it, and how easy the act was for Atropos to cut it.

"I thought this was the true me," I said finally.

"You are the Goddess that gives food, and you are perhaps the only Goddess that Zeus cannot bully into submission. Looking as you do is not about who you are. Reacting is not the same as acting either. It isn't about superficial changes, Demeter. It is about showing that you can do damage but that you are also in control of that damage. The longer you spread it without thought or demand, the harder it will be for your daughter to find her way back to you."

I paused thinking of their words. They sounded right, and yet I was resistant to them. "You know how this will play out, right?"

Atropos snapped another life, then turned to me. "We know the facts of life. We know the situations you will face, not the way you will choose to act around them. If we did, we could send the Erinyes before the acts. It was foretold that you would starve the world. It was foretold that you would be separated from your daughter, and it was foretold that you would reunite with her again." She turned to her sister and nodded slowly. "Show her, Lachesis."

The middle sister took out of her myriad threads a bright glowing line. It was the line of an immortal.

"This is your daughter," Atropos explained. "She is changing as well. You will see her again. Who she will be when you meet each other? Who you will be? That is up to both of you. One day you will exit this cave. Whether it is today or in a century, when there will be no life left, that is your choice. You need to consider what you will do with the power you wield. I can cut all the threads today, but if I do that, Clotho will not be able to spin new ones and Lachesis will not have any to measure. Our power, our importance, is in cutting the right one, at the right time, at the right interval."

"I don't understand," I began, but Atropos stood and nudged her sisters to do the same.

"Decide what you want to do. But know that one day, you will exit this cave. That is inevitable."

They never said anything else to me. They left me in the darkness of the cave to ponder their words. Exiting this cave and finding Kore were inevitable, but the how of those facts was not clear. I pondered over their words.

Their power was held because there was birth. If all died, none was born.

My power. What was the balance of my power? If I gave my all to humans and Gods, I was taken for granted. Loved, yes, but not respected. If I took it all in one go, then eventually there would be no life left and I would be powerless because no one would be begging for me.

The right time, Atropos's words rang in my mind.

The right time.

The right time to exit, I realized. When everyone was so desperate that their fear wouldn't be enough to stop them telling me what they knew. Humans would hate me if I killed too many. They needed to beg me, to try to win my good graces, knowing I could end them. What bargaining power would I have if all life was gone?

All the other Gods would have lost their power then. Their realms and dominions. If I took all of that from them, they would all hate me. If I came out of the cave at the wrong time, they either would consider me weak and easy to manipulate or so terrible that, like Father, I had to be sent to Tartarus so they could start over.

Seeing my daughter again was ironclad. But if I found her when everything she valued was gone and left her friendless and joyless, my own daughter would hate me. I stood up from my throne.

The right time.

I didn't know when the right time was, but I decided it was time to start walking towards the world again. The cave was long, the cave was dark, but the closest I was to its mouth, the better I would be able to understand when the time was right.

AUTUMN

I ended up staying at the mouth of the cave for a few human years, apart from periodically stepping outside, purposefully giving something back to the world to stop life from perishing completely. It was a calculated choice, not like the first time I had relieved humanity of the famine. The prayers to me increased and so did the demands from humans on my behalf to get my daughter back.

I wasn't sure what I was waiting for, but one morning, there was no other prayer uttered in all of Greece but the desire for the other Gods to help me find my daughter. I thought that was the time, the moment before the rope snapped and their pleas to help changed to pleas to stop me. That morning, I permanently exited the cave and resumed my active search for Kore, hoping that whoever would be able to tell me where she was would appear soon.

I began my second journey wearing my monstrous hybrid appearance, but the fear it caused wasn't helpful. No living creature approached me.

The Moirais' warning words echoed as a thought: Who would have the courage to speak to me if I just spread death and fear?

Throughout my life I had been terrified of facing my darker side. And yet, I felt stronger in its presence now. I didn't ever want to go back to the past me who was separate from it. I couldn't, anyway. And I wanted the face and skin I wore to reflect that I was in a new era of my life, a new era of my Godhood, even if I didn't know who I was going to become when my journey ended and Kore was again in my arms, safe and sound. I wondered whether I wanted to become an animal, or find my chariot wherever it had flown to and travel through the sky.

These thoughts stalled my search until I came to watch the humans. The old parents and the young children. Kore and I didn't look different in age. I moved my hands, still covered in horsehair all over, and rubbed my snake and serpent hair. My hands calmed their anger, turned them back into keratin, but not the colour I had before. Instead, the strands went grey and thin under my fingertips. I pressed my hand over my face, giving me again a humanoid face which would allow me to walk amid the human settlements easier and, finally, I scrubbed my skin to remove all the horsehair.

I dressed again in black, a sign of my mourning and grief over the loss of my daughter. I stared at myself in a lake nearby. I was me but I also wasn't. An old but not frail creature, I had become. My skin was marked all over with lines, resembling tree bark. My grey hair fell on my shoulders in waves, but hadn't lost its old shine and silkiness.

Yes, I thought, I was like this creature that stared back at me. Old but not ready to break. Wise. Unattractive but not ugly.

The reflection captured my interest, and I stood there for a long time, memorizing and meeting this new exterior I wore, this new skin that was now mine. As I watched my image in the water, remembering my daughter and tears filling my eyes, I heard a beautiful song which slowly drew my attention away from the water and myself.

I walked slowly towards the source and found a young nymph bathing and singing a silly tune of love. An epiphany came to me suddenly. Her song was nothing of importance, but the sight of the nymph and her beautiful voice reminded me in a sharp emotion that I wasn't the only one who loved Kore. I wasn't the only one desperate to find her. I couldn't be.

My siblings didn't come to help me, but my daughter had three friends. Three beautiful singing friends, ones that didn't chase after her and might decide to help me. How could I not have thought of them? It was even possible that Kore was there. They lived so far away from humans that they might have not even heard the prayers.

I knew that these thoughts were wishful thinking, but I also felt certain that the next right place to go was to them. How much time could I have saved if I had thought of going to them first? How much anger, pain and anguish could I have escaped? I had spent all that time travelling and drowning in my sorrow when I should have gone in search of allies. I should have gone to find these three friends my daughter had. I should have gone to find those creatures who loved Kore. They were weaker than my siblings, and I had always looked down on them, always assumed they were not good for anything but breeding children to my brothers. But, despite their physical weakness, they loved Kore.

If all they lacked was strength, I realized as I gazed at the singing nymph, then this was easily remedied. If they had the will to assist me, I could give them claws, wings and weapons beyond imagination to find Kore.

I hurried towards the closest seashore because, always to my surprise, Kore made friends with sea creatures. What were their names? I searched my mind trying to remember the last time I had seen the daughters of Akheloios.

They were pretty girls. Three sisters. My daughter played their mistress in their early youth, and they submitted as her handmaidens, caring for her with honest affection. They never came to Olympus. We only saw them when we went to the shore they used to live by, but I knew if I called them, invoking their love for Kore and their promise to me to care for her, they would hear. If I spoke their names, they would come.

Their names. Their names. What were their names? I cursed myself for never respecting nymphs enough to take notice of them.

Peisonoe. Parthenope. Molpe.

Their names rang in my mind as I reached the sandy beach.

"Daughters of Akheloios! Peisonae, Parthenope and Molpe. Your friend is missing. Your mistress. Her Mother is calling you."

The sea kept calm. "Kore is missing!" I yelled again, and all the earth shook from the volume of my voice. "Come to my aid!"

I stared at the waves, fearing that I was wrong to believe in them. I was ready to forsake and curse them even before the first wave reached my feet. But I sensed them responding instantly, as if they had been waiting for me.

It didn't take them long to reach the shore. Before I was finished speaking the words a second time, the three girls walked out of the water. Their dresses clung around their skin, accentuating their bodies, and they stared at me with wide eyes, full of admiration and immediate recognition. I opened my hands and they rushed to me, hugging me, even though we had never been close.

Their wet clothes soaked my skin. Their hair dripped with sea water and their smell brought me pangs of fright as I remembered Poseidon and the assault he had inflicted upon me. I closed my eyes and held myself still, knowing that whatever the God of the Sea had done, whatever smell he shared with the three daughters of Akheloios, it wasn't their fault. Their water nature was something they couldn't control, as I couldn't control being the Daughter of Kronos and Rhea.

"She has been taken, stolen," I whispered in their ears, and they nodded.

"We heard, Goddess," Peisonae said. "And we heard of your sorrow, but we couldn't find you. We wanted to come to you, but you were too far gone, and nobody knew where you had been."

"We even asked your brother, our God of the Sea, but he said he couldn't tell us."

I bit my tongue to avoid saying anything about my youngest brother. "I am here now, and so are you."

They nodded. They were such pretty girls. The water on their skin made them sparkle like fish.

"We have searched all over the sea," Parthenope said. "We searched every shore, the deepest parts of the sea beds, in case she was there, and asked every fish and every other sea nymph or sea God. We explored all the sea forests."

"Whatever is left of them," her sister said, and I couldn't resist a slight stretch of my lips. My power had affected Poseidon's world.

"Nobody told us anything," Parthenope concluded.

I examined their beauty and their honest, sweet faces, so eager to help me. I was struck with guilt for never thinking highly of them. There was something honourable in the way they loved my child. The way they defied their physical weakness for the sake of love and devotion.

"Will you then fly for me?"

They looked puzzled and stared at each other.

"We cannot fly," Molpe said. "We don't have wings of our own or shoes with wings like the God Hermes."

I nodded. Of course, I could see their physical inability to fly as they currently were.

"I can give you wings. Would you fly for me then?"

They stared at each other. Silent sisterly conversations took place in that glance. I knew it because Hestia and I once used to be that close. Once, but not anymore. I was silent, waiting for their decision.

"Will it be just wings?" Peisonae finally asked.

"Do you wish for something more?"

"We want to be able to keep our voices, that's all. So, we can find each other again," Molpe said.

Their demand was simple. Nothing too difficult for me to give them. I lifted my hand and Peisonae, always the bravest of the three sisters, took it.

The moment our fingers touched, I sent my power towards her. I moved like a snake under her skin, feeling her own faint divinity, barely enough to keep her immortal, but present. Mine was a stallion against hers. I could squeeze it out of existence so easily. Instead, I remoulded hers and by doing that, I enhanced her powers and changed her body. Her mind merged with mine, and I heard as a whisper all her fear of men. The way that both Gods and mortals had raped cousins of hers, and how she dreaded this happening to her.

The change was painful. She cried as she fell on the ground, letting go of my hand. Two large eagle wings erupted from her back, growing brown feathers which then spread onto her lower body, giving her claws and bird-like feet.

Her sisters watched dazed as she changed, becoming a beautiful woman-bird hybrid.

She brought her hands to her throat and pressed there, letting out grunts. "My voice," she said, and it came out as the most melodic and powerful sound I had ever heard.

"Your voice is more beautiful than ever, sister," Molpe said.

"Your voice is not simply for singing anymore," I told her. "Your voice is a weapon. Use it as you please against any sailor that looks at you in a filthy way." She turned to me. "I saw inside you. The fear. This power, this new form, is all your choice. I only meant to give you wings."

She nodded slowly, understanding who she was, and I wondered if she had lived with that fear the same as I had lived with my monster. She turned to her sisters. "Will you join me?" she asked them.

Molpe walked towards me and offered her hand. I took hers, and the intrusion into her body began. She was similar to her sister. The same faint divinity. The same love for music. There was no fear of men like Peisonae, but rather a desire to remain the same as her sister, to stay exactly like her, forever identified as one.

That desire and love sparked her change, and I watched as the wings appeared on her body, and light brown, nearly golden, feathers spread all over her. She screamed too, crying and panting as she changed. Her voice grew stronger. Her divinity changed as she became a new kind of being, one that hadn't ever really existed until that moment.

She let out a humming sound and smiled as she herself realized her own new-found power. Parthenope watched with her lips slightly parted at the creatures her sisters had turned into. She hesitated to lift her hand.

When I touched hers, it wasn't love for her sisters or fear of men that I was eye to eye with, but the fear of being left behind. It was the fear of being ridiculed or suddenly alone. Her hand wanted to pull back, but fear of loneliness overcame her fear of change. She was quiet as I let the change begin.

Prettier wings erupted from her body, and Parthenope remained more woman than bird. She took from what I offered the bare minimum, so she could stand by her sisters but also stay as much the same as possible. She wept without making a sound. Once her change finished, she stood, and her sisters came closer to her.

I caressed each of their faces, blessing them for agreeing to help me.

"Beautiful girls," I praised them. "You have the power of the most enchanting voices. Sing the tale of a lost daughter. Sing of my sorrow and fly around the world, telling any human, God, Nymph, Hero, demi-God—anyone—to find me if they have heard of anything related to Kore."

"We will," Peisonae promised. Always the leader of the three sisters, she flapped her wings and ascended to the skies first. Molpe followed her example.

Parthenope stood on the shore with me as she watched her sisters fly away. I put my hand over her shoulder, and she turned to face me.

"Your voice is powerful now. You are not nymphs anymore, but something different. I name your new being as the Seirenes. Choose whether you become heroes or monsters. You have the power to be something more than simply nymphs."

She turned to her flying sisters' vanishing forms. "Why tell only me?" she asked.

"Because you are the one that is the most nymph still. You fought the change. Are you sure you want to help me?"

The youngest siren looked at her sisters again and nodded. "Kore was kind to me. She treated us with respect, unlike so many other Olympian children. I want her found."

With these words, she flapped her wings and flew towards her sisters. I watched them as they experimented with their new wings, learning how to move in the air, and then I heard their beautiful voices. They began singing in loud, prolonged notes, and slowly their singing turned into words. They were singing of me and for me, and even I, who knew of the danger of their honey-like magnetism, felt their power.

Once they became small dots on the horizon, I knew the second ally I needed to find. The only other true friend Kore had. Even though the young boy who used to play with Kore in Boiotia was dead, Trophonius had retained his memories and affection when he became a daimon. I knew that because we had met the oracle spirit in Livadeia, where his transformation took place, and his eyes, despite having lost the spirited glance of his humanity, showed warmth when he last saw me and Kore. My daughter had worried for him and wanted to see him when we learnt of his fate. He didn't see her any differently than his playmate and she didn't mistrust his new deathly nature so even as a daimon, he remained her true friend.

I began travelling towards Central Greece. My plan with the Seirenes worked. Not long after they began their journey and singing of my quest, I started hearing it repeated. Every detail of my quest and my pain was known to all of Greece a few days after I left the seashore.

The humans were kind to me. I was treated with hospitality in all the villages and cities I stopped at, offered food and drink even from the poorest families. It wasn't only hospitality and kindness I experienced though. The humans, who had always loved me because I gave them a happy life, after the starvation they had endured, seemed to fight to win my favour. I had seen these behaviours towards other Gods, but I had never been the receptor of that glorified fear. The prayers to me increased, filled with more adjectives to describe my power. I wasn't only a Goddess of Harvest anymore. I was a Goddess that had the power of life and death over the whole world. Somehow that ability, which I had always possessed but never exercised, lifted me to a Great Goddess, a powerful entity that needed to be begged for her favour, offered feasts and boundless love.

On my behalf, humans prayed and sacrificed to all the other Gods for my daughter to be returned to me. My pain was the story everyone knew, everyone feared, and everyone understood. I didn't have any proof, but I suspected the humans understood there was a schism between me and the rest of Olympus and, although they didn't actively say it, they had chosen me over them. They had chosen to fight for me instead of against me.

I imagined Zeus suffered at the attention I stole from him. I could picture my littlest brother writhing in annoyance that although his plan to get me out of the cave worked, I remained a big thorn in his side. However, his pride forbade him from finding me. His pride forbade him to let any of his children or our siblings come to find me. But soon, I imagined even that would change as the tension in Olympus and the prayers demanding to help me increased inside the temples of all the other Gods, Olympians and Titans alike.

I wondered if even Hades might exit his Underworld kingdom because of it. The starvation and death I caused would lead to a massive workload for him, filling his kingdom with millions of souls.

I was on the outskirts of Argos, in the North of the Peloponnese, and was thirsty. I was very used to kindness and love by that time, that fearful glory offered to me by every house whose door I knocked on. I approached a small straw hut. I opened the small gate and walked inside the garden, admiring the pretty flowers, and how well cared for they were, a testament to the owner who helped them grow so strong with the tiny scraps of life I allowed in the soil. It was clearly a house that wasn't stingy with its kindness. I approached the door and knocked.

Slow steps reached my ears and a few moments later, the door opened, and I saw an old woman standing in front of me. She was frail, and her legs trembled as she held onto a wooden stick to stand. She lifted her eyes towards me, and I wondered how well she was able to see.

"I am thirsty," I announced.

Whether the old woman knew who I was, she didn't say. She only turned around and walked back inside her house, leaving the door open for me. I entered the hut, taking note of the floor bed and the small fire. Hestia came to my mind as I watched the tiny flame. The hearth, the home.

My eyes moved to the small figure of the woman as she brought me a small flask and handed it to me.

I examined it carefully, unsure what kind of drink it had inside. I was about to smell it when the door opened again and a little boy, no more than fourteen, entered. His hair was curly and wild around his head, and his body had clear signs of malnourishment. This was a poor house I had entered; I knew it.

"Who are you?" the youth asked me. I wondered whether he realized that I was the Goddess Demeter.

"She is a guest, Ascalabus." The old woman spoke for the first time. "A thirsty guest in need of our hospitality."

The youth snorted and walked inside the house. "We are on the verge of death, and you give the few things we have to strangers?" He turned to me and crossed his arms. "Well, take a sip and go."

I didn't like his attitude, and I was certain he had no idea who I was. He would not behave as he did if he knew. I brought the flask to my mouth and drank the flower infused water the old woman offered. It was tasty, made from the flowers in the garden. The love and care were evident in the taste and fragrance of the liquid. I enjoyed it and drank it all, gulping it down as it refreshed and restored my energy.

Before I was ready to return the flask to the old woman, my eyes caught the gaze of the youth. His eyes were wide open, his eyebrows raised, his mouth opened and terrible words came out. "You drank all of it?!" he exclaimed. "All of it! We have none left now!"

"Ascalabus, that's no way to speak to a guest," the old woman scolded.

"The guest ought to leave something for the host," the youth retorted. "She drank all of it and we have none left!"

My hands tightened against the flask. All his people begged for my favour, all of humanity was supposed to have learnt I was not to be mocked and ridiculed. That I was not the Goddess that they could always depend on. That I had the power and the will to be someone they had to respect, they had to fear and whose favour they had to compete to win.

"Do you know who I am, boy?" I asked the child, giving him one chance to win my forgiveness.

"You are the one who has made us hungry," Ascalabus said.

"Now, now," the old woman tried to interfere again.

"No!" Ascalabus shouted. "Our crops are failing. Our trees make fruit we cannot eat. It is all her fault."

"Our guest has suffered," the old woman tried again to reason with the child. "Apologize like a good boy."

"No!"

"He is not a good boy," I said and turned to face the youth. I lifted my hand and the teen stayed still as I approached. "He lacks hospitality. My brother, the King of Olympus, believes that to be the highest value."

The boy snorted and I watched how his mother—or grandmother—tried to stop him. At no point did she beg me to show mercy. She only spoke to the boy on my behalf as I watched his tantrum progress.

"I don't care," Ascalabus repeated. "I am hungry, I am thirsty, and she didn't leave any for us."

I could give them food. I could make their trees offer them fruit and their vegetables grow and ensure they had sustenance for an entire year. I watched the child and wondered why his rage was even allowed to exist. Did he believe that my thirst and his were one and the same? Did he imagine that his needs, his short life, had anything to compare with mine? Me, who had lost my child? Me, who had been denied the sun and the world from the moment I was born? How did this cheeky, rude boy dare to think that he had the right to feel anger towards me?!

"Well, then, let me help you, child," I said, and my voice came out cold. I put my hand on his shoulder before he had the chance to move or respond, and let my anger seep inside him. A tail tore his pants, and he screamed as he felt it move. Then his hair shed, and his skin began to change, becoming red and bumpy. His face elongated and his eyes transformed into those of a lizard. His rude tongue stuck out and split at the edge and then, with one last push of my divinity, he began to shrink until he was so small that he was resting on my palm. "Now, the world will have plenty of food for you, as a lizard though."

I turned my hand and let the small creature fall and land on its legs as it crawled towards the old woman. She stood still and stared at the lizard, the young boy she once had. "Your trees will always have plenty of food," I promised her. "For you and your new pet."

She fell on her knees. Ascalabus jumped on her, climbing to her shoulder, resting there. He hid under her clothes, terrified of how big and grand the world had become to him.

"If anybody asks," I began speaking slowly, "tell them that Demeter doesn't take well to humans insulting her grief or her hard journey."

The old woman held her mouth closed. Her hand was on the small bump over her shoulder, where the new lizard was resting. I let the flask fall on the floor and then exited the hut. I walked around the small garden, ensuring that, as I promised, the duo would have food. They would have the most food in the area, perhaps.

My work was repetitive. The labour offered me a beautiful feeling of tiredness, and by the time I finished, I was calm again. With that feeling of peace came the realization of what I had truly done. I had taken the child of another creature. She would never get the youth back, even if the lizard lived with her all its life. Ascalabus would soon even forget he once was a human and would abandon her and even start to fear her. I paused and stared at the half open door. I could go and reverse it. Apologize for the mistake.

But then what? There would be the story of how I fixed things. How my anger and my wrath were temporary and could be waited out. I could swear her to secrecy, to never speak of me but the child wouldn't keep his mouth shut.

I could fix it.

The old woman never came out of the hut. I never heard her utter a word and, I never went inside it again.

For the rest of the journey, I decided to keep away from humans for the most part. I even hid my divinity, walking without anyone noticing me much amid the smaller roads as I made my way to Boiotia to find Trophonius. I still heard my story being told but my epithets changed slowly. I was no longer simply the Corn mother. Humans didn't only pray on my behalf to other Gods. I heard them call me Carpophori, the fruit bringer, Potnia, the mistress, Aganippe, the Nightmare but also Erinys, the Fury and Brimo, the angry and terrifying.

The change shocked me and through these newly received epithets and titles, I had less love from humans but more respect. They prayed harder. They didn't simply pity me and fear for their lives. They feared me, and that fear wasn't only about food and survival. It was a deep fear of the entity of me. I was no more the mother that mourned and for that reason wasn't all giving. I was, as they called me, the Thesmophoros, a legislator of right and wrong, and they had to obey the laws I imposed on the world they occupied.

The faith around me was changing. Whatever kind of Goddess I used to be was no more, and I realized that the Goddess I once was would never walk upon this land again. Not even when I had Kore back to fill my heart with love, beauty and life again. To bring forth a revival in me and thus a regeneration to the rest of the world. I looked up at the sky. Why couldn't my siblings come to my aid? Why did they let me change so much? Who did they want me to be before they would consider me important enough to help?

It took a few more days before I reached Trophonius's residence. Ever since he had changed into a dark and chthonic spirit, he'd lived in a grove close to Leibadeia. I walked slowly amid the trees and all life moved away from me. The closer I got to the river stream, Herkyna, which cut through the small woodland, the darker the energy became. I felt chills of death as I approached his famous oracle region. I knew he would be sitting by the dark waters of the river, on a rock, staring with his odd eyes at the waters, seeing in the reflection of the light visions of the future.

I could hear the water now. The way it clashed against the small rocks, and the sound of its small waterfall close by. I was not far from the riverbank when I heard the barking of a dog.

"Is that you, Herkyna?"

The dog barked again, and I heard its running steps. Four legs which eventually turned into two, and amid the trees the young naiad appeared. Her sharp, dark eyes stared right into me.

"I am sorry for your loss," Herkyna said. The naiad born in the waters of the stream with which she shared her name had been another childhood playmate of Kore, alongside Trophonius when he was still mortal. I had guessed that the guard dog of the area would have stayed close to the son of Apollo.

I nodded and looked around the stream. "Is Trophonius here?"

Herkyna ignored my question and approached me. "I am very saddened by what happened to Kore. I hope she is found soon."

"I am here to ask Trophonius about it," I said again, trying to avoid the painful reminiscence of Kore.

Herkyna waved at me to follow her. We walked slowly next to the river. Wild dogs ran around the naiad, who transformed into a dog again and played with the other animals. We reached a small waterfall where I saw the flickering dark shape of Trophonius as the waters fell on his body. The mystical odd entity he had become. Herkyna ran to him, changing back to her humanoid form, and sat in the water by his legs. She rested her head on his knee and the daimon put his hand on her hair, playing with its strands and letting the water soak them slowly.

"Mother of my childhood friend. We were waiting for you to share in your pain for the loss of our beautiful friend."

"She has changed, beloved Father," Herkyna said. My interest piqued at the term.

"Father?" I asked, surprised. "Do not try to fool me, children. I was here when you were both growing up. I nursed you Trophonius, in your human life."

"Herkyna is my daughter. The world is a strange place, Mother of Kore, and sometimes a father and daughter are raised together until they settle into their rightful roles. I needed to change to a daimon to understand I was her father and for Herkyna to realize why she never knew any parents."

Time loops and mysteries weren't common, but I had no interest in examining the oddity of their relationship.

"Father and daughter then," I accepted, and my eyes narrowed at Trophonius again. "I know that after you cut your brother's head, you were lost in the Underworld. And when your body was found again, you were no more a human. I have only seen you once since then, because of the hunger you brought to free yourself. But I remember that despite the changes that occurred, you still loved my daughter. You remembered your childhood with her. Is that still true?"

Trophonius nodded. "We always remember your daughter. My descent in the Underworld was always linked with her future."

I hated oracles for never speaking with clear words. Always speaking double sided and uttering misunderstandings that somehow always came true but never warned of the future. I had no patience for any of the oracle games.

"I am here to ask for your help to find her."

Trophonius lowered his body and kissed Herkyna's head. "Your daughter and my daughter and I played together here. There was a goose incident, wasn't there, Herkyna?"

The naiad nodded. "Yes, we chased a goose and it got stuck amid some rocks. Oh, the poor bugger fought himself as we tried to free it. It refused to obey us and calm down. We kept trying. Kore had to lift the rock above it to free the bird and that was the beginning of the river, named after me."

Another time inconsistency. I remembered that the river was there from before we had met Herkyna and Trophonius, but whatever had happened to him had changed Herkyna as well, changing her identity without her knowledge, or understanding, even. I tried to think who her parents were, how I had met the naiad, but no matter how hard I tried, I came up blank. I only knew that Herkyna and Trophonius had played with my child when they were little. All three of them had been children at the same time, although I couldn't remember them playing together. Kore played with each of them as a child, when they were both children as well. And the river had been close to Leibadeia then, too. Something dark and mysterious had happened in the grove; the same energy that changed Trophonius into a daimon, had changed Herkyna's memories and identity, making her a daughter of the chthonic creature and birthing a false creation myth.

"So will you help me?" I asked them, ignoring the confusion behind their new state and narrative.

Trophonius stood and walked from the small waterfall. His body dripped water and he stared at me without seeing me. Flashes of dark shadows ran through his eyes, turning his flickering daimon body less human as his face further changed.

"You will see your daughter again," he spoke. "And there are more friends of your child who wish to help you. You should stay still and let them come to you."

I tried to think who else was a true friend to Kore but there was none.

"Where should I wait?"

"Anywhere," Trophonius answered. "Even here, if you want. The moment you stop searching will be the beginning of the end of your struggle."

Staying still had never been my plan. Waiting for someone to find me was something I felt my body refuse to do. "Will it take long?"

Trophonius turned to Herkyna, who turned into a dog again. "Just sit still and the help you need, a witness to your daughter's loss, will come forward. Anywhere you like. The place doesn't matter. Only the stillness."

I watched as he flickered, and Herkyna played by his side. The two began walking through the river and I sat at its edge, gazing at the dark waters. Sometime later, Trophonius returned alone and sat again under the falling water, letting his mind delve into the depths of his daimon state. I watched him, unable to keep my mind at rest. I had to stay still. The stillness was all that mattered, he had said. My whole body fought my mind. It wanted to move, to attempt to fight this terrible wait, the injustice of not knowing.

But each time I looked at Trophonius, I remembered his advice. I had walked. I had travelled to so many places without any leads. I had sent messengers all over Greece to find information for my daughter. Perhaps the daimon oracle was right. All that was left was to wait for information, to learn more about what happened to my daughter.

I tried to speak to Kore's old friend. I tried to ask him about his new life, if he visited the Underworld, if he could pass my regards to my brother down there, but he never responded. Only when I mentioned Kore, reminiscing to myself of my lost child, did he wake up and speak. Sometimes, he narrated stories of him and Kore, their games in this very land and the laughter they shared. At those moments, he seemed like a human, but they were fleeting.

Other times, he spoke in nonsensical riddles. "You will see your first-born daughter but never Kore again," he would chant.

"What do you mean by that?" I would interrupt his chanting, but he would never elaborate.

"Never Kore again. Never again," he chanted, and I was too tired to ask anymore.

We went through these cycles of silence, reminiscence, and madness for nine days and nine nights. During that period, Herkyna never appeared again. I never even heard her bark in the forest. On the eve of the ninth day, the sound of two dogs running in the water was heard.

I lifted my head and saw a dark brown hound running next to Herkyna's grey she-dog form. The brown dog continued running towards me as Herkyna headed towards Trophonius. The brown-haired animal placed its face on my lap.

"We should go for a walk, Father," Herkyna said to Trophonius, who stood up. "Leave them to talk."

Before I was able to question what she meant, the dog in between my legs started shifting into a woman. The Goddess Hekate was settled in between my legs. Her age was evident in her face and the gleaming of her eyes. We had once been enemies with the daughter of Perses, the Titan of destruction, and Asteria, a Titaness of the falling stars. Her family had joined mine at the end of the war, avoiding the pain of imprisonment on Tartarus. I watched her face as her eyes studied mine.

Her divinity was so different from mine when it reached me, in that manner I used to do with my sisters and brothers while we were in Father's stomach. I was struck by the intimate gesture. She was powerful, and faith around her was still strong, despite her not being one of the main Olympian Gods. Her power was dark and warm like mine. There was kindness in Hekate, but her links with the Underworld were always smouldering, as if she was made of a fire that made one cold instead of warm. The Goddess of Witchcraft, of Magic, of the Moon, of Ghosts and Necromancy. She was the abnormal unity of life and death, of the tenuous space those two states linked with each other.

Trophonius and Herkyna had disappeared. I was all alone with the Titaness.

"I don't know much," she began telling me.

"Anything!" The words came out of my mouth like a river themselves.

She sat with her legs in a basket next to me and rested her palms on her knees. "Someone took her," Hekate said.

"What?" I had never imagined anyone could be behind my loss. I had thought my daughter was magically lost, not abducted. "Did you see who?"

Hekate shook her head. "No, Demeter," she answered using my name with ease. She was my inferior in the order of the world. My pride ought to have risen in anger. I should have struck her, but she was there to help me, and Hekate wasn't a nymph. She was a Titan, daughter of Titans and old, older than me. My family might rule Greece after her own fell, but she was no child for me to scold.

And she had come to my rescue.

"I only heard her cries from my cave. I didn't think much of it at first. One often hears of female screams in the forest or by the sea, you know that like I do. You have always been very kind, Demeter. And a hard worker, much harder than most of your siblings. I have heard how labouredly you cared for all plants and all life in the soil. You don't deserve to have your child stolen."

"If you didn't see her, how can you know she was taken?" I asked.

She lifted her eyes to me and smiled weakly. "You know how. Because a girl's screams as she knows that she is losing her mother's protection and her innocence, is a sound that stays the same no matter the species. And I recognized the spot when I met one of the Seirenes and she told me your story, giving me all the details of the place and time of your misery."

I stood up and ran my hand over my hair. Taken. Abducted. Who had dared to steal my child from me? Who could hate me that much? Who could I have ever hurt like that? My mind kept searching for a culprit but came up blank each time.

I had never participated in the grudges that my brothers liked to insert themselves into. I rarely—if ever—got involved in human affairs or took sides. It made no sense that my child was stolen, but Kore's disappearance made no sense. It never did. My eyes landed on Hekate again.

Could she be lying to me? But there was no straight answer to this question either. Why would she?

Could this be a slight to start another war between Olympians and Titans? That thought had some basis. If that was the case, then Zeus was supposed to react as well. His complete absence from my quest made me doubt Kore's abduction had anything to do with a war declaration. If Kore was taken by a Titan, Zeus would know, and he would have intervened.

Zeus would know. My eyes widened as the thought formed in my mind. I brought my hand over my mouth, ready to let out a life crashing scream and wave of death as the realization took shape.

"He would have seen," I told myself. I lifted my gaze to the sky.

He was the God of the sky; he would have seen. He would have heard. This meant that Kore was taken by someone Zeus either feared and so he'd chosen to ignore the insult, or he had agreed to her abduction. My thoughts swirled because I didn't want to believe that Zeus would have gifted my daughter to someone without asking me, without even telling me.

But I also knew he would never allow an insult to damage his power. He would have waged war if someone had stolen our child without his consent. Not out of love, of course, but out of pride. That same pride was the reason he wouldn't have asked me. I remembered his wounded, hateful gaze when I rejected him after our one and only mating. How he had despised me because I denied him my love and complete subservience!

The more I thought of the situation, the more plausible it seemed that Zeus had agreed to it. It would be why he stayed away from me, keeping any of our close family from coming to my rescue.

"Hekate," I called, and the other Goddess looked at me with caution but without fear.

"Yes, Demeter?"

"If you heard my daughter, someone must have seen what happened to her. Someone that is always in the sky during the day."

Her eyes narrowed in confusion. I stared at her and wondered if she thought of asking my brother, but then they widened. Perhaps, like me, she had come to the same conclusion. Zeus was aware of everything but there was another deity, one who would talk to me if I was accompanied by another important Goddess like Hekate.

"Helios," she muttered.

"Yes," I confirmed. "Helios will have seen it. And you will take me to him!" I ordered and wondered whether she would accept this behaviour from me. She weighed her options, judged me, and we stood facing each other.

"OK," she finally conceded. She stood, water slightly dripping from her dress, and walked to the closest tree, snapping off two branches. She banged them together and holy flames burst on each of the two wood sticks. "If we are at the top of that mountain before his journey, he will see us, and you can call him to you."

I looked at the area. Boiotia was part of Greece, whose mainland characteristic was its mountainscapes. I followed her pointed finger and recognized the dark form her flame illuminated. Mount Helicon.

"We need to get going then," I said, and she walked ahead of me, illuminating the path with her flames, but also sending a warning to all life around that we were not to be disturbed. We walked fast, faster than any human could imagine, and before the middle of the night, we were nearly at the mountain top. A human would have needed at least four hours from Leibadia to reach the bottom of the mountain, but our feet moved the space itself, as nothing could stop me from learning of my daughter's abductor.

Not even a rock dared to be placed in the wrong space and delay us. Instead, all of nature, every tree, all the soil, worked to make our ascent easier, until we reached the peak minutes before sunrise. I turned to Hekate. On our way up, she had changed and wore her characteristic star crown, with its point and sharp edges framing her black hair.

"Why are you helping me?"

She turned to me, surprised. "Why shouldn't I?"

I had no interest in games, but Hekate didn't seem to play any against me. I had never known her to be a trickster. If she was, that myth of her character had never reached my ears.

"You get involved in Olympian politics, taking a side. And specifically, my side."

She handed me one of her torches to hold. "I am helping a mother whose tale of sorrow reached the depths of my being. I am helping every animal, every plant that needs you to survive. Like all other Gods, all prayers that reach me are of how much this plague upon the soil cannot continue. It is far bigger than Olympian politics."

She lifted the torch high, and I did the same. We saw Helios appear. His chariot was driven by his gorgeous, gold horses. Colours filled the world, and the sight was beautiful.

"Your side, Demeter, is the only one any Titan or God can take. Going against you means going against life itself."

"I am sorry," I told her, and meant it.

"Don't be," Hekate answered. "What other choice was left to you? If no one comes to your aid, you need to find a way to force them. I am the Goddess of crossroads and ghosts, Demeter. I know hard choices when I see them, and I know what resentment does to a being, especially one as powerful as an Olympian Goddess."

I was touched by her words. I had received pity for my pain before, which allowed understanding for the destruction I had brought upon all of Greece, but never before had I received support in my fight to get my daughter back. Hekate's words strengthened my resolve to learn the truth, to see this journey to its end and accept all the consequences it brought onto me. It was a crossroad, and it wasn't only mine. I had been misunderstood, devalued and insulted. I wouldn't stand for it. What self-respecting creature would choose to bow their head against such maltreatment? It was a choice, and I had made it and planned to see it through until its very end.

"HELIOS!" I called the Titan. His face moved towards the top of the mountain, and he nudged his chariot to turn. His light was sharp, even for my eyes, but I was strong and could face him directly. I gave the torch back to Hekate and then walked ahead as Helios landed on the rocky top and stepped out of his chariot.

"Goddess of the Harvest," he greeted me. "It is so nice to see you."

I had to endure his pleasantries, reminding myself that he wasn't a nymph I could cower into submission to get what I wanted faster. I nodded and smiled at him. "Your horses are as beautiful as ever."

He looked at them and smiled, his affection for the animals clear on his face. "Yes, but they are thin. Even for them, food is scarce."

That was a dig at me, and I welcomed it, allowing me to open the conversation I wanted to hear. "You know what has happened to me, don't you?"

His face lowered and he nodded. "I don't think there is anyone in Greece who hasn't heard. Your bird women have done a good job."

I owed a big debt to the Seirenes for their help. With their singing, they had managed to pass my message to all of creation.

I crossed my arms. "Hekate told me something interesting. I was wondering if you might help me verify it."

His eyes darted to the other Goddess. He was older than both of us, the son of Hyperion and Theia, both of whom were children of Gaia and Uranus.

"You are called Helios Panoptes, for you are able to see all during the day," Hekate said.

"I do see all," he admitted, forced by his ego to not devalue his importance and power.

"I told the Goddess of the Harvest that I heard her daughter's screams, that she was taken by someone." Hekate spoke softly, her eyes fixed on the other Titan.

Helios turned and looked at his horses. His whole body shone bright as he gazed at Boiotia. Even from a distance, the lack of my attention over the world was clear. There were sickly trees that didn't bloom, there were trees whose fruit never grew enough to be eaten. His horses were beautiful and strong, but so clearly in need of better nutrition.

"Well?" I pressured him.

His shoulders lowered slowly. "I know who took her." He didn't turn to face me as he spoke. He folded his arms and kept staring away, as if he wanted to distance himself from me and the effects of the revelation of his words.

"Who?!" I demanded. "Where is my child?"

"I have seen so much recently. So much pain, so much anguish. Everywhere I look, life is ridiculed. This world my family created has reached a disgusting and humiliating state. All because of a mother's grief."

"Who took her, Helios? A mother needs to know where her child is!"

He turned slightly to look at me. He pitied me. He feared me. I didn't care, I needed to know.

"Hades," he said, and my whole body went cold at the mention of my third brother. "He took her into the Underworld."

I shook my head, unwilling to believe him. I didn't want to think that my brother, who had been in the darkness with me, who had held my hand and calmed me so often in our childhood, had done this to me. Why? Why? How could he? I couldn't stop myself from trembling. My power was ready to escape my mouth, to turn into a scream which would destroy the entire world, but I held my jaw shut.

The Moirais' words came to my mind. Kore's return was going to be a negotiation.

"Thank you," I said to him. "Thank you for telling me." My voice came out soft and calm, as if there wasn't a rage that was spilling over, gathering like poison in my mouth.

My child, my girl, my guiding light was trapped in darkness. My brother had taken her there. Zeus had allowed her to be trapped in that darkness as I had been. Her own father made her a prisoner, as mine had done to me. She was denied light, the world, life and suffered who else knew what kind of injustices and cruelty. I didn't want to think my brother would hurt her. I didn't want to imagine the ways

IOANNA PAPADOPOULOU

he could change her. Flashes of Poseidon as a stallion came to my mind and I shook.

She was all alone in that darkness, that void of everything.

"Hekate?" I called the Goddess next to me.

"Yes?"

"As the Goddess of ghosts and necromancy, you can enter my brother's realm, right?"

Hekate nodded slowly. Hades's dark and cold world could only be entered by Gods and Goddess whose powers were linked with the dead.

"Please go to my child," I begged her. "Please go and be with her, as a friend. She is all alone down there!"

I tried to think which other Gods might know. Trophonius might be able. Perhaps he knew already and couldn't tell me. Hermes would be able to, but I doubted he would help me. The Erinyes would also be able to travel down there, but I didn't really know them. Nyx, the Goddess of Night. All the dark and brooding creatures I had avoided were the ones that had access to my child.

"Go, please!" I begged again. "She needs to have someone by her side, a friend. Someone that isn't just dark, cold and chthonic."

Hekate nodded. "Yes, I can do that," she said.

My eyes turned to Helios who had remained still like a stone as I spoke.

"Thank you, Helios. I owe you a debt for this kindness," I said, and without waiting for another word, I started running down Helicon. Like when I had climbed it with Hekate, nothing stopped me, but eventually everything was too much and too hard and I found my body changing. I was no

166

longer humanoid but a serpent. I crawled around the stones, feeling the soil under me drain from all life.

When I reached the bottom of the mountain, I turned back into a human, this time taking the form of a very old woman, dressed in black. My skin and entire body was covered in wrinkles and scars of life. I wrapped a dark shawl over my grey-brown hair and began walking again. With every step, I sucked back all the life I had given in the soil. This time it was not pain I couldn't control, nor lack of care. It was a clear decision that was sharply made. If my daughter was not to enjoy this world, to see it bright, colourful and blooming, then no one was going to.

WINTER

This time, my journey wasn't an aimless wandering. Though Kore wasn't anywhere I could reach, I knew exactly where my next destination ought to be. The next allies I needed to find, the ones who had always been by my side since their eggs hatched.

I found them at the location where my misery began, at the shore where Kore was abducted. I saw them basking under the sun, tired looking and hungry, and I was hurt by the hardships I had caused them. They were innocent and I loved them; after Kore and Hestia, they were my closest friends. I rushed to my serpents, even though ideas of fairness had no place alongside my motherly ache, and hugged them tightly, feeling relieved I was amid creatures who loved me, and I could hold onto and depend on.

"We will get her back," I promised, and they rubbed their bodies against mine. "I am sorry I left you alone for so long. I am so sorry."

My beautiful creatures didn't hold any grudges against me. They understood me without needing any explanation. They showed me all their affection with the same eagerness I was used to. I caressed their bodies, my hands frantically traced their scales, and I rocked my body around as they encircled me and kept me safe under their wings. They covered me completely, hiding me from Zeus's gaze. Within that small cocoon of their wings and scales, I planned how I was going to fight for my child.

It will be an ultimatum, I decided. I don't care if this causes a rift between Zeus and Hades. I don't care if it starts a new war or makes me a monster in everyone's eyes. I don't care about the cost. They will come to me. I will not go begging. I will not go and accuse. I will find a place and stay still there, waiting for them to realize they need to come and beg me to stop. And when Zeus is forced to come and see me, to look me in the eye and admit how he disrespected me, and promises to bring back Kore, then I will only allow the barest of life to come back.

"I want her back," I whispered to my flying serpents. "I don't care for anything other than to get her back in my arms."

These words became my mantra, my chant, and I whispered them in the hug of my beautiful animals as I took back everything, not leaving a single breath of life left in the soil. They tightened their grip around me, which would have choked a lesser creature, but I felt comforted by the tension of their bodies around me.

"Everything will starve," I muttered. "Everything will be death and darkness. If my child is to live in the Underworld, then all the world will be the realm of death." Nothing else matters but that they learn they cannot disrespect me anymore. They cannot ignore me anymore. They all need to understand that I will never stop. Zeus could make Chaos, Gaia, even Tartarus come to stop me, and I will never give in. This was a fight to the death, one where there were only two options, and the choice was all Zeus's.

If my daughter stayed in the Underworld, then I would kill everything, so I could become, by force, a Goddess of Death and gain passage to the Underworld. Then I would walk down there and face her abductor so I could take her back myself. That idea soothed me. It gave me an ultimate, desperate plan which ensured I would see my girl again. Even if the cost was dire, and I had to become the one to bring the end of the world.

There was a loud snap of wings and my serpents hissed all around me. A visitor, I realized, and I moved my head through my serpent's feathers to peek at the intruder. The sight of two manly feet wearing flying sandals confirmed his identity.

I softly nudged my serpents to lift their wings so I could leave our embrace. My eyes widened at their sight. Their scales had lost their shine and their eyes betrayed their tiredness, their hunger, and how close my beautiful beasts were to starvation. I had to feed them. I had to make sure those that were on my side lived. I couldn't let my animals die. But I also couldn't show that kindness in front of Hermes, who was surely sent by Zeus.

I caressed their heads, staring into their eyes and promising them with that look that I wouldn't let them die. They had no need to fear the consequences I would bring. Even in my ultimate plan, they would change with me, becoming chthonic creatures with me, and survive the end of life of all the rest.

"Father wants you to come to Olympus, Demeter," Hermes said once he realized I wasn't going to speak to him. "This issue needs to be resolved."

I stared at the messenger God and crossed my arms. "No," I said firmly. "He can come to me, and we can resolve this. Given that he started it."

Hermes's face contorted in anger, but he didn't say anything. He had been given clear instructions of what was to happen, and he hated me for making it all so hard.

"The world is dying because you are lazy and unwilling to do your duty," he reprimanded me. "Everyone is very disappointed with your behaviour."

I smiled at his words. "Everyone is disappointed that I didn't simply take the insult, am I right? That I didn't bow my head to Zeus?"

I watched as Hermes's fists tightened at my words. He glared at me with anger and perhaps even hatred. I crossed my arms and leaned against my serpents.

"What do you have to gain by doing this?" he asked, trying to speak as if he wanted to reason with me. He half spat the words, half asked me.

"I have only ever wanted one thing, nephew," I said, and I saw how, just like his father, he hated when I reminded him of my superiority in our family. "I want my daughter back. And I now know where she is. I assume you do as well. You have known for a long time now, given that you escort the souls down to the Underworld."

His eyes didn't meet mine. The answer was simple. He knew it as everyone did. There was only one thing I wanted.

"She is married now," he said to me in a whisper. "And I think she is happy with Hades."

"She was abducted," I spat the words out. "She didn't run away with Hades or agree to marry him. I didn't dress her as a bride or prepare her for marriage. I didn't speak to her as a mother does to a daughter so I could offer my blessing as she started her own family. So, allow me to question whether she is happy. If she comes out and tells me herself she wants to stay down there, I will stop."

If I could be reunited with her, I would be able to stay with her forever, never losing her from my sight.

"She is the Queen of the Underworld. She cannot just go in and out of her husband's realm."

I let out a snort at his pathetic excuse. "A Queen who cannot do as she pleases, cannot even visit her own mother. Now that sounds like a captor, wouldn't you say, nephew?"

His face contorted again at the term that described my higher rank. "I am not at liberty to make these decisions," Hermes finally said. "Father ordered me to take you up to Olympus. That is my task."

I shrugged. "That is not my problem, Hermes. I think it is yours."

He scanned the nearby area. I noticed then what had happened because of my sucking of all life. There was not a speck of green. The trees were scraggly dark branches and weak. Their brown barks had spots of diseases and mould over them. They were thirsty and starving themselves, barely alive.

"If you don't stop, soon it will be the point of no return," Hermes warned me. "Is that what you want? For your child to have no world to return to?"

"This is the only way for Zeus to understand he has no choice but to give her back to me. The only way for him to understand that this stunt cannot be repeated."

Hermes approached me and examined my face. "He is the King of the Sky, of Olympus. He can do whatever he wants," he whispered.

"Not this," I said firmly. "And when you go back up to Olympus, tell him that should he not hurry, all of life will be dead and then the strongest God will not be that of the Sky and Olympus, but Hades in his Underworld. And my daughter will be the most powerful Queen."

His eyes widened at what I insinuated, the length that I promised to take things.

"I was ordered to not return without you," Hermes repeated, and his eyes became those of a boy's begging for my help.

"Then stay down here with me. Take my side," I told him, and his body froze at the prospect. He shook his head and took steps back.

"I cannot turn against Father," he said, and he sounded sincere in his declaration.

"Why not?" I dared him further. "Zeus turned against Kronos, his father. Kronos against Ouranos. We come from a family of sons turning against their fathers."

He shook his head, as if it was filled with terrible thoughts he wanted to escape. I stood and approached him.

"You could be the new king, Hermes. Don't tell me you wouldn't want such a thing?"

Hermes shook his head, unwilling to meet my gaze, and then finally turned his back on me. "You will not come."

"I will not," I answered, even though his words weren't posed as a question.

He trembled. I saw how his back rose up and down in thought and his feet couldn't stand still, unsure whether he ought to face me again or run away.

"He will be so angry with you," he threatened. "He is already so angry. Nobody can talk to him. Not even Hera can calm him."

I let out a throaty laugh. "My sister could never calm him, Hermes. Their marriage is not of that kind." I laughed at the idea that Hera could have been the one to mediate her husband's rage. "And he should be afraid, not angry. He is the one who caused all this. The choice is his, not mine. Either my daughter returns and all is restored. Or all die, and he is the King of an empty world."

"He will never forgive you for this," Hermes said, and without another word, jumped up and let his flying sandals take him away. I watched as he flew away, wondering whether he would avoid Olympus for a while, but I saw him going straight to his father.

I wondered whether he would mention my offer for Kingship, for overthrowing Zeus. Despite the danger such a proposal represented, I wasn't afraid. Hermes was smart enough to know if he said such a thing, then Zeus would always look at him and his brothers with suspicion. It was no secret that when he heard the prophecy that Metis's child would be more powerful than him, he ate her whole to stop it coming true, birthing Athena himself by cracking his arrogant head open. And Athena was his favourite child. Hermes knew that and wouldn't risk his freedom, I was sure.

I slowly turned to my serpents, remembering my obligation to feed them. I needed them to survive, but my animals were carnivores, and I was the Goddess of the Harvest. I approached the closest tree and touched its bark, kickstarting its life cycle again. I watched as green leaves sprang from that one tree and many birds came to nest on its branches. Not long after, they hatched eggs, and I climbed up the branches and collected one from every nest. I infused the eggs with my power, making them as nutritious as possible, and fed them to my serpents.

My animals immediately looked stronger and brighter, sustained by my power and love.

I never returned to our cocoon of wings and scales. I lay next to them, our bodies tangled, as we waited for Zeus's response. I wasn't naïve enough to imagine he wouldn't try sending more representatives to change my mind. He was stubborn, and he had always misjudged women, thinking us weaker because of our motherhood, carrying his own prejudices against us for his own reasons. When it was a woman, Rhea, who saved him from Father.

He had tried to get me through his official messenger, and I imagined the next attempt would be emotional blackmail. I knew I would soon face my hardest challenge. I would have to deny the one other person I deeply loved.

It took longer than I expected, but eventually I heard her light feet as they walked amid the bare soil. She paused in front of the only healthy tree and closed her eyes, listening to the sound of the birds. My serpents went closer to her, and she embraced them caringly. She didn't speak, and we stood silent and distant, alone, and together in the way we had only ever been when it was just the two of us in Father's stomach.

The silence was painful, and I felt the need to reach her with my divinity, to feel hers and be comforted by her, to rest against her chest and hear her speak soothing words that would make everything more bearable. Simultaneously, I feared these words, the placation of my rage, because that was my greatest weapon in getting my daughter back.

Unable to decide what to do and what to expect from Hestia, I held still, and she kept only listening to the tree's sounds.

We stayed like that until the sun set and then she let out a loud sigh and turned to face me. She opened her arms and walked towards me. She enveloped me in her warmth, that constant flame of life which had always been her defining feature and the core of her divinity, but I was too afraid to hug her back. She tried to see me through our powers, and I let her see all I now was.

Her body went still as, for the first time, I made clear and visible the ugliest parts of me, the monster I had hid from her all our lives. After the cave, there was no hiding or fighting that part of me. It was me. We were Demeter, the one that would get their daughter back.

"Oh, my Demeter," Hestia said, and she lifted her hands and after a moment's hesitant pause, she caressed my nearly grey hair. This was the first time I looked older than her. I wore the face of an old woman, the skin and body of a battered-by-life creature, and she was seeing me, for the first time, as the dangerous being I truly was.

"Did Zeus send you?" I asked, hoping to avoid a sentimental conversation between us, one that might make me hate her.

She shook her head, and I was surprised by the answer. "He finally let me come to find you," she said. "He is very scared, our little brother."

I closed my eyes at her words. "I don't care," I said. "I was terrified not knowing where Kore was, and he left me in that state."

Hestia nodded as if she understood my pain. "What he did was wrong," she agreed, and I sensed the upcoming 'but' coming my way.

"But this is wrong too?" I spoke her words before she did.

She tilted her head slightly and caressed a string of my grey hair. "You know the danger," she said. "What will happen when everything dies? What will you have left to fight with?"

"He will not let it come to that," I answered, not trusting her enough to reveal my final plan was to become a Goddess of Death and live with my daughter in the Underworld, in a dark and lightless world, but at least together.

She smiled weakly. "He is scared, Demeter. And he is very unpredictable when he is scared. Hermes told him of your threat to make Hades the most powerful God by rendering everything dead. He is now terrified of that, causing him to make mistakes."

"Letting my daughter's abduction go unpunished was his first mistake."

I watched as her face lowered, and I realized there was something I didn't know. I wondered what worse thing could be left for me to learn.

"What is it?" I pressured Hestia. "What do you know that I don't?"

She lowered her hand from my hair and brought me in a hug. It was a different hug from all the previous ones I had ever received from her. She let her entire power, her entire warmth, envelop me, all her quiet power circled us, and I was suddenly sure that whatever I heard would be terrible if Hestia used all her power to keep still so she could utter it.

"As her father, it was his choice to give her hand in marriage, Demeter."

The words echoed in my mind. Each time they banged against me, a part of me changed again, growing angrier and wrathful in ways I had thought I couldn't become. I thought that I was always a mixture of warmth and cold, of good and bad, but as I processed Hestia's words, I realized I was able and willing to only be a monster, the same kind Father was to us.

"You were always so afraid of being a monster, Demeter. You need to keep your mind."

I tried to pull her away, but she held me tightly. I tried to escape her embrace, but she didn't make it easy for me. I could force our embrace to end. I was stronger and crueller than Hestia could ever imagine me to be.

"Let me go, Hestia," I said, and the voice that came out of my lips was not my own. It was like a serpent's hiss, like an eagle's threatening shriek or a lion's bark. "I don't want to hurt you."

"Do it," Hestia said and didn't budge. "I cannot let you destroy yourself. I love you too much to watch you lose all your goodness."

Another crossroad, the hardest I would have to face during my quest. This was something I didn't want to do. I didn't want to hurt her. I didn't want to make this choice and cross this road, but I also knew I couldn't stay still because I was a mother first and a sister second. I loved Kore more than Hestia and the choice, although painful, was clear.

"There is no goodness left in me," I said, and used all my divinity against her. She fought me, but I was stronger. I had the raw power of my anger; of all the life I had sucked out of the soil and all the prayers and sacrifices that were coming my way from every human begging for their lives.

Her family flame was nothing against my motherhood anguish. She was pushed away and landed on the ground, gasping and hurt. She looked at me, shocked, and I saw how determined she was to not give up. She stood and ran towards me, but there was no use. I evaded her.

She tried again. A third time. A fourth.

And finally, after the fifth attempt, she fell on her knees and cried. That sound shocked me as it reminded me of the first time I had heard her voice, when it was still a girl's, so eager to have a companion in the darkness, to end her loneliness. My arrival had marked the end of her isolation.

"I am sorry, Hestia," I whispered, and was torn because I didn't want her to hurt. I didn't want her to cry because of me.

She banged her hands on the soil and her divinity tried to grow. It tried to become stronger and bigger. She tried to change, but failed. There was not enough left of her to manage it. Her power came from the strength of family, from the strength of the home, the strength of family meals and from a portion of every sacrifice. But sacrifices now were of humans, family turning against family and killing one child hoping the others would survive.

Her power was spent, was weaker than ever before, and it was all because of me. It was because of what I had made the world into, and because she had raised me, the exemplary sister and mother figure who kept all of us alive and strong to her detriment.

"I am sorry, Hestia."

She cried louder. "Why can't I do anything?" I heard her whisper. "I am the first born. I am the one who saved all of you. How can I have nothing left to become!" Her eyes turned to me and for the first time I saw dark emotions mixing her love for me. I wondered if she regretted saving us? Saving me? Did she regret loving us? "You stayed nearly as long as I did, Demeter. How can you have so much more than me?"

The answer was simple. It was cruel, and it was one I didn't want to utter. I walked closer to her, this time determined to ease her pain.

"No!" she screamed, and I halted and kept my distance. "It's not fair."

It wasn't. "I wish you had become the Queen of Olympus, instead of Zeus," I told her. "None of this would have happened if you had been the leader. We were a family when you lead us." I meant every word as she cried.

"But why are we so different?" she repeated.

"Because I am a monster and you are not," I told her, confessing verbally what I had always feared and known. "You are the family that needs to be protected."

She wiped her eyes and sat cross-legged in front of me. "Zeus will replace me in the Dodecatheon. With his latest son."

The words shocked me. How could the rest of my siblings allow such a terrible thing to happen to Hestia? How could they allow her to be ridiculed after all she had done for us? "What?"

She nodded. "Dionysus, the son of Zeus and a human called Semele. He is very strong. He is meant to become the God of Wine, of wild frenzy, festivity, pleasure, and vegetation."

"Vegetation?" I asked, and I knew that it was selfish of me to focus on this. "So, he is trying to replace both me and you, if he can?"

"Zeus said he needs stronger allies. He needs every God and Goddess who rules beside him to be of the highest strength. I didn't make the cut."

I hated him for what he had done. I hated him for all he had done to us. I trembled in anger and tried to think of a way I could save both Hestia and Kore, a way that I wouldn't abandon my sister to her fate. I owed her a debt for the love she had given me, the power she had ensured I had to fight for myself.

"Then join me," I said, as the plan formed in my mind. "Let's join forces. Let's rebuild a world where life, food and family are the strongest. Let's overthrow Zeus, and then we can go and get Kore back, together."

She watched me amazed by the words I spoke, at the future I suggested to her, and within her black eyes, where some dark bitterness resided a moment ago, I saw the sudden appeal of my plan.

"We can't," she said. "Me and you, we can't do this."

I knew she was right. Just the two of us weren't enough.

"We could find allies. Zeus has many enemies."

She shook her head again. "That's another war. Like the one with the Titans. It is kin turning against kin, spilling our own blood."

"He started this!" I insisted. "He started it, and he needs to pay. Why does he always have to win, and we have to lose?!"

Hestia didn't disagree with me, but said, "Because thunder can set a house on fire."

I approached her and held her hands. "But it cannot make a family. It cannot make the soil give life and feed. We are not only the power he allowed us to have. We are also all its absence, and we are all the powers linked with that absence." I squeezed her hands, willing her to find all the hurt her withdrawal of her power could cause.

She pulled her hands away and shook her head. "I cannot," she told me. "I cannot."

"You can!"

She shook her head. Her dark hair fell over her face as her bun came unbound.

"I don't want to be the Goddess of Homewreckers, of kinslayers. I have always kept the peace, the balance. I don't want unfortunate and innocent creatures to die because of me."

I was about to say they didn't matter, that they weren't as important as us. That the world we would build would be fairer and kinder, so these lives would be a necessary sacrifice for this brighter future for their children. But Hestia wasn't a mother, she couldn't understand the inequality of love one felt for their child. She couldn't understand that drive I had for my girl.

"I will not stop, Hestia," I said. "Not even for you. I need my daughter back."

She looked at me in sorrow and lay on the ground. I lay next to her, and we slept, holding hands.

I woke up alone. I felt tired, ready to give up, despite my sleep. I walked to the tree and climbed, gathering all the eggs from the nest, bringing an end to that spark of life. As

I climbed down, all the leaves turned orange and yellow, fell on the ground, and the tree was left bare. The birds screamed for their lost eggs, but I felt I did them a kindness. It was time for me to leave this space and find another one to wait out the rest of this ordeal.

I didn't want to stay still anymore. To wait with nothing to do and watch. Instead, I decided, in a half-mad frame of mind, I would make my base somewhere I could draw strength and patience. Somewhere I could declare as a stronghold of my own. I climbed onto my chariot.

"Let's go!" I urged my serpents, and they danced up into the sky. Their wings flapped hard as they carried me higher into the sky, and I saw the devastation which had come upon this land. Greece was all in black, mourning as I was.

We flew around Greece until my serpents were thirsty and I pointed them at a seaside area in Attica to land. They followed my instructions and I soon stepped off the chariot.

"I think I know where we are," I told them as they moved into any pools of water from the latest rain they could find, and let their bodies absorb the moisture. "I will be back soon," I promised them, and placed all the eggs I had gathered in an open basket. "Don't eat them all in one go, am I understood?"

My reptiles didn't acknowledge me, but I wasn't planning to be long anyway, so I wasn't worried too much. In my old woman façade, I approached the town of Eleusis, eager to gather some freshwater before returning to my chariot.

It was one of the settlements that hadn't been completely wiped out from the starvation I caused, thanks to their proximity to the sea. They were able to feed themselves with fish, but despite that saving grace, I still saw that there were many sick people, and the lack of vegetation wasn't only killing their herds and limiting their food supplies. There was one more lack I had caused, which I hadn't considered. The loss of all plants meant there was no medicine for humans. So they died of diseases, lost babies in the belly, because of the lack of important nutritional elements and many other disasters.

I didn't walk towards the houses. Instead, I moved towards the edge of the city and found a well. I touched its stones and sat by its side, under the shade of a still barely alive olive shrub, looking at the water inside. It had been a long time since I had been so close to humans, since I had watched their pain and suffering, and I found myself unable to look up. I wasn't ashamed of what I had done. I didn't regret it, and if time moved backwards, I would do it again. I would do all again for the chance to see my daughter, but I was still saddened it had to come to that. Humans were simple creatures, with short lives and not enough time to withstand my feud with Zeus. They were small, and they were always treated like toys by Zeus, Poseidon and other Gods.

Toys and objects, like my daughter, who was given without consent. Angry tears filled my eyes, and I trembled with sorrow at her fate, what she was going through in the dark and joyless Underworld. I wiped my eyes quickly.

I wasn't like my brothers. I didn't do this out of boredom or arrogance. I was a mother, a desperate one, who needed to do everything she could, use any weapon she had, to be reunited with her child. I wasn't like my brothers. Nothing like them and their sons.

I sat there, slowly rocking, until the sound of sweet girlish voices and singing made me freeze. It wasn't her. Not her, I knew. I closed my eyes and listened to the high-pitched laughter, the way other female voices laughed in echo and the hushed whispers of their secrets.

The girly voices were coming close to me, and I stayed still, with my vision black, imagining it was Kore approaching me. That soon she would be close to me, and I would have the chance to hug her, hold her tightly and never ever again let her go. Never again allow anyone to take her away from my sight. My girl. My Kore.

My whole body tensed as I imagined that it would all soon be all right, even though my daydream was broken by my own knowledge that it wasn't her.

Finally, the voices were right next to me, and I opened my eyes to see four young girls carrying vessels and filling them with water. They all had brown hair and looked similar enough for me to realize they were sisters. I sat still at the other side of the well and watched them, barely registering their words, simply devouring the sound and all it reminded me of. That sweet girlish friendship and joy which I had always associated with my child.

The oldest of the girls noticed my gaze, and our eyes met. She was lucky I was in disguise, as such a direct look at my face could have blinded her or even killed her. But all her human eyes saw was the old woman, dressed in black with a sad smile on her face. Just a harmless, weak and frail old woman. Her sisters followed the eldest's gaze, and soon all four were looking at me.

"What's wrong, old lady?" the youngest asked, and before any of her sisters could stop her, she walked around the well and sat next to me. Her soft young hand was over mine, and she squeezed it with kindness and affection, so freely given that I worried for what terrible fate awaited this child in this cruel world. "You look so sad."

She wasn't my daughter. She lacked so much of Kore, but I felt such a stab of reminiscence as I looked at the kindness and eagerness to help in her eyes that I couldn't stop tears of sorrow forming.

"Oh, don't cry," another sister said and dashed towards me, followed by her other two sisters.

"It will all be OK," the youngest tried to soothe me, in an imperfect way of imitating the adults of her life.

"I am so lonely," I whispered to the girls, unsure why I showed such weakness and such honesty. They were humans. They weren't even heroes or Kings. They were simply girls, and yet I felt unable to stop my emotions.

One of them hugged me, and I let my head rest in the crook of her youthful neck, smelling her short life and the pain that awaited it.

"What happened to you?" she asked. "Tells us and we might be able to help you."

I shook my head and moved away from the hug. If she knew who she was hugging, she would be the one begging for kindness, not offering it. If they knew who I was and the power I had, they wouldn't ever dream that they could offer me help. Because they couldn't. They had no ability, no power, to help me, and their simple and small lives could barely make me forget my troubles.

Despite that, I let their hands touch me and their soft lips whisper words of comfort to me. I deserved it. I had earned this love and dedication and taking it didn't make me the same with my brothers and their sons. I could take it and still be different from those who toyed and used humans for their needs.

"What is your name, sweet woman?" the oldest sister asked.

"D—" I began speaking my name, but the word died in my mouth. How could I trust my own name and story to these girls? How could I make sure that Zeus wouldn't swing down, have his way with them, and make them fool-ishly think they were in love so that they would trust him with my presence in my sad and weakened state? I needed the entire world to think I was unshakable, in control unlike the first drought I had caused.

"Doso," I finished, making a different name for myself and spinning a new tale and character so I could keep re-ceiving their comforting interaction.

"Doso," the oldest girl tried the name in her mouth. "And what happened to you that made you so sad, Doso?"

I glanced at her face and saw that fleeting spark of youth, and Kore flashed again in my mind.

"I was born in Crete," I began my lie. "I was abducted by pirates. Terrible, terrible monstrous men who took me away from my home and my mother. How she must have cried and wailed when I disappeared! I cannot bear imagin-ing this." Tears filled my tears as I kept thinking of my sweet child. How Kore would suffer away from me. How the thought of me would fill her with sadness and misery as she would have learnt by now what I had done in the world of the living. Who I was becoming in her absence.

The two youngest girls let out a gasp at the beginning of my sorrowful lie, while the older two simply listened to me.

"I was a prisoner, left in a dark cell without being al-lowed to see the sun as they travelled, until we reached the harbour of Thorikos. More women boarded the ship, maybe prisoners like me, maybe of their own will, I never learnt.

Those terrible men went to find food, and I knew that this was my one and only chance to escape. But escape on its own wouldn't be enough." I stopped spinning my lie and stayed silent as I invoked my own anger from my truth. The terrible men of my life were many.

I am not sure how long I was silent. "Did you kill them?" the youngest girl asked in a whisper.

"Kallithoe!" the rest of the girls scolded her.

Her outburst made me chuckle. I shook my head. "That would have been too kind for men like them," I answered. "I was so angry for everything they stole from me. Everything they denied me, and the long, long time they kept me in their ship as a slave. So angry for the pain they caused to my mother and for stealing my youth from me." I felt my long-buried anger for Father, my bitterness for Rhea, my rage for Zeus, for Poseidon, for Hades, for the entire world that had allowed so much misfortune to come my way awaken. "They stole so much from me. No, I didn't kill them, sweet Kallithoe. I stole their ship and left them with nothing, stranded at the harbour."

"And did you go back to your mother in Crete?" another of the sisters asked.

That would allow a happy ending for my lie. Even in that fictional version of my tale of the separated mother and daughter, I knew I couldn't allow a simple happy ending to take place.

"No," I said. "I couldn't return home. I had to travel all over the world, as I fled those terrible men who never stopped trying to recapture me. I kept moving, never standing still until I came to this land, just to rest for a bit from my torturous journey."

The girls were quiet as I finished my lie, unsure perhaps if they believed me. If the lie that fell from my lips was plausible enough.

"And how did you feed yourself all that time?" the oldest sister asked. "What did you do as you travelled?"

I could lie further, spin a story of how I was a healer or had another secret art for survival, or that Gods showed me kindness.

"Terrible things," I said instead, letting that simple truth enter the tale of Doso.

"And you never had a family? Never had the chance to have a child?"

I shook my head and more tears flowed down my eyes, because I had known the worst pain of all, to lose a child.

"My name is Kallidike and these are my sisters, Demo, Kleisidike and Kallithoe. We are the daughters of Keleos, the king of Eleusis. If you come closer to the town, you will find more women your age with sad stories themselves. They could offer you hospice and refuge."

Kind and generous girls. I studied their faces and their sweet girlhood, so fragile and ready to be destroyed in this world they lived in.

"You are good girls," I said. "You have good and kind hearts. I hope life treats you well and you are blessed with good husbands," I let my power encircle their fates, whatever life-giving element was left in me, I let some of it touch them, "who will love and respect your goodness."

The youngest girl, little Kallithoe, stood. "Is there anything you want in life? Something that you think you could still have, even though those pirates took your youth away?"

I studied the girl and wondered if there was anything I could ask of this child that would ease my pain a little. The soft ease of my pain that their presence had brought me might give me patience.

"If there is a family, a house that needs a nurse for their children, I would be very happy to stay by their side, watch their children grow into strong men and beautiful women. The kind of work that is cut out for a female who has out-lived others her own age. I could take some newborn baby in my arms and nourish it well, watch over this child and do any women's tasks that need done."

Kallithoe turned to her eldest sister with pleading eyes. "Kallidike, can we, please?"

I wasn't sure what the young girl referred to, but I stayed silent as she pleaded with her childish innocence for what-ever favour she asked. Kallidike's eyes softened as she watched her little sister. She turned to me and walked closer, offering me her hand. I wasn't sure where she was going to lead me, but I knew that I had no reason to be afraid. I had no reason to fear any human. They could never harm me as they might a lesser Goddess or a nymph. But I felt that tak-ing her hand was a moment that the fates had predetermined, and that scared me.

Why did I think this young girl could have such power over the course of my life? Why would I imagine that she could be so important when she was only a girl, a human child, barely able to control her life in this world. I could see the faint evidence of how she was missing nutrients, all because of my war with Zeus, and her hand hung in the air as an invitation to take me to the next chapter of who I was going to be. I lifted my hand and took hers, standing up from the well.

That slight touch told me a lot about Kallidike. It told me of her desire to protect her family, but also to be kind and be the best example of who she could be, with all the gifts that the Gods had offered her. I also saw her rage at the plague that she was living through, the one I had caused, and that anger was honest like a harsh river. It washed through me, and I decided I needed to follow wherever her honest terror for the future led. I wasn't guilty, the realization surprised me again. I wasn't guilty for her pain and her fear, or her stolen youth because of the starvation I had caused.

I was hungry for it. I was hungry to see what it would turn her into, what she might do or say to me if she knew who I was. I wanted to consume that anger and youth that pulsed in Kallidike's veins and short frail life. I wanted her life, and other lives suddenly, to belong to me, and me alone.

"Old Mother," she began, using an endearing term for a woman she knew had no children or family. Another subtle kindness I found myself hungry for. Not the kindness per se but the drive that allowed it. I had never felt such a thing before for humans. I knew that my brothers, nephews and nieces, liked to meddle in their lives, to see how they could change the course of one's destiny, how much they could take from a human, as part of the worship they demanded, but I had never been involved in any of that. I had always been distant from humans, received their prayers and gifts, but there had never been anything extraordinary done in my name, a festival or a special day to me.

But, as I felt Kallidike's small life rushing through her veins, I wanted it. I wanted her life, not to take it but to own it, and that was a feeling that surprised me. I thought I had no other desire but for my daughter to be back by my side, but that was suddenly a lie. I wanted my daughter by my side and for our story to be significant, celebrated and mourned.

Kallidike spoke names of people I could help with their families. Good men and women, with respectable households who all were important in their community.

"What about Demophon?" Kallithoe asked, interrupting her sister.

The oldest sister sent her a warning look. "We need our mother's permission before we can invite Doso to our home."

Kallithoe looked pleadingly at her sister. Kallidike looked at me and then at the rest of her sisters. "If you wait for us here, we could go tell your story to our esteemed mother, Queen Metaneira and maybe she will invite you to come to our house."

Kallithoe nodded. "Since the Gods saw fit for her to meet us first," she added, trying to justify her kindness through the power of my siblings and myself.

"You have a younger sibling?" I asked them.

Kallidike nodded. "Yes, our mother recently gave birth to our brother."

"Our treasure baby," Demo said.

"He was born late, after many years of our prayers to all the Gods for a son to be the joy and heir to our parents."

"Kallithoe," Kallidike said her sister's name slow and quiet, but the scolding was present in her tone. "Certainly, if our mother agrees to allow your help to raise our brother, you will be the most envied and desired carer. Our mother is very generous to those who serve our family well."

I nodded, suddenly certain the next step I was to take was towards these girls' house and towards that babe who awaited me. I was going to build something here. Eleusis was going to become one of my most important places in Greece, I decided. My stronghold as I waited for Zeus to come.

"I will wait," I said to them. "Please speak on my behalf to the Queen and the King, sweet girls."

I sat on the well, under the shade, and watched them fill their jugs with water and walk away towards their palace. I filled the flask with water and started running, using my divinity to reach the spot I had left my serpents faster than any mortal could.

They looked up as I approached them. I let them come into my arms and kissed their scales. "We will need to stay here, my lovelies," I told them. "You can rest here, and I will come to see you often and give you food, yes my darlings?"

Their sharp eyes focused on me, and I knew they understood. I knew my beautiful animals trusted me. I left the water I had gathered for them, kissed their heads, and squeezed them in my hug, my secondary pseudo-children and beloved allies.

"Trust me," I told them. "This will help get Kore back."

I ran back to the well and just as I sat down, the four girls returned.

Pretty little Kallithoe skipped towards me and waved. "Doso! Doso!" she sang. "Get up! Mother wants you to come! She wants to meet you!"

Kallithoe took my hand, and I followed them towards their home. Despite the little girl's innocent and friendly chatter, my attention was focused on Kallidike and the way she walked ahead. So angry, I thought, and I was again overcome by the hunger for that emotion. I wanted her, not in the sexual way my brothers would, or with the pettiness with which Hera would control her. I wanted her like I wanted Kore, as an extension of who I was, of who I could be.

As a believer in me, my pain, my power, my plan. My eyes moved to the rest of her sisters. I wanted all of them that way: Mine, loyal first and foremost to me, loving me blindly in a way I had never before craved from humans. A simple sacrifice and a prayer wasn't enough. Their fearful prayers because of my devastation weren't enough either. I wanted more. I wanted them to be my special people, my believers, my champions. I looked around at the stones that made up the houses of the people. I hungered for all of them. Mine. Mine.

This place, I decided then and there, would be my sanctuary, a stronghold of my power. I wouldn't be a simple patron deity to them, as Hera was to Argos or Athena to Athens. No, this place would be the centrepiece of all my story and how I came to be the victor.

These people, these girls, their families, were mine and would join me in making sure that neither any human King nor any God, even almighty Zeus, ever forgot I was to be feared as much as to be loved. The panhellenic sanctuary of Demeter for all those who would decide to live under my protection, taking my side over the rest. I looked up at the sky and could see Zeus's eyes on me.

We walked through the streets, and I noticed the paint had washed off on the walls. Another loss from my absence. Without flowers, there were few ways to make colours. Through the houses I sensed that one in two were empty of life. Even though the human population of Eleusis was still surviving, it had paid a heavy price. The closer we got to the palace, the better kept and grander the houses were. The streets were getting wider as the palace became clearer to us. It was a beautiful building, and clearly all care had been taken to fight against the impact of starvation and lack of resources. However, it was barely managing to keep up appearances. I could see the patchwork to fix issues instead of the full-scale repairs it once would have had, when times were better.

We reached the palace, and the girls quickly led me to the room where the Queen received her guests. It was a cool room, with large windows, and as it was nearing sunset, the white stones were tinted orange by the sun. Kallithoe let go of my hand and ran to her mother, seated in her throne with her youngest babe in her arms.

Meteneira was a beautiful woman, clearly blessed from Aphrodite with sexual virility. Despite having birthed at least five children, she had retained an element of youth that she couldn't have, given Kallidike's age, without divine support. Her hair had few white strands amid her light brown locks. I watched her as she kissed all her daughters' foreheads and then the girls kissed Eleusis' miraculous little prince.

I stood in front of the throne, slowly watching their familiar bonds, and I was filled with painful jealousy, remembering my own child and family. My daughter who was taken from me, trapped in darkness like I was as a child. My eyes filled with tears, and my divinity darkened as my sorrow rose, mixing with anger and despair at the injustice I was dealt.

"Oh, poor old mother. You look so sad," Metaneira said and stood up from her throne, holding her son in her arms. She walked down and approached me. My eyes moved from her face to her baby's. He was awake, and his eyes were fixed on me, curious and aware that I was different than his mother, but not how. I smiled at him.

"I have had a very difficult time," I said to the Queen. "Unfairly and cruelly treated."

I liked the baby and suddenly wanted to hold him. For the first time since this terrible ordeal had started, I felt my heart calm at the sight of him, human, yes, and weak as a mortal, but still beautiful and warm. He reminded me of Kore, but the pain of the memory was less bitter because of his innocence.

My cheeks flushed from an inner heat.

"Oh my," Meteneira said, and she moved away. "You are glowing with the Gods' grace and power. Your skin is emanating holiness," she whispered, and all her daughters agreed.

I wasn't sure what they saw to bring them to that conclusion, but I didn't correct them.

"Your son is beautiful," I praised her. "Just like your daughters."

"Would you like to hold him?" Meteneira offered.

"Yes," the words left my throat before I could register the question. I wanted to hold the baby, to feel his life, soft and warm, against my chest and smell his newness. My arms opened and the young baby was placed in them. His head rested on the crook of my elbow, and his pretty little eyes were fixed on me. I kissed his forehead, and the contact made my heart flutter with the closest I had felt to happiness since I lost my girl.

I returned him to his mother, immediately missing his warmth and smell. "I would be honoured to care for such a good prince as your Demophon."

Meteneira motioned to a woman, no older than thirty, who ran towards her Queen. "Iambe, bring a chair for Doso to sit."

Iambe obeyed and soon came back with a heavy wooden chair, decorated with beautiful and expensive linen. She placed it in front of Meteneira's seat and I stared at it.

"That is so luxurious," I said to them. "That is no chair for someone like me."

The rest of the women looked at each other and then to their Queen. I lowered my head. "That is the chair for an important guest, not someone of my station," I lied and waited to see the Queen's reaction. I had to judge Metaneira's strength of character and how she responded to pressure. I wanted to see if she was a mistress that wouldn't be too troublesome for Doso.

"You are an important guest," Metaneira insisted, but the baby in her arms started crying. She turned her back to me and started bouncing Demophon in her arms as she tried to calm his cries.

The baby, though, wasn't calming, and I was still standing. Iambe, the servant who had brought me the chair, acted without needing to be told what to do. She took the chair away and came back with a plain wooden stool.

I took a seat and sent my divinity towards the mother and crying son, softly calming, and numbing the baby to ease his wailing. Soon after, Demophon was calm and Metaneira turned to find me sitting in my new seat. She smiled at me and positioned herself on her throne again. Her daughters sat next to her or around her feet. I watched the way she absently caressed her girls, the way Demo rested her head against her knee, and the way she smiled at Kallithoe's whispering.

Four wonderful daughters, a beautiful baby. I was over-come by grief, envy and deep sorrow. My body ached all over as I watched them. I didn't want to become Metaneira, I didn't wish to take her place, but I felt the loss of my Kore stronger. How much had happened since the last time I saw my daughter? What was the last word she said to me? The last word I said to her?

What was the world and life like before she was stolen from me? I could barely remember anything of that old life now. I only knew I missed it and recoiled at the fear that it was forever lost to me.

"Old mother Doso," Iambe softly spoke in my ear and then, to my amazement, she didn't offer any words of con-solation or showed worry. Instead, she whispered a joke in my ear. I didn't find it especially funny, but the effort was such a surprise, the attempt to make me smile so direct that I laughed.

Laughter, an act I hadn't exercised much in my life, never after my daughter's abduction, was infectious. My en-tire body relaxed and soon it turned real, as a self-healing practice to make me relax and forget the terrible situation of my reality. Iambe was laughing with me and soon, like an infection, Metaneira and her children were laughing too. Even little Demophon was giggling.

"Iambe is very funny, isn't she?" Kallithoe said. "Did she tell you the joke about the old man?"

I nodded and the young girl giggled at the memory.

Metaneira squeezed her youngest daughter's cheek and turned to Iambe again. "Bring us some wine, please. We need to offer Doso something as our guest, and my throat is dry."

I coughed loudly and shook my head. "There is a better drink for that," I said, and without waiting for Metaneira to accept my offer, I turned to Iambe and directed her to mix water, mint and meal. I sent my divinity to nudge the human into submissiveness and the other women into quiet. We stayed silent until Iambe returned with our drinks.

I accepted the drink and took a sip.

The rest of the meeting went smoothly. Metaneira showered me—or rather the human Doso that I impersonated—with compliments. It seemed that despite my appearance and desire for only simple things, she saw that I wasn't a simple woman. She had no way of understanding my true nature of course. So instead, she thought that I was the daughter of a noble, stolen but so evidently gracious in my movements that I had to have noble blood in my veins, my line blessed by the Gods.

I didn't contradict her. I allowed her to build up an image of me that made me more trustworthy and desirable as a carer for her precious son. By the end of our meeting, I had agreed to care for her child, to raise Demophon to be the more honoured prince of Eleusis and bestow upon him the grace that Metaneira saw in me.

Soon, before I even knew it, I was alone with Demophon in his nursery. I lay on the small bed and placed the babe on my chest. His fickle mortal life was so visible to me, but his weakness didn't stop the mother in me feeling relief at his touch. He turned his face and made sounds against my chest, his toothless mouth trying to eat or gnaw at my flesh. He knew I was someone special. He knew I was someone who would keep him safe. I lifted him higher until we were face to face. We gazed at each other, and I felt the need to own him as I wanted to with his sisters. I wanted his innocence, his blind devotion in a way that I had never been interested in with humans before. I wanted to be the beginning and end of the world for that little creature.

I bounced him and he smiled and giggled. Soon, I was up on my feet, and we were dancing. The sweet prince, the first favoured human child of the Goddess of the Harvest, the Goddess of Food and fertility in the soil. The bringer of good seasons. Sweet little Demophon knew he was chosen for a special destiny by my side.

I rested his little body over my chest, his head was supported at the crook of my neck as I hummed and danced with him. My eyes dilated and for the first time in my life I experienced what humans call imagination and daydreaming, but we Gods call foreshadow and planning. I was dancing with Demophon, with his sisters, another young boy, and the King who I had never met. All around us there were more humans, but we were the core of the festivity.

Soon my Kore appeared and was dancing with us. She was more beautiful than I had ever seen her. Her eyes were sharp, and she looked suddenly like a different person, a different kind of daughter.

I swirled around on the spot, clutching the baby tightly, feeling his tiny life, so easy for the Moirai to snap.

In my frenzied dance, my eye glanced over a girl's face that was so much like my Kore's. But it wasn't her. My Kore was next to me, dancing close to me but never properly with me. I tried to find that other girl's face, the one whose hair was a bit darker and wavier, but her face was like my own, like Kore's. No matter how much I searched, I never saw her again.

My turning around must have scared the baby. He vomited all over my clothes and started crying. I stopped, and the vision that had overtaken my body ceased as well, fading as the room came into existence again. The smell of the retched-out food came to me, the smell of the poo and pee from the baby's bottom and his desperate crying.

I held the baby in my arms and lifted him higher. His eyes were out of focus, but soon they settled on me. The more I gazed into his eyes, the surer I was that he knew my identity. He knew to respect and fear me, and his crying ended.

I smiled at him and soon he obeyed my need and smiled back at me.

"There's a good baby!" I praised him, and he calmed down, becoming again the pleasant and comforting creature I needed. I was a mother and knew the weakness and need of babes. I didn't blame him for his bodily functions. "I went too fast. You are not ready yet for that," I said to him, but still couldn't find it in me to apologize. I could only explain to him his failing. I forgave him.

I placed him on the bed, securing him with a pillow so he wouldn't roll away. Once I changed my clothes, I picked him up and washed his little body, changing him into fresh smelling linens.

I lay with him again on the bed and watched him as he slept. My eyes fixated on his little chest and the rhythm with which it rose and fell as he breathed his life away, always a step closer to the moment that Lachesis would decide the point of his death and Atropos would use her scissors to end it. I caressed the baby softly. How terrible it must be for his mother to know that her child would die. How terrible it must feel for poor Metaneira to know that all the children, her pretty girls and this perfect baby, would perish and travel down to the darkness of Styx and Hades's world.

I found an odd feeling of sympathy for the mother, who had shown me great hospitality, even though her home was impoverished and there was barely enough food to survive. My brothers and even my sister Hera often rewarded kindness and favours towards their favourite humans. They often bestowed upon them strength, wisdom and intelligence, and if they proved themselves worthy, using their gifts as they ought to, offered them good wives, descended from other deities, or in some rare cases even made them immortal.

The idea struck in my mind as I looked at the small fire that was nearly dead. I stood up and added new wood to it, urging the flames to grow stronger. This fire, this hearth of the house, was where my Hestia held her power. Not for the first time, I remembered my sister and her sorrow at our last meeting. I wasn't surprised she fled my proposal. I knew there was something that could have pushed her to make a leap of faith and change her destiny, but whatever that was, I didn't know if she would ever find it. Each creature had a path of transformation in their lives, at least one.

Still, my sister was here, in the fire, keeping me company even if she couldn't fight alongside me. I moved my head closer to the flames and let it lick my face. The fire felt like soft kisses over my face, and it warmed my heart and eased my pain all over again.

The baby made a sound as a harsh dream filled his little mind. I got to my feet and held him in my arms and slowly walked to the flame and showed his little face to Hestia's proxy fireplace.

"Isn't he beautiful?" I whispered. "I think he will be mine, loyal to me," I added. "Him and all his family. All of Eleusis will become mine."

The baby woke up and stared at the fire.

"He can tell you and I are here, but Demophon is too little to betray our identity. No, he is loyal to me." I raised him up and watched him smile as I needed him to. My heart eased and I knew I wanted to repay the gift of the comfort he gave me to this land that gave him life, to the King and Queen, the four princesses that led me to him and the comfort that made my pain more bearable. I closed my eyes and let his warmth and smell, and Hestia's soft fire kisses, reach my deepest self.

I allowed it then, just in the land of Eleusis, for some life to return to the soil. Not a lot, not so much that it would make more humans come. It was just enough to make some medicine, just enough to save some unborn babies from malnutrition, and just enough for a few more people to survive. That was my first gift to Eleusis.

The second gift, I decided as I held the baby up, was to make their prince immortal. I could imagine the type of small God he could be. I could see him as my attendant on Olympus, residing alongside me and Kore when the palace of Demeter was finished. I smiled at him and moved his body close to the flame.

The fire licked his body, and my power kept his skin safe and unburnt. It only strengthened him as I allowed my power and the power of his family's hearth to protect him. I held him upon the fire all night, and in the morning, before anyone else was awake and ready to begin their day, I fed him a few drops of ambrosia, the food that made Gods, and held him tightly against my chest. I breathed out all over him, tickling his sensitive body and imparting the coolness of my power that balanced the warmth of the hearth from the night before.

That was how I would make him an immortal, my first human prince.

My days with Demophon were a medicine to my pain. Kore always crept into my mind. I saw her face in every shadowy corner and couldn't bear to look at her. Her eyes told me that she was trapped and waiting for me, her lady mother Goddess, to save her from the darkness, while I was playing with a human baby. I couldn't bear to imagine what she was going through in her imprisonment, but I knew that this was the last stand of our shared trial of separation.

It was here that I would keep humanity mine, would erect a cult all about me. Here in Eleusis I would make my stronghold and let all of humanity and all of life die in the rest of Greece, maybe even the whole world. If what it took for Zeus to give in was for only the people of Eleusis to be left standing, humans loyal to me and sacrificing only to me, then so be it.

My brother was a stubborn creature, a stupid and prideful man, and that was why I was sure that he wouldn't bear for one daughter to cause him to lose an entire kingdom. Whatever alliance he had made with Hades, he wasn't willing to lose his realm to keep it. He would let thousands die. I would too, for my girl, but I now was standing still and waiting at the final stop for Zeus to come to me. I was showing him that I could make my own realm of power, and that my patience was nowhere near spent.

One way or another, I was going to be reunited with my daughter.

In that precious time I had with Demophon, Zeus often crossed my mind. I returned to that night before we started our war, when I had been plagued by the question of how we, the ones raised together, had decided to follow a little brother we knew nothing about. We, all of us, had made him the King of Olympus.

I felt the presence behind the door before it opened. I moved away from the fire. Demophon's body was burning hot in my arms, even though his skin was untouched.

"Come in," I said.

The door opened and a young brown-haired boy peaked his face inside the room I shared with Demophon.

"Hello," he whispered, tiptoeing into the room. "Mistress Doso," he greeted me and bowed, without any grace, and then approached me. "My name is Triptolemus. I came to meet my brother."

Brother? I looked at Demophon in my arms and then turned my attention to the boy. He was no older than fourteen. He was tall, with a head full of curls that ended at his shoulders. I tried to find Metaneira's features in his face, or any similarity with the princesses, but there was nothing to betray their relation.

He walked closer to us. His shoulders were wide like a man's but sleek like a boy's. He was in that awkward stage between childhood and adulthood. He moved his hair to rest behind his ears. At that moment, I saw the validation of his identity. His eyebrows and the shape of his nose and eyes reminded me of Keleos, the King of Eleusis.

I lowered the baby to make him more visible, and Triptolemus approached even closer. He brought his face close to his little brother and tried to hold the baby's hand.

Demophon grabbed his thumb and tried to bring it to his mouth. Triptolemus laughed as he wriggled his hand away.

"All of Eleusis is so happy and proud that you are here, Mistress Doso," Triptolemus said. "Our one precious prince is growing stronger and bigger every day since you got here. He seems to be growing faster than any other child."

I had heard that gossip when I was taking Demophon out for a walk. The divine power that was infused in his body was the reason his upbringing was accelerated. It wouldn't matter if the child grew beyond his years once I revealed myself, but I needed to be careful while I was hiding my identity.

"The Queen told me Demophon is her only son," I said.

Triptolemus didn't seem surprised or even uncomfortable with the words.

"I am a bastard," he said, without much care or thought. I had been told that lineage and family meant everything to humans. All my siblings narrated stories of the importance their special humans placed in proving their identities, proving their divine links by completing great tasks of glory or acts of supreme ability, all to attest to being their parents' children. I had, perhaps wrongly, imagined that bastardry would be a shameful and painful subject for humans, in ways that it wasn't for us Olympians and Titans, who coupled freely without the need for marriage.

But this boy didn't appear to mind his status or feel any shame in admitting it. I didn't know how to respond.

"How come I have never seen you before?"

He lifted his face from the baby and crossed his arms. "I was on a long hunting trip. To bring back meat to Eleusis."

"Ahh," I said, losing interest in the conversation. The issue of starvation had been the most boring and unpleasant subject that the humans talked about constantly. My aid had slightly helped but the nagging never stopped. I found that what from a distance I had perceived as cries of despair and pleas for mercy, when I experienced up-close felt rather different. It filled me with dreadful annoyance that these creatures, which we had made special and chosen by our standards, made by our hands, were so incapable of suffering in silence, of making anything in the world with their own hands.

Helpless. And yet, I didn't want them to perish. I was never close to them as my other siblings. I didn't ever think of them too much before losing Kore, but her absence had changed me. I had gone through many phases, from monster to hag, but my time with humans had changed me again. I believed that it made me more of a Goddess, seeing how much better, stronger, and smarter I was than those creatures. How much more like animals they were than any other Olympian wanted to admit. How could my nieces and nephews have become Olympians, hold such power when half of them came from this species?

I thought of all the affairs between Olympians and mortals, and I suddenly felt it disgusting. They were so incapable of understanding our differences. Humans were incapable of being on par with someone like us. It was rape just for that reason. Even when the human accepted a God's or Goddess's love—Aphrodite after all had never shied away from human flesh—it could only be rape when they couldn't understand what we were. Or rather, they thought they could, thus they believed they loved but we didn't. We, I was certain, could see and sense the disparity of abilities, and yet so many of my siblings still went ahead and coupled.

Triptolemus finished speaking of his meat-related activities. "You should head back to bed," I told him. "I need to clean the prince and feed him."

He nodded and, after placing a soft kiss on Demophon's head, he kissed my hand. "Mistress Doso, thank you again for making our prince strong."

I watched him walk away and found myself beginning to feel enamoured with this new child of the King I had found. Perhaps it was the King's seed that made them all so desirable, because I felt that there was something I wanted to take from Triptolemus too.

I turned to leave the baby to rest on the bed so I could bring water and new clothes. As I turned, I was faced with a full shadow. I saw, within that dark corner of the room, thousands of eyes, noses and mouths, all ones I recognized in an instant. It was pulsing, that darkness, moving in and out of its spot, as the flame, where Hestia's presence hid to keep me company, danced as it ate the wood the servants placed for it.

"Kore?"

The shadow remained silent. It stared at me, wearing my daughter's face, but was monstrous, not loving, kind and joyful as my girl was. It reminded me of myself in the cave, the darkness and the despair, the presence of that monster in me, which I had fought all my life until then.

I wasn't sure whether what I witnessed was a play of my imagination or a vision of what was happening to my child. Was Kore being consumed by darkness, battling her own inner monster? Could my girl have had a demon like me, pulsing darkness under her skin? Could my daughter have a dark side that was getting stronger and hungrier in the Underworld?

I shook my head and closed my eyes tightly. No, my child was pure. She didn't have anything violent in her. I refused to believe that. My Kore was the purest, brightest, and most beautiful part of the world, filled with kindness, girlhood, and life. There was nothing of her that could even remotely be at home in the darkness and death of Hades's kingdom.

"I will save you," I promised the dark corner. The facial characteristics faded, and I turned back to Demophon. I lifted him and squeezed him in my arms. I held him tightly, breathing in his youth, innocence, and life. I held onto him. He was the only spark of light and joy in my world.

He was mine. I let my fingers dig into his flesh and my power emanated from me to him. His little body struggled, but the ambrosia and the ritual over the fire had made him stronger than the average child. He was in pain, but he was strong enough to endure me and I needed him, the essence of what this little baby was, to keep my goal and plan intact. A plan that I didn't really know or understand. A plan that changed with every turn of my journey.

How pitiful must I have appeared to Zeus? Never willing to stick to one decision.

Did I have a plan? Or was I simply reacting still? Was I still dancing to the tune that my brother played? Did I simply move in accordance with what his own moves dictated? Trophonius had once said that all would become clearer and easier if I stood still. What if Hekate wasn't the only gift that stillness would bring me?

If I stayed here, waiting, and standing still, would my brother be forced to come and face me? Would me staying here show him and all his allies that there was no other path? That I wouldn't change my mind?

I wished to feel pain and despair as humans do. In the knowledge that I could one day be reunited with my child in death. But as an Olympian, a supreme being, I was denied such pleasurable consolation. I was to live forever, in some form or another, even if one day the Olympians fell and another child by Zeus took over, restarting the world once again.

I felt Demophon's little body tremble in my arms and I moved him away from my breast. His small life was so fickle.

"Don't worry, little prince," I whispered to him. "You are a favourite of the Great Demeter. You will be sculpted into history. The boy prince who became a God because he eased the pain of a suffering mother. You will not suffer the mortal pain of death, but the everlasting superiority of Godhood, by my side."

I would stand still. I would stand here, in Eleusis. I would stick to this plan, sucking out of Demophon and his siblings all the life I needed, all the joy I lacked to keep my courage high. Whether it was what the Moirai dictated or not, I would make this land my own, my stronghold, and face my enemies here. Here, where I had this family to keep me standing still.

I wish I could have said that my resolve never wavered. But I often experienced the same doubt. I often felt the need to move again, to start searching for a way to enter Hades's realm. I made thousands of plans to fight my brothers, to find Hades and demand an answer from him for the injustice he had caused me. Each time, I held onto Demophon and his presence; his growth and slow making towards Godhood kept me standing.

Each time, I approached the four princesses and heard their laughter, their girlish giggles, or secretly watched Triptolemus, appreciating his dedication to be the person life ordained him to be. Not an heir, not a prince, but still the son of a noble King. That family kept me standing still.

I made sure the door was closed and no sounds of servants could be heard walking outside and picked Demophon up. I slowly undressed him and started the ritual of his God making.

He slipped slightly from my hands when the cry of Metaneira reached my ears and the door flung open.

"Demophon!" she screamed and ran towards me, as the child was losing his safe holding in my arms. If I stopped touching him, the flames would consume him. I saw Hestia reaching her power to protect the child too and together, we reacted fast enough for me to grab the baby again.

The damage was done though. Everything was ruined.

Metaneira reached me and pushed me onto the floor, snatching the child away from me. His flesh was hot, even though it wasn't burnt thanks to my power. She cradled the child against her chest and shot me angry looks.

"You will pay for this!" she threatened and moved away from the door. "I showed you kindness and you tried to burn my son. My only son!"

I stared at her in silence, and for the first time I felt a rage towards humans. I wanted to punish this stupid, pathetic little creature who ruined the precious balance I had found. All my gratitude for the children she had birthed, those who filled my weary and pained heart with comfort, evaporated. She had ruined everything.

I imagined my brother watching from Olympus. I saw his face, that smirk, that pompous look as if he was telling me, Yes, Demeter, you never get your way. I always win. All my efforts to fight myself, to keep the world happy, had been answered with the abduction of my daughter, the disrespect and ridicule of my rape. I had changed so much, becoming something that I never wanted to be and still, still, even after all this pain, this anger, and this change, I was still denied the ability to choose what happened in my life. What other God or Goddess was like that?

"No more," I whispered, but Metaneira didn't hear me amid her ranting of curses and threats as she cradled the baby. I ran my hand over my face, shedding the age that I was hiding behind. The wrinkly skin changed into smooth, sun kissed youth. I looked at my hands and they slowly changed from the rough and pained hands of a creature at the end of their life to the youthful hands I used to associate with myself.

Metaneira had grown silent. She had walked to the corner where just a few days ago I had seen Kore trapped in darkness, distorted from her happy self to a deadly creature, the Queen of the Underworld that Hades wanted to change her into. She held the baby, Demophon, against her chest and I saw how his life and fate was marked by her impulsiveness and weakness.

"You stupid woman," I said to her. I ran my hands over my hair, changing it from silver white to light brown. "You denied your son immortality. I was going to spare you the pain of knowing that your child will die, and you ruined everything! Mortals," I spat the word out, realizing how little I valued it.

Why had I tried to be different than Zeus? Why had I tried not to take from humans what I needed all those years? Why had I simply offered without playing? Why had I not taken what I wanted simply because this was the realm that I ruled and these humans, Metaneira and all her family, were my subjects. Why did I bother to pretend to be Doso and hide as a human amid them? When I had the power and the right to demand their hospitality and devotion.

"Mortals. Demophon has no choice now but to die. He will travel down to the waters of Styx, meet my brother Hades and lose the sweetness of life. I would have made him unageing and deathless. He would have been the first hero of Demeter, but now he cannot escape death and fates."

He began crying and I found the sound hard to bear. It was annoying and ruining the moment of my revelation.

"He will always draw pride from having slept in my hug, from having sat on my lap, even though he will never be my attendant at Olympus or my companion. But he will age. Years will move around him, and he will be powerless to do anything against that. And, when he is in his prime, the sons of Eleusians shall wage war and fight each other continuously at the same time every year."

There had to be a price, I decided. A price for having thwarted my plan. Demophon himself had to pay it because he was part of the family that hurt me. His family had to carry a burden to commemorate what had happened to me and the insult they inflicted upon me.

Metaneira tried to speak, but her fear of me was so strong that no matter how many times she opened her mouth, her jaw closed silent again.

"I am Demeter, the one who brings the sweetest gifts, who brings food and prosperity as much as hunger and disease. And you will order your people to build me a grand temple, with a majestic altar in the middle. All the people of Eleusis will build it, offering me their hard labour, their sweat, their tiredness to show me love and as an apology for your actions. It will stand over the hill of Kallikhoron. And then I will instruct you how to treasure me, Demeter, with the proper rituals and acts."

This will please me, I thought, but I didn't know for sure. All I thought was that I couldn't return to my wandering. All I could see was Zeus's face mocking me. I would stand still. I had to see this plan through, this self I had chosen, to the end of my time. This plan of making Eleusis and all its people mine alone. While the rest of the world was dying without me, these people would only be mine!

I felt my power envelop me. Light radiated out of my body, finishing off any touches of Doso that had been left on me. No more ugliness to hide behind. No more age to shield me from the cruelty of the world. No more. No more. No more hiding. No more changing.

I transported myself to the clearing with my serpents. I had visited them often in my time with Demophon. I even once showed them the baby. Their eyes looked at me and there didn't need to be any words for them to understand that something had went wrong. Their eyes softened as I was once again the old self they had known since they hatched from their eggs. I sat down in the clearing and they wrapped their limbs around me.

I heard horses approaching sometime later. I stood taking care of a tree, which was the way I ensured my serpents were able to feed themselves, when the sound of the horses' breathing reached my ears. The serpents were the only children I had been left to fend for. I had held their eggs in my hands, after all, and I was the first creature they saw when they broke the hard shell and claimed their right to the world. Like me, I had thought then, they came out of the darkness to glorious light and life.

The approaching presence of humans made them hiss and prepare themselves for battle. Their bodies tensed as the sounds became louder and louder. I decided I didn't want to wait for whoever wanted to find me. It was no God after all. I prepared my animals and stepped onto my carriage.

"Let's go fly, my beauties," I urged them. "Let's go see what this city looks like now."

They didn't need more encouragement. They flapped their wings, and we were airborne. I leaned, without much interest, against the edge of my carriage and watched the tops of the black-brown trees and the bare mountains on the far horizon. Their bodies had transformed into ugly black heaps of soil instead of their previous green shades. I listened to the flapping of the nearby sea, and the wind blew softly against my skin. Helios was halfway through his journey and his light felt like a cruel joke to me. We flew in circles, aimlessly, until we approached Eleusis and I noticed a large white building erected.

"Go there," I ordered, and my serpents flew down towards the building. There were still people building as the new temple wasn't complete and we were greeted with screams. From the corner of my eye, I saw men, women and children move away. There was only one man standing.

King Keleos, who I had briefly met a few times as Doso, stood still.

My serpents landed on the white marble that made the entrance of my new temple and I walked slowly up the steps to reach Keleos. He lowered his body slowly, until he was bowing to me.

"Goddess, allow me to thank you for the kindness you showed my son, Demophon," he said. "As you instructed, we have built you a temple on the hill of Kallikhoron."

I studied the man who was still bowing and slowly looked around. His four daughters appeared at the edge of my sight, all of them bowing again. Metaneira, holding baby Demophon, who just a while back I had squeezed and clung to for strength, stood close to them. I saw Triptolemus as well, a boy on the verge of manhood, behind all of them. The seedlings of Keleos were all here.

For me.

"I will reside here," I promised him, but made my voice sound louder so that it echoed all over Eleusis. It reached the ears and hearts of all the citizens, noble born and not, and my words etched themselves in their minds and hearts. "I will stay inside this temple you made for me. I will teach you the ways of my worship and bless you with my power. I will stay here until my daughter is returned to me." I tapped Keleos's shoulder.

He tried to hide his fear, but I didn't miss his soft twitch at my touch or the hard beating of his human heart, always a beat closer to death.

"You will be my priest, King," I said to him. "You will lead and learn the ways of my proper worship, begin practicing new rites of passages so the world will never forget my story and the injustice that the other Gods did to me."

He nodded, even though my words weren't a proposal but a command.

"All your family will join these celebrations in my honour. Your daughters." I paused for a moment and glanced at Metaneira. She clutched the baby in her arms, whom she had condemned to death. I felt a vile feeling of disgust towards her. She had been blessed with beautiful children, but she was the curse that they had written over their bodies. "And both your sons," I added. Metaneira lifted her face in surprise.

She turned slowly to Triptolemus behind her, who looked shocked. I didn't wait for her to speak or react any further. I lifted my hand and invited the other boy towards me.

"Come, Triptolemus," I commanded, and the boy walked slowly towards me. I looked Metaneira straight in the eyes as I told her with all my power that she had lost the chance to make her son my favourite, but I would still have a son of a King as my own. The one she hadn't birthed.

Triptolemus reached us and bowed, with less grace, next to his father.

"We will reside in my temple together," I instructed the boy who, to his credit, also hid his fear well. "And you will learn my story, and become my hero."

I offered my hand to him and, after a quick glance to his father, he took it.

"You will be my first hero. The one that all history will remember, a Goddess's favourite. Honoured by your peers, respected by your descendants and admired by your family for the privilege of being my attendant, while I reside in the Temple and wait for my daughter to come back to me."

I squeezed his hand and walked back to my animals. They stared at Triptolemus, and the boy was divided between his fascination with my serpents' beauty and his fear of their muscular bodies. He followed me as I set them free, untying them from the carriage. They stretched their bodies and moved to lie on a few rocks, lazing against the scorch of the sun. I took Triptolemus's hand again and walked into my half-finished temple.

Inside the Temple we were alone. The young boy stood still as I inspected the main space. He was afraid. His little life flickered as he followed me amid the shadows of the new home I had claimed.

"Did you know I have a daughter?"

He nodded.

"She was stolen from me. Her absence is the reason I am like this. That's the reason for all the misfortune that has befallen the world and all your people."

Triptolemus stayed silent, just waiting for a direct question to speak. I let go of his hand and walked around the altar that I had commanded Metaneira and Keleos to build for me. I could see the blood that would run over it. I could see the animals that would be sacrificed in my name, the way their life would end as their blood left and spread over this altar.

"Don't you think Zeus is at fault?" I asked him.

The boy opened his mouth and tried to find an answer. His eyes drifted up to the sky, but he failed to utter a word. Terrified to enrage me and my brother, he was lost as to what course of action could be the right one. I watched him from the corner of my eye as he struggled to find a way to react.

He lowered his body, bringing himself on his knees and his face on the floor, his forehead touching the stone.

"I don't blame you for what has happened," he said. "You are fighting for your child. You should fight with all the weapons you have at your disposal."

It wasn't an answer to my question. He cowered against insulting my brother, but I didn't hold that against him. I had often cowered against Zeus, and I was far stronger than Triptolemus would ever be.

The people of Eleusis kept working on my temple, and some women and men had entered its inner life, becoming my personal servants and priests. I was surprised that the King, Keleos, had also decided to be active in the daily rituals of my worship. They brought me food I didn't enjoy eating and they filled the temple with words of praise and devotion to me. They rarely spoke to me directly and even more rarely looked at my face.

Keleos's daughters visited me every day and brought little Demophon with them. Whatever joy or comfort I had drawn from the little baby was mostly gone. I caressed his soft body, and he was obedient as ever, always eager to be pleasant to me. He didn't cry when I ordered him to be sweet, happy, and cute, and he didn't complain when I held him too tightly. But there were no more secret dances between me and him. He was mine still, but I didn't like playing with him that much anymore.

Triptolemus and Keleos became my closest companions in that period of waiting and building. The King to show his piety towards me, and Triptolemus because he was the only human who dared meet my gaze. I tried to use Keleos's older son the way I had once used Demophon, but

Triptolemus didn't allow for daydreaming. He obeyed me always, answered my every question, but his gaze always hid within it a harsh honesty. I hated him for that constant reminder, and loved him for it. He focused my mind, and for that he was my favourite, even though he didn't shower me with gifts and praises.

My first Olympian visitor didn't take long to come. The Temple had barely been completed when, in the middle of the night, as I watched Triptolemus sleep on a small straw mattress close to me, I heard the soft tapping of feet. I immediately knew they were no human's.

I walked towards the exit of the temple to find Iris standing in front of the entrance, looking at the structure. She was wearing her usual loose white dress, hiding most of her body shape, adopting an androgenous style. Her two large eagle wings stretched out from her shoulders.

"I am not coming," I told her, because I knew there was only one reason why she was here. She was another messenger God, one of the most prominent and official. Hermes was too important for every menial task, so it fell to Iris to fulfil most communication needs between us Olympians.

"Our King orders your return to Olympus, Goddess Demeter," she narrated her message. "I have been tasked to take you."

"I am not coming," I insisted. "Not without my daughter. I will never step back on Olympus without Kore."

Iris didn't seem surprised by my words. I wondered if even there was a spark of excitement at my rebellion. She hadn't been our ally in the war with the Titans and had worked hard to build her reputation amid the new ruling order. I knew she didn't like Zeus, as she was a close friend of Hera and blamed my brother for her mistress's jealous rages and misery.

"Is that the full message you want me to relay to him?"

"Yes," I said.

I knew she would say it word for word. Unlike Hermes, she wasn't actively trying to be in his good graces, partly protected by Hera and partly because it was her divine duty to say the words as they were spoken. Hermes might have feared losing power, but Iris had more duties than power and for that she was freer to be a good messenger.

It was a short visit. She nodded and flew into the dark sky, going straight to Olympus to relay my message to the rest of the Olympians and all the other Gods who were hiding by their side. I wondered if Hestia had told Zeus that this was a futile attempt, that there was only one way to appease me, and that was to bring me back my child.

I was visited by many Gods and Goddess the next few nights. Each of them came to plead with me. They alluded to my beauty, my peace-making and life-giving skills. They whispered that I was so kind, and they always loved me. I asked each of them if they would support me against Zeus in getting my daughter back. Each of them lowered their head and remained silent. Some tried to plead again, but after a few days they all seemed to come expecting to be turned away. Still, they insisted on pressurising me to become obedient and placid again, as I used to be. To be the Demeter they had always known.

"No more," I said to them, and they all left defeated.

After a few days of silence, I heard the soft tapping of steps again. I wondered what deity had decided to come see me today, to change my mind and make me obey. I walked outside to find the only person I never imagined would come.

"Hera?" I asked. My surprise couldn't be hidden when my little sister turned around and stared at me.

"Your temple looks very good," she praised the work of the Eleusians. "I might need to ask a King to build me one. The Queen of Olympus cannot be outdone in grandness and majesty."

I didn't care at all whether she had a better temple than me. She had always been the one who cared about such things.

"Are you surprised I am here?" she asked directly. "I definitely am surprised I came."

"Why did you come?" I asked. I knew there would be no pleading from her. She wouldn't shower me with praises and soft words. It wasn't in Hera's nature to be like that.

"Officially, to convince you to come back," Hera said. "That's what I told Zeus."

I lifted one eyebrow at her. "But that's not the reason?"

She cocked her head to the left and examined me. She looked suddenly like a girl, even though she had matured long before me. "I came to talk to you as a mother. As a sister."

"And convince me to come and obey?"

She shrugged. "I know this will never happen," she said. "But I wanted to talk to you, nonetheless. About Kore."

My body went frigid at the mention of my child. "My daughter was stolen from me. As her mother, I was owed to be consulted for her wedding. My permission was to be asked. I am Demeter, a daughter of Kronos and one of the first Olympians! I fought and won alongside Zeus. He had no right to do as he pleased with my child! My one and only child."

There was a flicker of knowledge in her, but I didn't care to chase it. I didn't want to learn that she probably knew of Poseidon's parasites that came out of me.

"It is a good marriage, Demeter," Hera said once I finished. "What marriage would have been better? Or were you never planning to allow her to marry? Was she to simply be a girl because you couldn't let her go?"

I gaped at Hera and, before I could stop myself, I sent my divinity towards her, forcing it upon her and demanding a closer connection as Hestia and I used to do when we were in Father's stomach. When Hera was terrified of being lost amid that union. She didn't let me in, but neither did she get angry at my attempt to hurt her.

"These bursts of anger are not going to help you, Demeter," Hera warned me.

"Are you saying I was a bad mother? That I enslaved my own child?" I demanded, ignoring her words.

It was so unlike us to fight like that. We had grown apart slowly after her marriage. Zeus's influence on her chipped our relationship bit by bit until antagonism became the deciding factor of our relationships.

"I am not saying anything like that," Hera answered calmly. So unlike her usual bursts of pride whenever she was confronted. "I threw my son away, Demeter. I am not the one that can pass judgement on motherhood."

I had judged her when Hephaestus came to Olympus and that story had been revealed.

"What are you saying then?"

"I am only saying that Kore wasn't given away to a mortal King, beneath her station as Zeus's daughter. She holds one of the most powerful positions. Queen to an entire realm."

"My daughter is not you." I don't think I had ever uttered harsher words to Hera. I don't think that I had ever spoken with such disdain and disrespect to her ever before. "To love power and the men who hold it."

I was expecting her to be angry and attack me herself. I expected her to shout insults or threaten me. She, who had always held her head high, looking down on everyone else, closed her eyes and her face contorted in sorrow.

"I didn't, Demeter," she whispered, her words barely audible.

She let her divinity leak out of her, like a small, weak stream, and it reached me. She had never opened herself to me like that before. I was terrified suddenly, as it softly tapped onto mine, asking for whatever truth it hid to be allowed entrance in my mind. I hesitated, but eventually allowed a small opening for our natures to meet and, perhaps for the first time, a truly honest conversation to take place between us.

"That night in the clearing, I lied, Demeter."

My mind went to our night conversation when she declared her love for Zeus and her intention to marry him.

"Why?" But I knew why and didn't need her to say it. "He raped you?"

Her small nod was so slight that I nearly missed it. But I knew I spoke the truth, because her divinity spiked not in anger but sorrow and regret. All this time, I had mistaken her anger for bitterness that Zeus hadn't loved her as he promised, because of her shattered pride and being constantly surrounded by her husband's bastards. Many of these bastard descendants were stronger than her own, becoming major Olympian Deities over her own children.

"Why did you marry him then?"

She let out a laugh and I felt the anger in her divinity change to sadness and melancholy. "Because without him, what would I be? I had no allies to help me, Demeter. So, I decided that I had to make the best of the situation. I became the Queen of Olympus, the Queen of the Sky and the ridicule of all females, constantly betrayed by my husband, whom I didn't even love."

She withdrew back to herself. I tried to hold her close, to keep our conversation open and fragile.

"I am sorry," I told her.

"The plan was spoiled before I was even married. The first person he betrayed me with, the night before our marriage, was you, the sister who had tried to keep me from marrying him," she added. "But you were smarter than me. You used your sexual intercourse to gain a freedom that will never be mine. I thought I could be the most respected as his wife, but I should have asked for other things, as you did."

I didn't understand what she meant. How could she have known of the deal that Zeus made with me after our one and only contact? "I am not free."

"Freer than me," Hera said. "You are not tied to any man." She turned around and showed the world. "I don't have the power to force a war all on my own against Zeus. I don't have the power to make life die as you do."

We stared at each other, and I felt a deep desire to reach her, hug her and keep her close. I wanted to convince her to stay by my side. To join my fight. But something else tagged at my mind before I could do that.

"Why do you think that the marriage is good for Kore, then? After what happened to you?"

"Because it is a good marriage. It is a powerful position, and if Hades is truly as mad for her as everyone claims, she has even more power in the Underworld realm than I do as Zeus's legal wife. If she can hold Hades infatuated with her, she will be in control of his whole dominion."

"But why does it have to be this way?! Why does her power and importance need to be defined by the man she marries? I don't want that for her."

Hera crossed her arms, and her face once more took on her usual expression of pride and all-knowing look.

"You always talk about Kore in relation to you. Have you noticed that? She is always an extension of your state of being. Your happiness. Your sorrow. Your wounded pride. It isn't simply about getting her back. It is about ensuring that your power and position will never be diminished again. Zeus, even though he doesn't admit it, is afraid of you. He didn't expect you to be able to last this long, he didn't think you would actually be a threat, and that is why he gave Kore away without telling you. He never expected you to react as you did. You might be the first female that has battled him to such an extent, and he is unable to strike you down."

"I am not doing this to win any wars or negotiate any political power in Olympus. All I want and care about is that my daughter is returned to me."

"I know, that is all you care about."

There was a hidden element behind her inflection of the word you. Was it an insult? Was it knowledge of something I didn't know? I wasn't sure what to make of it.

"I have said what I wanted," Hera said, interrupting my thoughts. "I think you should help your daughter retain control of Hades. Guide her in how to negotiate her position in the realm, to gain power within it the same way you have, help her become a powerful Queen. That was all I wanted to tell you."

Before I had a chance to say anything else, she vanished away to Olympus. Her words rang true in my mind, and a traitorous thinking whispered that I had done the same thing in so many ways. I had exchanged my body for power. Hera proposed that I helped Kore ensure she had more power, but I didn't want that for her.

I had always shied away from the other ways that I could describe my sexual intercourse with Zeus. A transaction, a ritual, a show of obedience, and the last of the ways I could call it was prostitution. Even if I had done it to keep myself safe, to keep myself strong. Even though I had only done it once, the act was uncomfortably similar to the concept of offering sexual pleasure to gain something of value in return. There was never any desire between me and Zeus. There was never any love, nor other feelings that pushed me to him. And, unlike Hera, I did it of my own free will.

I couldn't hold it anymore and I screamed. That scream echoed all over Greece, and I sucked out life again. I searched within the soil for the barest seed of life and strangled it. I reached all over the sea and killed any sea plant. All of Greece, maybe all the world, ruled by Gods I had never met and didn't want to meet, would die before I had my daughter back.

I didn't want to think about what Hera had suggested. I didn't want to negotiate and find a silver lining. The time for that was long gone. I didn't want to be thought of as weak. I didn't want to be placated. I wanted my demands met, and I wanted Zeus, who had infested my family, slowly drawing wedges between us, and nurturing sick habits in my brothers, to see that I wouldn't bow down to him.

"No more," I screamed up to the sky. "No more!"

Who was I talking to? My siblings who had forgotten our early life? I found myself hurt all over. How could Hades, the brother I had loved the most, do this to me? He, who had always kept the farthest from Zeus, acted in the same way. How could I have been so wrong about my own brother? How could Hestia not fight alongside me? How could Hera not have told us the truth when we could have still pushed Zeus out? How could Poseidon, that boy God who promised to save me, become my rapist? How could this have happened to me? To us?

"No more," I yelled, but it was a lost battle, and I knew it.

How could I have stood and watched Zeus take command of my family, wonder why he was made leader, and kept my questions to myself?

How could I have slept with him, making my power linked to him? Linking my daughter to him?

It was a lost battle now. It was too late.

The next day, my power was different than any other time I had caused starvation. I felt every bit of food in the world but the town of Eleusis turn to mould. Every tree died, every plant died. I made Greece a wasteland. I made Greece the realm of the dead, subtly inviting my brother, the King of the Underworld, to take everything. I had become truly mad, truly deadly. I deserved to be the mother of the Queen of the Dead.

I looked up and saw Helios's shocked face as he flew through the blue sky, looking down at in terror. There had only been one other creature who had inspired such fear in others and that was Father. I had become Father's daughter in legacy, not only in flesh. I had dragged the world into darkness, as he had swallowed me into his own stomach. I deprived the world of hope, as he had deprived me of light. I took away the future, as he had eaten mine away.

The messengers came again, this time all day. They pleaded and cried. They begged.

"No more," I answered each of them. "I am no more the Goddess I used to be. My demands will be met, or we will all lose."

Some threatened me. "You will not come unscathed out of this. You will invoke a new war."

"There is nothing worse that can happen to me than to be separated from my daughter. All this will end if she comes back to me."

The people of Eleusis were mad with fear themselves. They had never been visited by so many Gods and Goddesses before. I saw them hide behind the doors of their houses. I saw the ones serving me in the Temple fall on the floor and hide their faces whenever a God or Goddess appeared. The men also told me that many animals and small creatures like Nymphs had settled at the outskirts of Eleusis. That was the beginning of the war, the beginning of my last battle with Zeus regarding Kore, and I had started gathering allies. It was the final test for Zeus, showing more clearly and more blatantly than ever before that I was not going away, and his rule wasn't indefinite nor indisputable.

SPRING

Days passed, and humanity was closer to extinction than ever before. Already, other animals had been lost from the world forever. My visitors had stopped coming to my Temple, and life at Eleusis had returned to a semblance of peace, albeit a fake one. Wherever I walked, I saw forced smiles and the terror still present in the eyes of the humans who surrounded and served me. However, their fear didn't overshadow how grateful and in awe of me they were, because stories of how fast people were dying elsewhere reached them every day. They knew the only reason they had enough to live on was my presence and grace towards them. So even though I felt how forced their manners were and their fear of what else might happen between me and my brother, I also sensed the relief they felt that I had chosen their kingdom to make my final stand against Zeus.

Each morning I looked up at the sky, searching for signs that Zeus was coming to speak to me and put our custody battle to an end. Each day, his absence made it clear that he needed more of life to die before he would realize that there was no other way to end this but to come and face me. Some days, I expected him to come for a battle, thunderbolt in hand, while others I expected him to appear tired and accept my terms. Neither happened.

I stretched my hand to Triptolemus, who took it obediently, and we began walking towards the fields where my
serpents rested. He greeted them with respect, and my animals moved their faces closer to him, allowing him to caress
their scales. The boy rested his face against their bodies. I
watched as he kissed them and felt a tinge of happiness at
the sight. I was fond of Triptolemus, who had eased his fear
around me, although he never allowed himself to forget that
I was his superior.

The sound of wings made my serpents hiss and ready
themselves for battle. I looked towards the sky and saw Hermes flying towards me. I wondered if it was another
summons to Olympus, and I prepared myself to refuse his
offer. I prepared to close my ears to any segment of logic he
might say to me to convince me to take even half a step back
from where I was.

I was standing still. I had decided that. It was Zeus's turn
to react.

The sun made the messenger God appear as a dark figure. Helios's power shone bright, making me struggle to see
Hermes for a moment. I put my hand over my eyes to cast a
shadow and I realized Hermes wasn't coming to me alone.
In his arms, a female was hanging.

My serpents, having sharper eyes than me, let out a
sound of joy and went flying towards him. Hermes was
holding the most beautiful and special woman in the world.

She jumped from Hermes's arms onto my serpents and
their bodies danced with each other as they fell. Their wings
flapped and guided their joined bodies towards me. I opened
my arms and she fell into them.

"Mother!"

Her voice. I had missed her voice so much. I held her in my arms and breathed her smell, forcing all my power towards her and screaming with all my being that she was mine and returned.

"My child!" I cried, and tears of joy ran down my face. The sensation of having her again in my arms, of being close to her, was one that I had never experienced before. Every moment of joy that I had ever experienced was small and insignificant compared the feeling of having her in my arms again. Seeing the light at my birth, my freedom from Father's stomach, meant nothing compared to the feeling of relief, completeness, and joy that her body in my arms gave me. My divinity rushed over to her, in that most intimate way that us, Gods, engaged in. I enveloped her in my power, and she circled me with hers.

My serpents joined our embrace and squeezed us tightly, making us complete.

I didn't even realize how my joy had leapt out of me. Rather, I smelled it. Roses, lilies, daisies. Their scents reached me. I felt the grass beneath my feet and the sound of the bees dancing all over me. I heard the prayers of joy reach me. All of Greece sighed in relief as life was returned into the soil and the harsh years of starvation, pain and extinction came to an end.

All of humanity, all animals, all plants, all creatures upon the land joined in my celebration. Order had been restored. Life had returned. Mother and daughter were finally reunited, as they ought to be.

The tighter I hugged her, the more my divinity pushed towards her and hugged hers. She was still the rejuvenation I remembered, the joy of my life. She had edges that were harsher, parts that were colder, but she was still a child of nature, my child. I would help her heal all scars from the ordeal. I would help her reclaim all the bits of herself that Hades and Zeus stole from her. All that mattered was that we were together again. United.

I don't know how long we held each other. I don't know how long it took me to gather the strength to move an inch away from her and look at her face.

"Kore," I cried. "Look how beautiful you are! You changed!"

She had changed physically, too. Her face had lost some of its childish fat. It was my daughter, there was no doubt of that, but she was older, wiser, and stronger.

"We both changed," she told me and placed her hands over my cheeks, like I used to do to her when she was a little girl.

I kissed her face many times, caressed her hair. "How are you? Did he hurt you? I am so sorry for not being able to save you from that. I am so sorry that you had to experience the darkness. I tried to spare you that pain, to keep you in the beauty of the light."

Kore let me speak without interrupting. Once I finished expressing all my regret and shame for failing her, she smiled at me.

"It is all right, Mother," she comforted me and kissed my forehead, as if she was the mother and I the child.

Hermes had stayed and watched our reunion. He made a small coughing sound. My serpents hissed as if to scold him for interrupting the moment.

"Father said that he will send someone soon to escort you both to Olympus."

I had promised that only with my child next to me I would step onto Olympus again. I still wanted to scream and vent for the pain his father's actions had caused. But Kore beat me to respond.

"Thank you, Hermes," she said.

I watched as her eyes narrowed at him and Hermes shifted in his stance. Something was said between them, but I didn't know what. I didn't know what they could possibly have to say to each other. My daughter's expression turned darker and nearly threatening, until Hermes flew away and we were left alone. I felt then a deeper change in her. Her divinity was stronger than ever before, but it was no longer that spark of light I had felt in my stomach when she was conceived. It was cooler, darker. It reminded me of Hades. It reminded me of the monster I had lived with most of my life, the Dark Demeter I had merged with to become whoever I now was.

It wasn't just some spots that had changed. It was as if all she was to me was perfectly mixed with this other side of power she now possessed. In my joy and excitement of our reunion, I hadn't noticed this change. Or I had assumed that whatever harsher part of her I felt when our divinities mingled was simply a bad memory.

However, I could clearly see now that she was changed in much deeper way.

"Triptolemus," I said and turned to find the boy hiding behind trees. "Run to the city and tell them the good news. Tell them to spread the word that Kore has returned. Mother and Daughter are finally reunited."

My daughter's eyes moved towards the young boy, who stood up and began running away.

"Mother," she began and turned her face towards me.

"Tell me everything that happened to you!" I demanded. "Everything!" Something was done to my child. I sensed the trap that had been laid. Even though she was returned to me, our fight to stay together wasn't finished.

Kore took a deep breath and began narrating the tale of her abduction: How she had approached the flowers and Hades appeared from the earth. How he grabbed her and shoved her onto his golden carriage led by his dark horses. How the earth swallowed her, closing above her, closing off the light under which she had always lived. How she screamed and didn't want to go. How scared she was.

"The Underworld was scary at first. Very cold and dark. It was the saddest place I had ever been. The souls, the dead roamed around the place. So sad," she described Hades's kingdom. "I didn't think there could be anything worse. Hades wanted us to marry the same night I arrived."

"The night he stole you," I snapped, and my daughter didn't say anything, only continued her tale.

She spoke of her marriage a few weeks after she arrived in the Underworld, their first night which was thankfully not as violent as I feared. "I felt different after that, Mother," she said, and the words were bitter. "Like, I was no longer Kore anymore. Not only Kore." Her divinity spiked as she spoke, and I was shocked to see a hint of thrill in her narration of her life as Queen.

"But I missed you so much," she finished, and the words soothed my heart. Our bond was beyond anything Hades could have corrupted. "I was always so sad because I couldn't see you. And my sorrow was so great that it took me a while to notice the dead had changed. That they were dying faster than ever before and some even welcomed the realm of the dead because they were freed from the hunger that plagued the living world. It took a long time for the news to reach the Underworld. I heard my own story narrated, my abduction and what happened to you, sweet Mother." She took my hands and kissed them many times. "That my absence had broken your heart so much that all of life was dying. I was so sad to be away from you, to not be able to hug you and take your pain away."

I squeezed her hands. "I was fighting for you. To give you your freedom back."

"I was so happy when Hermes came and told me that Father had spoken with Hades and I was allowed me to leave Erebus. I would have the chance to see you again. And you to see me, to bandage the scars in your heart so that the world could be healed."

"Zeus let things reach this point. He allowed your abduction; did you know that?"

She nodded and lowered her head. "Hades told me," she confirmed.

"And then you came here? Is that all that happened?"

Her eyebrows narrowed in thought. "Yes, nothing else," she said. One of my serpents rested their head onto Kore's lap. She lowered her head and kissed its scales.

"I missed you too," she whispered, and the animal shivered with delight.

"We all missed you, Kore," I said. "The entire world felt your absence."

Her caresses stopped and she looked up to me. "Mother," she began, and I knew something terrible would be uttered from her lips. I wanted to put my hand over her mouth to stop it from being said. I lifted my arm, unsure whether I would caress her face again, or cover her mouth. Perhaps Kore understood that I was conflicted and lay backwards, out of my reach.

"I am not Kore anymore," she said quickly, as if she needed to say those words and free herself from that final part of her tale.

I didn't understand what she meant. I didn't know who she could be, if not my Kore. "Of course you are. My daughter."

She shook her head. "I mean my name, Mother. I am no longer called Kore. That title belongs to the past. I now have another name."

"Another name?" I stared at her. "Who changed your name?"

"No one, Mother," she insisted.

What kind of trap had Hades set? What had he done to my child to make her deny the name I gave her?

"Hades did nothing, Mother," she said, as if she was reading my thoughts. "I changed. I became something else. I am no longer the same girl. Our natures aren't like those of animals or humans. They aren't like those of trees and flowers. We change, we shift in ways that they, perhaps because their lives are shorter, don't."

I did know what she meant. I had changed a lot during her absence. I was a different entity, a different Goddess than the one she had last called Mother.

"And what is your name now?"

"Persephone," she said. The name sounded beautiful as it came out of her lips, nearly melodic. But it was a dangerous name. I watched how her entire being changed just by uttering the sounds. It was a tiny change, a small shift, but words had power, especially the words of our self-identification.

"The one who brings death." I translated the meaning of her name. "How could someone as kind and pure as you hold such a dark name? You were born for the light and beauty of this world, born to bring me joy and give meaning and shape to my life."

"Kore was born for that," she replied. "I used to be her. I remember how it felt to be so innocent, so protected." She paused and stared at me. Her gazed hardened, suddenly resembling her father and the Dark Demeter I had met in the cave in Arcadia. "So naïve. Enamoured with flowers and pretty songs. I, now, am the one for whom the world nearly ended."

"Persephone." I tried the word and she smiled. "Do you want to be this kind of being?"

"I already am," my daughter said. "You are different too, Mother. You might still call yourself Demeter, but your epithets have been amplified. You are now called Erinys, Melaina."

I couldn't deny her words. We were both different creatures. It didn't matter that I had changed to get her back and she had changed to survive the world of the dead. The result was the same, and we had no other option but to obey our natures, follow them and see what paths they might force us to face. Or rather, we would see what dilemmas our new selves would face and, depending on our choices, we would both change again.

"I have a temple in Eleusis," I told her, changing the subject. "Would you like to see it, Persephone?"

I stood up and offered her my hand. She took it and I pulled her up. She wrapped her arms around my back, and I did the same.

"This will be a major site for our worship," I said. "It will be one of the most important celebrations in all of Greece."

"It should," she agreed. "My mother is the Goddess Demeter, the mother of the earth. A daughter of Kronos and one of the original Olympians. You are due a concrete and dedicated cult in your honour and power."

The people of Eleusis greeted us on their knees. They rejoiced and began a celebration at the news that my daughter had returned. We walked amid the people, both of our divinities bringing fruits forth from the trees, and making the soil grow life, wild and superb. I was glad to see that whatever change had occurred, there was a part of my Kore which still existed. My power was still strong in her. I let myself hope that with time, right by my side forever, she might change back to the Kore I lost.

"Persephone," I called her name. It came out of my mouth with difficulty, like a foreign parasite. I wasn't sure if I was meant to make it feel at home with me, accept it as part of the natural order of my life, or to fight it to extinction. "These are some of my favourites," I said, and introduced her to the four daughters of Keleos. "And you remember Triptolemus. He is my companion and attendant in the temple."

She nodded and fixed her gaze on the young boy. Triptolemus lowered his head and bowed to both of us.

"Goddess, I am glad you have your child back. It is only right."

I nodded, and we continued into the Temple.

The next few days went by fast. Persephone and I were inseparable, and although I often caught glimpses of expressions that I didn't recognize, my heart was softer just by being closer to her. But complete relief still eluded me. I couldn't let my feelings ease. I had her back now, but what if she was taken from me again? That thought ate inside me, transforming into a new monster that resided at my core. I panicked each moment she was out of my sight, even if I could hear her voice or smell her; the idea that I could do anything and she would be lost again, maybe this time forever, made my body tremble with fear.

I had to find a way to ensure she was never taken from me again. That Zeus would never allow anyone else to set eyes on her. That he would never dare to make any decisions about her without my consent and permission. These thoughts controlled my mind as we spent those first precious days together.

I knew that soon we would be summoned back to Olympus. My return would officially mean my rebellion against Zeus, my disobedience against the King of Olympus, was over. I had won my girl back, but I knew my little brother's pride wouldn't allow for my victory to be simple. I had to be on my guard for a long time. Perhaps for the rest of time.

Together with my daughter, we taught the people of Eleusis the ways to worship both of us, beginning a rite that would continue until the end of time, or perhaps until there was another Godly rebellion, and the world order was reshaped again. Keleos, eager to establish himself as one of my favourites amid other Greek Kings, ordered for all of Eleusis to follow my commands.

We participated in the first celebration and were worshipped in body and spirit by all the people. During that first and momentous celebration, I bestowed many gifts to all my favourite humans. I whispered good luck to the four girls who had brought me there, kissed Demophon one last time, remembering the comfort his little body had given me once, and finally, as I stared at Metaneira, I bestowed the greatest gift to Triptolemus.

"To the bastard prince of Eleusis," I declared, "I give these newly hatched winged serpents."

Persephone carried the babies in her embrace and gave them to Triptolemus. He held them in his arms and was startled by the present and the honour. His eyes darted up towards my own, completely unafraid for a moment, and then he knelt in front of me. He placed the baby serpents on his lap and bowed deeply, kissing the edge of my dress.

"I am not worthy of such an honour," he whispered, but I could tell he wanted to keep them.

"As with all divine gifts, they come with responsibility," I said. "You will be my hero among men, my chosen representative and messenger. I have been teaching you of the secrets of agriculture, the practice of farming, cultivating the soil for the growing of life within it. This will be something all humans will need to learn to do better from now on."

I turned to Keleos. The moment he felt my gaze on him, he stood up and walked next to his son. He put his hand over his son's head, and I could see the pride that shone on his face. From the corner of my eye, I could also see Metaneira, the fool who denied her son the opportunity to be a special creature, a God, overshadowed in history by Triptolemus.

Her face betrayed the pain of injustice and wounded pride. It was a good expression for her to wear.

"King Keleos, you shall help your son raise these serpents. Once they are grown, you will build a chariot for Triptolemus so he can begin his mission for me. He will fly all over Greece, spreading the knowledge I have passed on to him."

The King bowed. "It is an honour to our household," he said. "I will do all I can and must to support Triptolemus in his duty to you."

"Thank you," Triptolemus added.

I didn't speak to them again. Persephone and I watched as the humans exercised the rites we taught them, dancing mock battles. Their faith reached both of us as we sat on our modest thrones.

Persephone leaned closer to me. "We should establish more ceremonies and mysteries in your name, Mother."

I nodded. I wanted it. I wanted more of what the people of Eleusis had given me. Why had I not worked on claiming their time and dedication sooner? What had stopped the previous Demeter from demanding worship in the format of my choice? What had made me timid and afraid to stand on the ground and demand of the humans I fed and kept alive to move as I commanded and dictated?

"We definitely should. To both of us," I squeezed her hand and she smiled at me. Her expression broke the spell for a moment. There was greed in her eyes, power-lust. I had never thought my sweet and innocent child would ever wear such a face. But she was Persephone now, not my Kore, and we had both changed from the simple family duo we once were.

Once the celebrations ended, Persephone and I went for a walk around the area. Our steps left behind them a trail of flowers, of beautiful smells and sounds of all the animals that sprang to that new life our mere feet bestowed. There was a pandemonium of life wherever we stood. As we crossed the now green plain of Rhario, our escort appeared in front of my temple. Most humans were asleep, tired from the festivities. The few that were still awake didn't say anything. They didn't have to. Their duty would be to declare our departure to the rest of Eleusis.

"Daughter, grand-daughter," Rhea called us. "I am here to take you back to our King, Zeus. There is a great celebration in honour of your arrival back on Olympus. Come!"

Persephone was aware of my own difficult relationship with my mother. I had kept her away from Rhea as much as I could, not because I feared her, but because I didn't want to share any more with her than I already did. This was something Zeus knew, and he had decided to send her to bring me back, signalling that I was right to fear him. He was mad, and even though he was forced to do as I wanted, a new bitter petty fight would start between us. He would try to spoil all my joys from now on.

It didn't matter. I squeezed Persephone next to me, pulling her even closer. Nothing mattered apart from being with my child. Everything else I could endure.

"Let's go," I told my child. We walked slowly towards Rhea.

Her eyes travelled between me and Persephone. "You have changed, both of you."

"We had to," Persephone said. "To survive."

244

"Come," Rhea said again. "Zeus calls you back to the family of Gods. Obey his will and increase, for the rest of time, the food which gives humans life, so they will shower us with gifts, pray our magnificence and obey our commands."

Persephone squeezed my hand, signalling her own consent to the offer. I put my arm around her shoulders, kissed her pretty and flower-scented hair, and nodded my agreement as well.

SUMMER

Our arrival was indeed greeted with great honours. All the Gods who had visited me, begging, and threatening me to obey and stop my rebellion, were present. The ones who had called me selfish and cruel because I demanded for my daughter to come back. Now, they celebrated my return, praising Zeus for reuniting me and our daughter again. We walked through them as we made our way to Zeus's throne, where he would receive us. They offered us flowers which I had allowed to live again, offered us ambrosia and sweet fruits, and hugged us.

All of them had come to stop me from fighting for my daughter. The hypocrisy of their well-wishing and love enraged me, but Persephone held me close. Each time I felt I'd had enough of it, that I wanted to remind them how they had tried to stop my fight and none of them had stood by my side, my daughter held me close and pulled me forward. She was better at dealing with the hypocrisy. She nodded her head to their wishes, spoke confidently of how happy she was to see them, and we continued our way towards the heart of Olympus, where Zeus's throne was.

Hestia, now forced out of the Dodecatheon, but still too important to be standing at the gates for our arrival, ran and hugged us first. I held her close, kissed her cheeks and squeezed her in my hug. Persephone did the same.

"I am so glad you are back," she told my daughter, who kissed her aunt in return. We continued further and were greeted with the sight of the rest of the Olympians. Zeus stood and looked down at us. He forced his lips to stretch, showing us his teeth, declaring that his anger was still present for the humiliation I had forced upon him. Athena, his most beloved child, stood close to him, wearing her proud helmet. She also looked at me in scorn. The one who had no mother and was allowed to never bear children, to never suffer against men's injustice because of her place as the King's favourite child. My eyes settled on Poseidon after, the little brother who had found me in my darkest hour, only to steal from me the last shred of strength and dignity I had left.

"Sister! Daughter!" Zeus called and stood up. "Welcome back home," he opened his arms, inviting us to a hug. Persephone didn't wait for my cue. She walked towards her father and allowed his arms to envelop her in a hug. I fought with all my strength not to rush and push her away. I couldn't stand that he was touching her, that he was calling her daughter and pretending this was a happy occasion for him. It made me want to spit poison on his face and watch it melt, revealing to everyone how ugly he was.

Zeus's eyes were focused on me as he hugged Persephone. I had to do this, play along with this game so this part of my life and story could be put to rest. Once he let go of Persephone, I moved closer and allowed him to put his arms over my shoulders. I kept my face impassive as he pulled me in. His face rested on the crook of my neck.

"We will talk about this," he whispered to me, and I couldn't help but smirk.

My eyes moved to my other sister, Hera, who kept her gaze firmly away from mine. Once our embrace ended, he put his right hand over my waist and his left went around Persephone's shoulders, allowing the rest of the Gods gathered to see us united. They clapped and wished us well, saying nonsense of how wonderful it was for a daughter to be reunited with both her father and mother.

I moved slowly away but retained my smirk. There was a moment when our eyes met, and I wondered if all pretences would be dropped then and there. He hated the look on my face, and I knew he also feared me, just a little. He feared pushing me, because he knew I had become a different person to the sister he had once dominated.

"It is good to be back on Olympus, little brother," I said, loud enough for all the other Olympians to hear us. His eyes twitched at the term, one that he didn't tolerate, and I insisted on using.

He turned to Persephone. "Drink for the return of Kore and Demeter!" He lifted his cup, and the rest of Olympus did the same. A wave of cheers followed.

Persephone took a filed cup of ambrosia and lifted it. "Thank you, Father!" she said. "Thank you for arranging for Mother and me to see each other again." She took a sip and lifted it again. "And for giving me the opportunity to introduce myself again to Olympus. I am no longer called Kore. As the wife of Hades, the Queen of the Underworld, I am now called Persephone."

There was silence as the news spread over all the attendants. Hera turned slowly towards me. Our eyes locked and she smiled, as if she understood something that I didn't. It irked me, but I had never been a wife or a Queen to anyone, and perhaps that was now a distance between me and my child. And a connection between her and Hera, the two Queens of the Gods, one of the realm above, and one of the realm below.

"To Persephone!" Zeus said, reclaiming his cool and drinking another big sip of his ambrosia.

At his approval of the change, the rest took their sip. "To Persephone!" they hailed.

My daughter held her head high and smiled at the assembly. Her face betrayed a pride that I didn't recognize in the child I had raised. That glee and delight in the attention she received, the power her new name betrayed. It was a happiness I couldn't join in. I had barely learnt to appreciate this kind of power and found it uncomfortable that my daughter was so at ease with it. It was hard to accept that she and I, who had been so similar and close for so long, a dual existence since her birth, had such a critical difference.

My fragile secret wish that with time I could turn her back to Kore, that simple and pure girl I loved, crashed inside me. Persephone didn't want to become Kore again. I had to admit that. It was evident from the way she announced her new identity at each chance she had. It was my duty, my task, to love Persephone for herself, not only as an evolution of Kore.

The celebrations lasted for days. Gods, Goddesses, nymphs, demigods and any other immortal creature that was on Olympus drank until they were overtaken by a frenzy. The worst of all was Dionysus, Zeus's son who replaced Hestia as an Olympian. He walked about with vines on his hair and offered wine to everyone who was close to him. I drank little, watching in quiet how Olympus continued to pretend that Zeus had been kind and generous, the wise All-Father, instead of a proud man that was left with no option.

I went for frequent walks alone in the gardens, seeking quietness to collect my thoughts. It was no surprise to me that during one of these walks, Zeus followed me. Without any witnesses to his anger, he grabbed my elbow and pushed me against the wall.

"How dare you do this?"

"I should be asking that," I retorted. "How dare you make a decision about my child without my consent! How dare you marry her to Hades without my permission!"

He began laughing. "Your consent? Your permission?" he mocked me. "Why should I, the King of all Gods, the King of Olympus, the God of the Sky, the most powerful of all, have to speak to you about strengthening my alliance with my brother."

His divinity came at me, hard and cruel as he was. It stoked me hard like one of his thunderbolts, but I was strong too and could take the pain. My own divinity rose in me and went at him. It went like the feeling of starvation I caused, like the absence of all life, like the monster I had merged with. He was surprised to see such darkness in me. His face didn't manage to hide it.

"What did you become?" he asked me. "You disgraced yourself. You have lost all the beauty of your womanhood."

It was my turn to laugh. "My womanhood?" I approached him. "I did what I had to survive. I did what I had to in order to get my daughter back. You should have known that my obedience to you was only through her. Whatever I am and whatever I have done, however the balance of power has changed because of our custody battle, it is all your fault and your choice."

He didn't engage with my words again. He lifted his finger threateningly. "Never humiliate me like that again."

He started walking away, but I sent my divinity after him. He stopped and turned to look at me again, unable to hide his anger.

"Did you send Poseidon to find me in Arcadia?" I asked.

He didn't say anything. He simply stared at me, stunned at the question and perhaps uncaring of the answer.

"I don't know what you are talking about," he said, he lied.

"Did you send Poseidon to chase me, rape me as an attempt to break me? Because my initial reaction wasn't passive as you wanted? Because I didn't bow my head to you and your decision, all-seeing little brother?"

He didn't respond. He turned around and walked away, fleeing from my truth.

"Did you get angry that it didn't break me? Did you get angry that my reaction forced you to speak to the Moirai, to send them to me?" I taunted. I could see he wanted to lunge at me, force me against the wall again, make me feel like a piece of trash compared to his power.

But he didn't take my bait. He kept walking away and I decided that it wasn't maturity or wisdom that made him ignore my accusation, but fear. Fear of what would happen if our rivalry continued, fear that I would end the world, just to spite him.

Over the next few days, Persephone and I resumed our usual duties while we were on Olympus. We ate alongside the other Gods. We joined in the extended celebratory mood of the reunion of the Dodecatheon. However, I felt eyes always on my back. Everyone was wary of me, unsure as to whether to relax in my presence or to be ready for a future feud. It seemed that my hug with Zeus appeared as hollow as it felt. I ignored their gazes and the feeling of tension they gave me as they pierced me from behind. Instead, I turned to the comfortable occupation of my old work. I walked all over Olympus's palace gardens, adding new flowers amid the existing ones Persephone and I had revived.

It was a pleasurable surprise that my daughter sought my company. She no longer chased after her friends and tried to find excuses to be without me in their presence. Instead, it appeared that with her newfound strength and confidence, she and I grew to be closer as well. We went for walks and talked. Sometimes we spoke of the future and the plans we had for new temples we would build, or the kind of gifts we might bestow on princes that we chose to have under our protection. Triptolemus was simply the beginning of our journey. Other times, we talked of the past and discussed the changes that had taken place on Olympus.

"Artemis keeps staring at us, have you noticed?" Persephone mentioned as we strolled slowly along a narrow wall path at the outer edges of Olympus.

I had noticed her intense gaze. "Don't mind her," I said. "They all stare when we turn our backs."

She linked her arms around mine and leaned closer. "I think her stare is different. I sense puzzlement rather than simple fear. As if she knows something that nobody else does," she whispered.

I shook my head. "She keeps herself away from most things, preferring to roam through the forests with her nymphs and animals. I doubt it."

Persephone stopped abruptly. "Just be mindful of her, Mother."

I smiled at her, touched by her worry for me. I had lost the young girl who depended on me for everything, who pouted and rebelled against me but, even though I missed Kore with all my being, I was starting to appreciate the allyship that the woman Persephone offered me. I nodded and I saw her relax as we continued our walk.

We walked down the steep narrow stairs of the wall and reached a small garden I had built for Kore—no, Persephone—to play in when she was little. I remembered how she had cried that she never had a place for herself to do as she wanted. I never let her have her own room, so I made her this garden, where she played with her friends as I stood at the wall, watching over her.

During our long walks, we even saw again some of the nymphs who used to be my child's friends. Their faces lowered in fear of me when we approached them and, although they were kind and happy around my daughter, I could also see a sense of fear towards her as well. Her new name carried with it a feeling of doom, of death, and her new title as the Queen of the underworld only intensified that fear. Most Gods had never been to Hades's realm, and their entire natures were completely separate from the world below. Even when our path crossed with them, Persephone didn't seem inclined to leave my company for theirs.

Other than the walks and conversations I had with Persephone, I spent time with Hestia. Even when we were alone, we never spoke of the conversation we'd had when she had visited me. I didn't press her. I was tempted to push for an answer as to why she didn't stay by my side, but I couldn't bring myself to open those wounds. On the few occasions the Dodecatheon was gathered to make an announcement, hear lower deities' complaints, bestow silly presents, or bless a marriage during my stay, I was shaken by grief to see Dionysus in her place. She was filled with grief as she watched us from a few steps below, knowing that she used to be one of us, one of the greatest. The insult hurt her, even if she chose to swallow her pride for the sake of peace.

I often tried to speak to Hera during those few days I was on Olympus, but each time I thought I had her cornered her, she escaped me, or her daughter, Hebe, appeared and pulled her away for urgent business. The only time we met was when the Dodecatheon was together and she stood right next to Zeus.

Even as we stood there, she avoided my eyes. Zeus was speaking to a demigod about a request he made, but I wasn't paying any attention to them. Instead, I had turned my head, looking at Hera, whose face was set to look straight ahead. I often wondered how did she do it? How did she manage to stand next to the person who had hurt her when she was so young, who continued to hurt her pride and diminish her beauty, and manage to look at him without disgust?

The demigod bowed and I thought the ceremony was over. I was ready to dash to Hera, grab her by the arm and force her to go for a walk with me. I would call for Hestia to follow us, even, but someone else walked into the open-air space where we held our audiences. I assumed it was another demigod or a nymph, but a quick glance showed that it was a daimon. All thoughts of Hera vanished from my mind. I turned my complete attention to the newcomer. The room grew silent, as it was a rare sight for such a creature to walk to Olympus. He was a creature of the realm of

Hades. He had no reason to come here, to seek advice or command from Zeus. His eyes went straight to Persephone, who was standing alongside Hestia, and he slowly bowed to her.

"My Queen," he greeted her, and Persephone nodded in response.

He avoided my face, intensifying my fear and suspicion that his arrival was an omen of bad things. He quickly looked towards Zeus and fell on his knees.

"Zeus Kronides, most high and most honoured God of all, I have come on behalf of your brother, Hades, the King of the Underworld."

Zeus glanced towards me, as if he knew to be afraid of whatever he would hear and must act upon. We both knew it had to do with my daughter, and he knew that if it was something I didn't like, I would start trouble all over again. I would end the world for Persephone, her new name suddenly ringing truer than before. It suited her new place in the world: my love for her knew no bounds and held no mercy.

"I haven't seen Hades in a long time," Zeus said. Our brother rarely, if ever, left his realm. "What news of him do you bring, daimon?"

"Askalaphos." Persephone introduced him to us.

The daimon lowered his body towards her again. "He ordered me to remind you that there is a rule in the Underworld. The proper way the balance is maintained between the realm above and the realm below. Anyone who has eaten the food of the Underworld needs to return to it."

As soon as the words were spoken, I yelled, "No! No!" I walked quickly towards Persephone. I grabbed her arm and held her close, clutching onto her fiercely. "You will not separate us again."

The daimon didn't seem as afraid of me as he had earlier. His eyes were focused on Persephone.

"My Queen," he began. "I was there when you ate those pomegranate seeds, just those few, only six, and for that reason, your husband decided that you don't need to spend the whole year with him. Just six months of the year."

"And the other half?"

His eyes moved towards me finally. "Here, in the realm above, with your honourable mother. It is only right, as you are still a Goddess of nature, along with your position and power as our Queen."

Persephone nodded as if she agreed with him. I shook her next to me.

"No!" I protested.

My eyes darted towards Zeus, and I was ready to fight again. Everyone who surrounded us held their breath. Dread was written on their faces; they were so clearly terrified of what I would say or do.

"I don't accept this!" I declared. "No!"

Zeus looked around, unsure as to how to react to my growing anger, the eyes looking at us, and the soft ultimatum that our brother had put him under.

"The rule exists so the dead don't come back to plague the living," the daimon said.

I spat on the ground and sent my divinity, the essence of myself and the core of my power towards the terrible creature.

"My daughter is not dead. My daughter is a God! I don't accept this."

"The balance between this realm and Hades is a precious and sacred one. Life and death must not mingle," Zeus said.

I couldn't help myself. I spat on his feet.

"I don't care," I said. "I will not allow this."

Before my little brother had a chance to answer me, I turned to the daimon and lashed towards him. "You vile creature," I cried and started my punishment. I forced my power over his form, taking control of his nature and changing it.

I made him smaller and covered him in scales. "You pathetic creature," I insulted him. "You will live forever under rocks and shadows." His body turned brown and green. By the time my rage was finished, he was a lizard. A small, weak lizard, and without much thought I walked towards him and kicked him, sending his small body flying away from Olympus.

Everyone was looking at me, shocked. Their faces betrayed fear towards what I had done—had I declared war on Hades?—and amazement for my daring. Maybe even admiration for being so strong, for loving my daughter so much.

Zeus stood and sent one of his thunderbolts flying towards me. It landed in between my legs, cutting the edge of my dress.

"Persephone will return for six months of the year to her husband," he declared in a final tone. "I will need to go and speak to our brother, to make sure he knows that your transformation is your act alone and not a refusal."

"I refuse," I told him coldly.

He lifted another thunderbolt. I readied myself for his attack. I watched how he tightened his hand around it. The sparks of electricity surrounded his entire arm, and I stood still, calling to the ground where my power lay to help me endure his attack, to be ready for my counter move. The rest of the Gods stood still. They let no sound out.

That stillness was why Persephone's simple act of standing between us was even more startling.

"Mother," she said to me, ignoring Zeus. "It's OK. I will always come back to you."

She walked towards me, as if I was the one ready to attack and not her father, and hugged me. Her body was cold. Darkness had slipped inside her and changed her from Kore to Persephone all over again. Her breath was filled with death. It reeked out of her.

I slowly caressed her hair. My eyes moved to Zeus, who lowered his thunderbolt. I didn't manage to stop my smirk and his rage flickered in his eyes. He was humiliated. He was made insignificant by Persephone's choice to speak to me, to plead with me instead of him.

"We have changed, sweet Mother." Persephone spoke in my ear. "We are not the same creatures that once walked in this place. We are not the same Goddesses."

"I can't live without you," I whispered as I hid my face in her hair. "You are my joy."

She squeezed me in her hug and then moved away. "We are different creatures now. There will be more joys in your life from now on. More pleasures."

The world had been erased as I stared into her eyes. "Nothing will ever compare to you."

She gave me a half-broken smile, knowing perhaps that my words were true. "I will be with you half the year," she promised. "But I am the Queen of the Dead. I cannot go back to being Kore."

Since our reunion, she had insisted that the change was more than a name. Her self, her identity, had moved away from the child I used to know. I had been standing on a ground that was shaking, splitting in half, and yet somehow still balanced. But the shaking was over. The world was split in half. There was the before and the after, Kore and Persephone.

"No going back then," I said, resigned, and moved away from her. I stared at Zeus and stood in front of Persephone. "I will be withholding my power for the six months that my daughter is away," I told him. Another warning, another threat forced upon him. "Only when she is with me, will I offer life in the soil. The rest of the time, I will simply maintain the barest of life."

"But the humans need you," a soft voice spoke amid the crowd. I didn't recognize it. It was an insignificant voice, a nymph maybe.

"Then do your fucking job," I snapped. "This is the new reality. There will be six months of hardship and cold. There will be six months with no food production, no flowers. Find the way for the animals you protect to survive it. Humans included."

I turned back to Zeus. "No going back," I repeated. "A reminder that should anyone break this deal, should anyone try to keep my daughter away from me for one more day than necessary, life will perish."

I didn't wait for him to speak. I turned to Persephone. "I will go pick up my chariot. Say your goodbyes and then come meet me."

She nodded, and I didn't fear that she would be lost when I returned. Kore was easy to snatch, easy to hurt, but Persephone, as the daughter of the King of the Olympus, a Queen in her own right and the one for whom Great Demeter nearly ended all life, had nothing to fear. Her name, the ominous threat of impending destruction, betrayed the danger that would come to any fool who dared to hurt or cross her.

I ran away from Olympus, feeling freer from its harsh political life with each step further away. My feet took me quickly towards Eleusis where I had left my winged serpents. I found them waiting for me, tended by Keleos and his children. Little Demophon had grown since I was last here, able to crawl around my animals. Triptolemus was playing with the winged serpents I had gifted him, already grown enough to move on their own, daring their first small flights.

They fell on the ground when they noticed me.

"I came for my chariot," I declared.

There was another celebration in my name, which lasted all day and all night. My chariot was filled with gifts of all kinds. None were gifts that mattered to me in any way, but I still took them. They were tokens of my importance, my power. My ownership of this place and its people.

"Keleos," I approached my King-Priest. "For the Eleusynian Mysteries, there is one more part of story I want you to add." I narrated to him what the decision was for my daughter. I warned him for the repeated periods of lack of food they would need to prepare for. "Share my story," I ordered when I finished. "Make sure all of Greece knows so they can rejoice with me when my daughter is back by my side each cycle of the year."

"And what shall we call the two periods, Goddess?"

I paused, pondering my answer. "Four periods," I decided. "Spring for when my joy for being again with my daughter is the strongest. Summer for when I am still with her, but her departure comes close. Autumn for when I have just let her go. I will not take everything away at once. I will simply not tend to the soil. And Winter," I finally said, "for the darkest and hardest time of the year, right before Persephone is back, the moment I have spent the most time away from her."

His eyes betrayed his fear of the cycle of seasons I described. Life was never going to be the same. I would never be the same Goddess, as I would never again have the sweet girl who had filled my life with light and joy back.

"No going back," I declared again.

AUTUMN

The days went by too fast. I had heard humans speak that phrase often. Eos had said the same thing, speaking of her Trojan lover getting old. Six months of the year with Persephone wasn't enough for me, yet I was expected to let her go. I had refused to acknowledge the time, to mention it to her or myself until she announced that we ought to go to a certain location on the last day of the sixth month. I didn't try to avoid it. I could have fought harder. I could have started it all again, but a certain look she gave me told me that she wouldn't stand by my side, killing off all the plans I could have made. That look didn't even let me speak a word of them.

Persephone wanted to see Hades and the dark Underworld kingdom again.

I held her hands tightly as we walked. She led me to the only place that linked the living and the dead realms. We stood staring at the entrance of the cave passage. The light abruptly stopped, and a pitch-dark void began. She looked towards it and smiled.

"It calls to you?" I asked her, unable to hide the pain I felt. It wasn't only that she was leaving me, that I would need to spend six terribly lonely and painful months without her, but that she had changed enough to be called somewhere I couldn't follow. She wanted to be somewhere that I didn't.

She nodded slowly. "It is part of who I am," she said, understanding my confused sadness. "I can't change that. I am its Queen." She raised her hand and waved towards the void. I followed her gaze but couldn't see anything. Another change between how we perceived the world.

"Is Hades there?" I asked.

She shook her head. "He will wait for me in the throne room. Penthos is there. Thanatos. Geras. Phobos. Limos. Nosoi. Hecate is just behind them, waiting for me. All the Gods that usually stand close to the entrance. And our pup, Cerberus."

"The three headed dog? You call it a pup?"

She nodded. "I am the Queen. He is my dog too."

"I cannot see anything. It's as if the world ends at that point."

"It does for you," Persephone said and turned to me.

We hugged each other tightly and, at that moment, I feared I wouldn't be able to keep my end of the deal. I would never let her go. She didn't push me away. She simply let her hands fall, ending our embrace and, even though I held onto her tightly, my strength was too little to keep her. The memory of her gaze and her clear desire to return to this new place she belonged to made my own hands fall down. I caressed her arms as they fell slowly, inhaled her odour, and it filled me with warm strength to endure the pain.

"Goodbye, sweet mother," Persephone said. "I will see you soon."

I watched her walk willing and eagerly towards the end of the world, the void and darkness which I had tried to save her from. It was as if she walked across an invisible line as her body entered. She paused and looked back at me before she was fully consumed. Half in and half out. Exactly what she was. A creature that belonged to both life and death. She smiled one more time at me, with her still visible hand blew me a kiss, and then turned back to the void and walked through it fully. As her body vanished, all feeling of her was lost to me. It was like she wasn't anywhere to be found, the same feeling I had when she had been stolen from me.

I don't know how long I stood and stared at that darkness, hoping to see something inside it. Or to be given a sign that would let me know she was well. Helios came and went many times before I was ready to start moving again.

I contemplated going to visit Hestia, but I didn't think I could stand being close to Zeus. I wondered if she would come down to walk with me, but discarded the idea quickly. Hestia wouldn't be the answer to my problems.

I didn't immediately make all life end the way I did before. This time I simply stopped helping, but life was enduring. I watched the plants slowly die, turning orange and yellow. Their leaves fell, but they still managed to stay alive as they shed parts of themselves to keep their roots and core alive.

I walked slowly amid them, watching their slow dying. I thought watching them would be painful. I thought I would struggle to resist helping them, but I was numb to their pain. I simply watched, finding myself enchanted by their dying instead of sad about it.

I still had the option to return to Olympus, spend time with Hestia, Hera and my nieces and nephews, but the idea was rejected as quickly as it entered my mind. I had no interest in facing any of my family. I had no desire to take part in their celebrations of life, not when I was missing the most important part of my own. There was no point to it.

All creatures avoided me during my travels, perhaps understanding that I had chosen solitude. I heard their running steps as I walked slowly. I didn't have any specific place in mind to go. I simply followed the dying colours that sparked my interest. I knew I was in the Peloponnese, but as I had avoided humans as much as they avoided me, I had no indication of my specific location.

All I did was follow the trail of death, seeing it as a manifestation of my sorrow, my slow suffering and difficult waiting for my child.

When my eyes landed on a healthy green trail, I was initially shocked. It was small, nearly lost amid the oranges and yellows, but it was unmistakably life within the soil which sustained the colour. It was life within the soil which I hadn't allowed to exist. The only other one who had the power to do that was my Persephone, my Goddess daughter of Spring, but she was gone, in her death-filled kingdom alongside her dark husband.

I stared at that green streak and examined the power that gave it life. Similar to mine but wilder and more violent. An amateur attempt at life, but a rival to my power if I allowed it to grow further. The fear of this existence, this threat, pushed aside my pain and I changed my course.

I stopped following the trail of death and instead I followed that tiny spark of life that persisted against my power's absence. It was small, barely visible in most cases, but that green colour managed to spring up here and there. Badly made, rough and clunky, but getting better the closer I got to it.

It was a huge shock to me when I found myself in a section of a forest that was nearly all green, completely unaffected by my sorrow and pain. I couldn't stand the sight. I couldn't stand the existence of such visible defiance. The absence of my power was the only leverage I had against Zeus, the only way to ensure my daughter would return to me in six months.

I actively smothered the life that was growing, ensuring the greens turned to yellow both to make sure no other creature followed this trail of life, and to hide the existence of my rival. I had to reach them before anyone else, subdue and end them before Zeus realized there was a creature that could replace me.

I found myself in familiar places as I followed the green leaves. Discomfort and fear settled into me when I saw wildflowers around the banks of Ladon. The river where I had washed my old self away after Poseidon's attack.

I wished more than anything that I was wrong, but as I followed the trail, I found it leading straight to the cave where I had hidden during my terrible pregnancy with the monsters Poseidon had infected my body with.

I recognized the horse immediately. He was still outside the cave, now fully grown. I stared at my beast of a son and saw no recognition. I was just another God, of no importance to that animal who only cared for the grass and flowers it chewed.

"Where is your sister, then?" I asked as I approached him.

I couldn't help but touch him, slightly pulled by the part of myself inside him. I felt less for him than I did for my loyal serpents, but I couldn't deny that he was a beautiful beast, even though he seemed to lack all sense and reason.

He had always been the less troublesome of the two children. His neighing was nothing compared to the needy demanding nature of the horrible girl. Greedy and always unsatisfied like her father.

I let my hand fall off his back and turned to the mouth of the cave. The grass was so green here. With every step I took, the soil around my feet instantly died, turning dark and mouldy. The more I walked and spread my power, the darker the area became. She fought me though. She brought back to life everything I killed, for an entire day. We continued our dance of death and rebirth in an endless loop, but the terrible child never dared to face me.

Helios had vanished by the time I heard footsteps.

"Finally!" I exclaimed. "Come and face me. Let's finish this."

I sent my divinity searching for her but instead found a different kind of creature approaching me through the forest. A Titan. He was one of the younger generations and I didn't recognize him. Even when he reached the clearing in front of the cave, I didn't know him.

The horse did, though. It neighed in pleasure and galloped towards him.

"Hello, Arion," he greeted my son, who neighed in frantic happiness around him. I watched in silence as they embraced and their faces nuzzled against each other.

He eventually walked closer towards the cave. "Daughter!" he called, but there was no answer. "I have returned." I watched as he waited. The darkness accentuated his features through sharp shadows all over his face. He turned to face my horse of a son. "Any idea where your sister has gone, Arion?"

The horse neighed as if it was able to answer. The titan sighed, and it was then he noticed the destroyed plants.

"What?" I heard him mutter. He went on his hands and knees and examined the destroyed grass, the evidence of my work. "How can this be?"

I resisted the urge to come out, showing off my abilities. I needed him to lead me to that terrible girl, to get to her unprepared. Her own divinity, smaller in scale than mine, worked to restore all I destroyed, and we were still locked in a battle.

The young titan continued to observe the grass, dying and resurrecting in a constant loop. He stood up and looked around, worried.

"Daughter!" he called again. He dashed into the cave, and I wondered if I should follow him. I exited my hiding spot and watched the dark mouth of the cave.

Arion approached me, resting his face against my back. I turned sharply towards him and moved my hand as if to hit him. But my hand didn't make harsh contact with his face. It simply touched him. I had no war with this beast. I had no need to hurt him as I had refused any responsibility of raising him.

I looked at the sky and took a seat in the clearing again. The horse chased the healthy grass, eating some before I destroyed it.

"She will exit the cave," I whispered to myself and the horse. "Sooner or later, she will appear. She will tire of this battle."

Her tiredness came weeks after we began. And even then, she didn't appear to me herself. The young Titan, the one who called her daughter, exited the cave.

"Goddess Demeter," he called me before his form was visible in the light of Helios's power. "Is that you?"

I didn't answer. Simply continued to destroy all that the terrible girl created with the gift that she had stolen when she lived inside me.

He walked further and his face became known to me. He was a fairly good-looking Titan. Humanoid, rather than monstrous, but rather weak. There was no glow over his skin as with Helios. No extraordinary strength rested in his muscles and bones. However, the more I studied his face, the more surprised I was to see concern, instead of the fear I expected.

"Are you here to harm the girl you abandoned?" he asked, and I was taken aback by his directness.

Arion ran to him again, affectionately neighing and nuzzling his neck.

"She is threatening me," I stated. "Who are you?"

Fully under the light now, I saw he was dressed as a warrior in the hoplite manner: sturdy, thickly made linen linothorax instead of the bronze I would have expected of a Titan. Horsehair decorated his helmet. He held his spear in his one hand, but no shield in his other. He stood tall, as if he wanted to appear of equal footing to me while he approached me.

"My name is Anytos," he introduced himself. "I have raised your daughter since she was an infant. She is called Despoina by all but her closest people." I expected him to offer me his parentage, as all divine creatures did. Instead, he spoke of the child he had adopted, as if that was the defining element of his identity and place in the world.

"Despoina," I repeated. "The mistress. A bold title to hold. I have no desire to hurt her. But I cannot have her keeping nature alive here when I have stopped it everywhere else. She is putting my daughter's return at risk with her behaviour."

He didn't seem to listen to me. "She doesn't want to rival your power. Just dominion over Arcadia. Just this small part of land to exercise her power."

I sent my divinity towards him like a snake. He was so weak compared to me. He had no way to resist me. He fell on his knees as my divinity strangled and overpowered him. I could transform him into a snake or a lizard, or a pig. I could change his nature, his bones, his flesh. All of him.

I pondered over the choice, when the power that I had come to squash came at me, protective and fierce. This was the first direct contact I had with that terrible girl since she exited my body, and I was startled to find such a clear resemblance of my tormented youth in it. I glanced at Anytos.

"Oh, you love him, your dear adopted father?" I asked loudly and made the titan scream louder. "Come and save him!"

She tried to get plants to strangle me, to get them to grow fast and quick. She wanted the strong barks to keep me prisoner when she came out. But I turned all the life she created into mould, not letting them rise above my ankles.

"You think you can best me?" I mocked her.

My eyes sharpened and Anytos let out a shriek of pain as I slowly began changing a small patch of his skin, letting snake scales appear on one finger.

She didn't try to attack again. Arion, the beast-boy, was upset. He stayed away from us, a coward at heart, lacking the mind to find solutions to his anxiety, but his neighing betrayed his discomfort at watching Anytos suffer.

I saw the small flowers grow as the terrible girl appeared at the mouth of the cave. She stared at me with such anger, such contempt, such wild emotion that I was startled because I felt like I was looking at an image of my younger self, when the monster was not merged with the rest of me. When only Kore's existence could quieten it away.

She also reminded me of Kore. Despite her anger, her girlish face betrayed her precious youth. Her hair was a wild bush around her head, and she was wearing a plain dress, like the one Artemis preferred, easy to move in and without any decorations.

"Let him go," she said, her voice a mix of a plea and a command.

I made him gasp with pain before I released him. "There you go."

I walked past Anytos, who was still on the ground, towards her. She didn't flinch, but I knew, because I had been her once, how she felt and what she thought of me. She feared me. She hated me, and she was immensely curious about me, something she hid and hated as I did towards Rhea.

"You heard Father," she said when I stood in front of her. "I am no rival to you. I just want to take care of Arcadia and its creatures. They will respect and worship me in return."

I shook my head slowly. "No, you will not do that. I am the Goddess of Agriculture, of life in the soil, and I declare that while I am away from Persephone, life will be harsh."

"Why should the people of Arcadia suffer because you don't like your daughter's husband?"

Her harsh defiance startled me once more. That part of her wasn't from me. I had always pushed my anger and feelings down, for the small freedoms I wanted, the only ones I thought I could have. But this terrible girl, this little mistress of Arcadia, spoke up. Even though she had no safety net of power, even though she had nothing but a weak Titan and a beast brother on her side against me. Various answers formed in my mind: 'You are too young to understand', which would enrage her, or, 'I can't live without my daughter', which would hurt her.

I settled for a different kind of answer, one that was about the place she held so dear. "Because if this place isn't affected by the lack of food, word will spread, and other kingdoms will come for it. And then there will be war."

She pondered my words, trying to decide if what she knew about humans and life could match the warning I offered. She shook her head finally.

"That's not why you don't want me doing this." Her eyes focused on me, piercing me with her sharp and angry gaze. I saw so much similarity between myself and her. So much of me was in her that I couldn't understand how that was possible. "You are afraid of me," she said.

How could she, the child I cast away, be so much like me and, as her answer suggested, be able to read me so well too?

I laughed hard. Partly because it was funny to be afraid of such a young child, barely aware of all she could do and how the world worked, and partly because it had been fear that led me to her.

"Daughter, do not speak like that. It is an offence to the Great Demeter," Anytos scolded her.

She shot him a look of youthful resistance, childish scorn even. "But it's true," she insisted and turned back to me. "I know it is. You are afraid that Zeus will use me against you."

I kept on laughing. That was exactly my fear. "You are the daughter of Poseidon," I began, but she shook her head.

"I am the daughter of Anytos, one of the Kouretes. Keep your great parentage and legacies and politics to yourselves. They hold neither value nor interest to me."

My laughing stopped as I examined her. "Whether they do to you now, doesn't mean they won't in the future. Neither does it mean that others will not force that value and their interests on you, little girl. They will use it, whether you accept it or not. We cannot deny our nature."

Anytos, recovered partially from my attack, walked closer to her. I watched in silence at their small touches, the comfort and worry they betrayed. Arion galloped towards them. She caressed her brother and father and looked back at me.

"Let them come, then," she declared, as if she had the power and ability to wage war against the way the world worked. "I will tell them that they have no interest to me. I would not be Despoina if they did."

"Names change," I warned her. "My daughter changed from Kore, the maiden I raised, to Persephone, a Queen whose name invokes fear. We are not like humans or other creatures. Our natures are not as settled as theirs, as we have more power and freer will than them."

She was about to react, to let her youth betray how little she knew of her own self, but her father turned to her and kissed her forehead softly. Her words died on her lips as she allowed that soft act of paternal care, so foreign to me. Father never offered that to me; the only experience I had of his mouth was being swallowed. Neither of the males I had lain with treated their children in that way. I couldn't think of a single God on Olympus who would offer such a tender expression of care. Even Zeus with Athena had never done such a thing. He would kill for her, yes. He would take vengeance on her behalf, punish those who insulted her, and intervene if he feared she would come to harm, but nothing like the simple act which Anytos offered that terrible girl.

"Stay with us, Great Demeter," Anytos said as he caressed her hair and played with its loose strands. Was their relationship erotic perhaps? I knew that Zeus had no qualms of sleeping with his own children. I had always feared he would try something like that with my own girl. Could Anytos, even though he called her daughter, also have her as a wife? "And we can come to an agreement, hopefully, about the future of Arcadia."

The little mistress turned her face away and folded her hands.

"Daughter," Anytos spoke to her as if she was a small child, further confusing my understanding of their relationship. "Will you promise me that you will not let anything grow until an agreement is reached?"

She pinched her lips in a pout. Her light brown, nearly gold eyes shone in fury at the request, but one look at her Father turned that anger into trust. That was another emotion that I had never seen on anyone's face for a very, very long time.

"I promise, Father."

Anytos turned to me, putting his hand around her shoulders. "Daughter has a small temple, where we stay. Would you like to stay there with us?"

Her temple was a modest building in Lykosoura, in the south region of Arcadia. It was still under construction, but the main part was completed. It was a new settlement, built amid trees. The houses were unfinished, too. Made mostly of stone, the only building that betrayed any wealth was the temple. It reminded me of the early days of humanity. It was located at the highest point, allowing it to act both as a space for worship but also a vantage point in case of attack.

Despoina walked comfortably amid the humans, without treating them as equals. She held a distance, and they clearly saw her as superior. Anytos was the same.

Arion didn't come with us. Despoina and I agreed to allow the grass in the clearing area to grow, so her brother could have food. The area was too small to be noticed anyway.

My confusion about their relationship continued as I saw further signs of affection and loyalty between them, but no clear evidence that they were lovers. Instead, they reinforced their familial bond, always referring to each other with their family titles. Did I envy her? Did I feel that she, born out of pain and violence, had no right to such a loving relationship? Did I wish for what she had for my daughter? For me, even?

They offered me a room, large and full of food and gifts, the grandest in their small unfinished centre of worship. It was nothing like the places I had stayed before, but I accepted it without comment. It was the best they could offer. I had expected her to approach me, but instead she kept a firm distance.

It was Anytos who talked to me and tried to bridge the gap on her behalf. We walked each day, mostly in silence because I had no interest in all he wanted to tell me, and he couldn't understand what I had to offer. The only similarity we could find was the love we had for our daughters.

"I thought you were brave to fight for your child," he said when we first broached the subject. "I know you had to do it all alone. Your daughter was lucky to have a mother as strong as you. Most of us, parents I mean, wouldn't be able to do that for our children."

I hadn't considered myself or Persephone as lucky, but he had a point. How many other mothers had forever lost their children, drowning in grief and powerlessness? I was lucky to be able to fight for her, even if I had to do it all alone.

"I suppose," I conceded. But I didn't like the meaning behind his words, the privilege he seemed to suggest lay behind my success. Was it a privilege to become the chthonic creature I had fought all my life to not be? Flashes of various faces of animals, nymphs and humans flooded my mind. Their terror as we fought against the Titans, as we split the earth in games and as we drove their leaders mad because they had slighted us, because they had dared to not play the role we cast them into.

I had tried to deny that I was the same as my family. I had tried to deny that because I had the ability to change the course of life for others, I automatically had the right to do it. But I had done it. I had decided for Triptolemus to be a hero, for Keleos to be a priest. I had decided for that little boy to be a lizard and for his mother—or was it his grand-mother?—to live alone. What else would I decide for lesser creatures because their behaviours weren't to my liking or because I needed them to act a certain way?

"No more," I said, and Anytos turned to look at me. "No more." I felt my skin harden, like the thick fur I used to wear during my time in the Arcadian cave.

I didn't speak another word. I walked away quickly, heading for the dying and bare nature that reflected my pain and loss. I desperately followed the trail of death, walking in pursuit of something that would offer me relief, that would mirror my emotional state. I made some plants die faster, I made the oranges and red brighter, and the leaves fell in colourful heaps. The moment of their slow perishing was beautiful.

It was like a storm of my own creation, a storm of oranges, reds and yellows. My storm of leaves didn't start fires like Zeus's thunderbolts, neither could it drown and destroy the landscape, but it was still a storm of death. It was a storm of the dying. My trees and plants shed parts of their bodies to preserve a core of what they were, to extend their life.

When I returned to the temple again, it was night. I saw the terrible girl sit cross legged, examining a crack on the stone. I approached her slowly and noticed that her attention wasn't on the grey stone itself, but what had managed to be born inside it. I watched her divinity flicker as she tried to hide her experiment. Her hands glistened as she guided that wild life to defy the hardness of the stone and come out.

She made it bloom into a soft purple colour and then she clapped her hands as if congratulating the plant she had created. I took a step closer, letting my presence become known. She turned to me and clenched her fist. The purple flower died instantly, turning brown and dehydrated. We stared at each other, neither willing to speak first.

My eyes went to the dead flower, clear evidence of her experimentation and joy over her life-giving ability. I once used to feel the same, acted the same. How long would it be until that terrible girl faced enough of the world's cruelty and had to give up her girlish games? Would I ever again feel the joy of making a new plant, building it from scratch and watching my creation bloom into beautiful colours?

She stayed next to her dead flower as I walked past her, returning to the room in her temple. Her eyes followed me, and I was filled with a strange desire to turn back to her and show her my power, demonstrate to her the levels to which I could go in my plant growing. I didn't know if I wanted to do that to humiliate her or to inspire her, and that lack of clarity forced my steps and kept my back turned to her.

I spent the night pacing my room, pondering over the sight of Anytos's daughter experimenting with the power that only I and Persephone possessed. I wondered what I would do if I saw her again. Would I see more of that power in her?

When I exited the temple, I saw Anytos sitting on the steps and gazing at the sky. He explained to me that his daughter was gone.

"She went with Artemis," Anytos said, even though I hadn't asked for an excuse over her absence.

Artemis, the wild daughter of Zeus, the twin of Apollo, who preferred to run with girls amid the trees instead of boys. Persephone's words rang in my mind. She had warned me that the Goddess of the hunt was looking at me weirdly, and the information clicked in place. Artemis had known of Despoina, of the potential she held, and the danger she posed to me. Or perhaps she had noticed, long before I even knew the terrible girl had survived, that she resembled me more than even Kore used to.

"Arcadia is filled with wild beasts. It is a place that Artemis would love to hunt." I said, as if it was of no importance.

However, if Artemis knew of the brat's skills, then what had stopped her going to Zeus and presenting her as my replacement. Was she not aware of the potential? Had the life-giving power been a recent manifestation?

Anytos and I walked together in silence, unable to find a common ground to discuss, but also unable to find an excuse to keep apart. I kept thinking of the various scenarios related to this unexpected link between Despoina and Artemis, which brought her much closer to Zeus's attention. I wanted to ask Anytos for information on their relationship. I craved to learn how long they had known each other, and how well, but the words died in my mouth. Each time I was ready to begin the conversation, my mouth snapped back shut. Why was I afraid? The next three days continued like that, filled with tense silences as I walked next to Anytos.

When that terrible girl returned, the situation changed. I saw her walk into Lykosoura with Artemis by her side. My eyes locked with the other Olympian, who met my gaze with excitement and mirth. She nodded slowly and then turned to Despoina. Anytos's daughter looked at me too, then turned to say her goodbyes to her companion. Artemis didn't enter the city. She stood, bow in one hand and the other placed on her hip, as she watched Despoina approach us. It wasn't surprising; Artemis didn't like humans much, preferring the company of her animals, apart from her select group of virgin pretty girls she ran around with, rolled on the grass, and bathed with. It seemed the mistress of Arcadia was one such companion.

Once Despoina was closer to us, Artemis looked at me one more time, with a faint smile on her lips, and then turned to leave. Despoina glanced at me as she walked but didn't speak to me directly. She moved towards Anytos, opening her arms to be enveloped in his embrace.

"Father!" she greeted him. She wrapped her arms around him and then linked their arms, pulling him away from me.

"Daughter," he scolded as she tried to separate us. "You should greet the Great Goddess."

The little mistress turned her eyes towards me, and she struck me somehow again. No matter how many times I saw her face, the likeness between us startled me, the similarity with my lost Kore, despite the harder edges, unnerved me. It bothered me that simply by existing, by being, this terrible girl whom I had cast away the moment she was born, she insisted on being linked with me. Artemis must have known from the first time she set eyes on her that she was mine.

"I didn't know you and Artemis were friends," I said, wondering if I could learn more about the extent of their relationship and the new dangers it posed to me.

She crossed her arms. "We are both loved by the Arcadians. She will have a statue next to mine in the temple. And father of course," she added quickly and smiled at him.

"I see." Her words didn't answer any of my questions, nor did they alleviate any of my fears, but I didn't want to discuss her relationship with Artemis with her. The uncanny similarity we shared made me certain she would see right through me. If I tried to fish information out of her, then it would become clear to her the power she could have against me. I couldn't risk her understanding the danger she posed to me and Persephone.

She stayed silent but examined me intently. I wondered whether she was going to speak further. Her eyes were calculating. She was weighing her options over something. I looked at her suspiciously, trying to understand what trick she might have prepared. I should have trapped her when I first saw her. I should her grabbed her by the hair and pushed her into the darkest depths of Tartarus, the closest to death I could force upon our kind.

Her lips stretched into a smile, full of girlish meanness, suddenly reminding me of Hera. I had seen it so often on Nymph's faces, on Hera's daughters as they played mean pranks on one another, testing their capacity for cruelty.

"I heard something about your daughter," she said. "Perhaps your stupid period of death will not last long, since her husband will tire of her soon and send her back to you."

The desire to strike her was immense. The grass around our feet turned dark as I sucked all life out of that soil. She looked at it and made it spring back to life.

The idea of that terrible girl speaking like that about my daughter, my Persephone, made my skin crawl in anger. My divinity lunged at her as my body moved to hit her. I would have changed her into an ant, or a pig, or a lizard, if Anytos hadn't stepped in front of her, shielding her with his body.

"Apologise, right now!" he demanded. I couldn't see his face as he stared at her.

"I thought she might like to hear the rumours that go around about her child." She sidestepped her father to face me again. "We are quite secluded here and news always reaches us last. Artemis told me, though, and I thought it was only proper to tell our esteemed guest what is being said."

Anytos stood in front of her, unsure what to do and how to protect her. He would have no power to stop me hurting her. All he could do was give her some time, suffer for a moment on her behalf. But no matter how much I wanted to hurt her, I couldn't shake the fear that her words were true. I was secluded here, but games of power and reputation were still being played in the world. Kore had never been part of them. She was too perfect, too attached to me, and I had no enemies then.

But Persephone was a different story.

"Speak," I demanded, caging my anger to listen to her. "Anytos, step aside and let your daughter say what she wants."

He obeyed, but still was a step too close to Despoina, in case I changed my mind.

"Your brother, the God of the Dead, loves another," she said.

He wouldn't dare to have another lover after all he put the world through to take my child. "Says who? Did he tell you himself?"

She shook her head. "Artemis met a naiad called Minthe, who is his lover. She has been speaking to all willing to listen about how she will take Persephone's place by his side, and your daughter will be banished from his realm. So, you will get her back and there will be no need for your period of mourning and loss."

To them my actions seemed certain and direct, but I was at a complete loss over what I wanted to do or what even I ought to do.

"I will be back shortly, don't break our deal while I am gone," I ordered them. I directed a dark and threatening look towards Anytos, forcing his daughter to step in front of him for protection. I knew she got the message that if she broke our deal, her dear precious father would pay the price.

I left Lykosoura and walked aimlessly around the dying colours of the Arcadian woods, not knowing what choice to make. If my daughter's marriage ended, I might get her back. Despoina's words were correct about that, but still the prospect of Persephone's ridicule was terrible. What would the world do to me and my daughter if we were rejected like that?

Who would next think they could have a go with her? How would she show her face in Olympus again?

Who would she turn into if Persephone, the Queen of the Underworld, failed in her existence? I was certain that she wouldn't revert to Kore, but become something different, sadder and even darker. Would I risk her becoming such a creature? Would I risk making such a choice and further separating my daughter from the spark of light that she had once been?

These thoughts travelled into my mind as I roamed aimlessly.

Hera's face came to me. Her sad life, her anger and pitiful vengeances against humans and nymphs, most of whom, like her, Zeus had raped and then threw away. Her position as the Goddess of Women and Matrimony, but trapped in a shallow marriage and seeing all women as her prospective enemies instead of her charges to protect.

Help your daughter, my little sister had urged me. Help her in her marriage.

I was certain I didn't want my daughter to become like my sister.

I hurried to Mount Erymanthos in Arcadia, where I found my serpents scattered amid the mountain peaks. The oldest one had stayed with my carriage and called its siblings and mate to gather back. Once they returned, I mounted my carriage.

"Fly, my loves!" I ordered, and they soared into the sky. I watched them dance in the air as their wings flapped and their lean long bodies moved like they were crawling through the air. They circled the clouds, and my carriage glided around them.

They were my beautiful creatures, my gorgeous animals, my symbols. I felt such pride in them, and such comfort. They were so steady in my life, so constant. My mind travelled to when they had first been born from their eggs and had stared at me. Kore was just born, and she was sucking at my breast as their eggs opened and my magnificent serpents emerged into the glorious light of the world. They fluttered around me, moved to rest next to my child, becoming my children in their own turn. They had carried us for aeons of happiness, always keeping a watchful eye and always patient to wait for us to return from work.

I remembered how Persephone called Cerberus her pup, how eager she looked to return to the Underworld, wanting it as much as she wanted to be with me.

I watched the world below and I resolved that I had to find this nymph. I had to do as Hera said and help my daughter in her marriage. I had to make these decisions based on what she seemed to want instead of how I could keep her closer to me.

I had to truly accept, even though I had said it many times, that Kore was never coming back. I had to accept that my daughter was Persephone and, as the woman she had become, I would never again have her as a child stuck to my side again.

I had to protect Persephone, the only child I had left.

The image of Despoina flashed into my mind, but I pushed her away. She was just a terrible girl that lived in my flesh and ate from me, not my joy and light. Not my world.

It took a few days to locate Minthe. The nymph was stupid to be telling everyone her love story as I only had to follow the trail of rumours to catch up with her. It helped that I was flying while she was walking.

I saw her bathing in a small river stream, showing off her naked body to the world. Her breasts were glistening with the residue water drops as she stared at the bright blue sky. I looked up as well. Was my brother looking down at her? Or one of my nephews, deciding whether she was a meal they wanted to sample?

"Let's land there," I suggested to my serpents, and they moved towards the large flat rock. I stepped out of my carriage, took off their harnesses and jumped down.

"I will be back," I promised them. They stretched their long bodies over the warm rock and let their wings rest as they lazed about. I stood watching them get comfortable as they entangled their limbs together and went to sleep.

Once I was certain they were comfortable, I headed towards the stream where I had spotted Minthe. I walked slowly amid the tress that surrounded it, listening to her soft humming. I approached to find her sitting at the bank, still naked. Her hair was dark brown and her skin pale white, as if the sun barely ever touched it. She looked nothing like most of the people of this land, whose skin always bore Helios's effect on them. If she indeed was Hades's lover, I imagined she lived large parts of her life in his dark world, where Helios's power was never present.

Would my Persephone grow to look like that each time she exited his world? Would her colours grow darker and her skin paler the longer she distanced herself from Kore, the longer she aligned herself as the dark Queen. Once innocence is gone, it is lost forever. I didn't want that for her, but I had to stay firm to my decision to do as she wanted, not as I did.

I walked slowly until I was standing right behind the nymph. Her hair dripped water which fell on my sandals, but I masked my entire presence, keeping her unaware of how close I stood.

"You claim to be better than my daughter," I stated in my lowest voice and moved my leg towards her, not as a kick but as a soft tap.

She shrieked and jumped into the water, as if its shallow depths could help her hide from me. I waited as she turned towards me. Fear was plastered over her face. I could feel her weak, barely immortal self tremble at my presence. She tried to understand the situation, she tried to find a way to escape, but she quickly realized that there would never be a way to escape me in the forest. Each tree, each bush, every bit of the soil would tell me where she was.

"Great Goddess Demeter," she finally greeted me, and her voice came out in gasps, as if she was barely able to speak in my presence.

I eased my masking and let my power reach her. My divinity overflowed hers, overtook her body, and she watched her hands in puzzlement as if unable to recognize them as her own. They weren't really hers while I stood so close. Her flesh belonged to me, her nature was mine to change, should I want to.

"I heard you say you would be a better Queen than my daughter," I repeated. "That my brother would soon replace her with you."

She looked at me and I could feel her thoughts as she trembled to make words reach her lips.

"I was Hades's companion for so long," she said finally. "Since I was just a young girl. I lived in the Underworld as his aide, helping him run the realm, keeping his bed warm and pleasing him in any way imaginable."

I saw her story then and I did pity her. She was taken by a Great God, one as powerful as me. In his presence, did she ever feel whole? If my short closeness to her made her doubt her flesh and her own hands, what did Hades's constant coolness do to her? How much of herself could she be, constantly under his power.

"But he made my daughter Queen, not you," I said. "And I will not have my daughter ridiculed by anyone. Not by you, a pitiful excuse of a being, and not by him. He stole her from me, he brought cold and death unto the world above for her. I will not have her ridiculed like Zeus ridicules Hera with his constant infidelities."

She looked at me like a scared animal. She looked at her hands again, as if she still didn't understand who she was and who they belonged to. I let my power reach her further and she was such a blank canvas, as if her entire self had so little value. She had been moulded by others, lived and perhaps born in one of the five rivers of the Underworld. Or, like me, was she born in this world but for Hades's pleasure taken into darkness and moulded to suit it.

"I was with him before," she said. "I was with him always. I love him! I want to be with him! She didn't want to go. I was there when she first arrived. She was scared and hated the place; she feared him."

This was the part of the story that I had never learnt. That first moment when my daughter was still Kore and she had been dragged into the darkness of the world.

"Tell me what happened," I ordered Minthe.

My power slipped further into her, and she trembled again as I took over her nature. There was no resistance, as if she was used to others overtaking her existence, overtaking her body and mind, and she moved like a puppet to their fingers' movements.

"He didn't notice. Hades spoke of you a lot, too, how he loved you as well when you were together in darkness. He said he always knew that you and he were linked because you shared the coolness. He was sad you chose the world above instead of the realm of the dead, but when he saw Kore, he knew it was all for a reason. He knew the darkness had passed from you to her, and she would be the one to join him in his palace. He waited until Zeus consented, and then he took her."

"Hush now," I ordered, and Minthe was left with her mouth hanging open, ready to speak another word but paused by me. I crossed my arms and found myself puzzled about my role in Hades's tale. We had been very close, but after he became the ruler of the Underworld, he had kept himself away from all our family, including me. I had kept myself away from him too. I didn't want to go into darkness again, to lose the colours of the world, but he had never invited me either. I had never had to make such a choice. Perhaps he thought the invitation was implied. All I needed to do was ask.

I imagined my daughter, who had never known such coldness, terrified, and I clenched my fists. Minthe let out a deep throat gargle, as if I was strangling her. I eased my hold on her and her eyes blinked slightly and her mouth closed. She was still paused, still waiting to be told what was next for her, but free enough to be comfortable.

"Go on," I allowed her to continue. "What happened next?"

"The first few days were a chase. I was still there when she tried to avoid Hades every time he approached her. She tried to leave, getting lost all over the Underworld, mixing with dead souls of famous Kings and Heroes, begging daimons to help her, but it was all to no avail. No one would dare help her while Hades wanted her there. She begged me to help her, and I wanted to. I told her how I loved him, how I had given up so much to be what he needed, and she promised me friendship. She promised she would never take him from me." Her face spasmed in sorrow and anger. "Liar. Traitor," she spat, and I instinctively hurt her because I couldn't allow such words to be said about my Kore, even if she deserved them.

"How did she become Persephone?" I asked her. "When did that happen?"

She shook her head as if she didn't want to remember. I pressed myself over her more and she went rigid. Her eyes grew blank as I forced myself into her mind and made her speak.

"The night before their wedding, there was a feast. I was made to watch, to be a witness to it. I brought cups of wine and food to all. She never took anything, refused to eat and drink, and she was growing weak because of that." My Kore had tried to remain the sweet and innocent girl I adored. She had tried to remain the daughter I raised. "It all changed when they danced. He had never danced with me, but he danced with her. They moved in circles, their fingertips touching, and he let her take control. He let her lead. Dark, night flowers sprang amid their feet as they danced. They were hers, she brought them into our home. Each flower born amid their feet changed her. Her hair grew darker, her skin shone in the dark, and her eyes…" she paused and tears rolled down her face, as if she didn't want to say.

"Her eyes, what?" I ordered her, and she fought me as I tried to force her to speak. Her first resistance to my over-taking. It wasn't enough for me. She didn't have enough power nor enough will to fight me.

"Her eyes grew sharper. Her gaze matched his, and then the flowers started dying, becoming nature in death, and the only place they would grow was in the Underworld, in that dead state. She changed the palace, and he let her."

"Or he couldn't stop her," I said, in defence of my child.

"He let her," Minthe insisted. "And then their dance ended, and she fed him three pomegranate seeds. She put her fingers in his mouth and he sucked them, biting her slightly as well and his eyes changed too, as if he was changing for her too. She opened her lips, and he put six pomegranate seeds in her mouth, and she sucked them too. It was a horrible sound, the way her lips met his skin, the way she laughed after that. The way she looked. The next day they were wed, and I was asked to come to the world above."

"And she became Persephone?"

She nodded. "At her wedding she called herself that. Queen Persephone. The one to be feared for the destruction she would bring to the world."

I watched her shake as if she didn't want to remember, and I felt pity but not guilt for forcing her. She was such a simple and fragile creature, cast away because a new love story began and her own was meant to lessen in importance. I moved my hand over her dark hair and caressed it, tangling my fingers in between the strands. I understood her, and I pitied her. She had been stripped of everything she ever had.

But I didn't allow these emotions to grow. I was a mother. I had one and only duty, and that was to my daughter. Such insults couldn't be allowed, and I knew as I watched the nymph that she would never let her sorrow go. She had nothing left but that sorrow and her hope that one day she would be able to reclaim her life. Like me when Kore was stolen.

Anytos words rang in my mind. Not everyone can fight for what they want, for those they love.

I kept stroking her hair, and with each movement, strands fell on the ground. She was still under my power, moving as my fingertips ordered as I began to remove, layer by layer, all that Hades had instilled upon her. I removed her dark hair and her pale skin. I removed her pretty breasts and pink lips. All I kept was her green eyes. Each touch took something from her until she was left just a small green bulb, barely alive. I gathered soil around it and wrapped it carefully with layers of mud burying her newly formed body in the nearby soil. Close to the native floating waters of her original nature, but far enough to keep her safe from being drowned. Close to who she was, and hidden from what she once was.

I touched the soil and her now-green limbs came out of the ground, following my instructions as she searched for the sun. They grew high and bloomed in lilac colours. I made her beautiful, finding within me not just joy at this new plant I made, but a sense of moral duty because she wasn't just another plant. I made sure my divinity would stay enough for her to survive the winter and have the chance to live again by the time spring came.

"I will be kinder," I promised. "This form will not hurt you as the previous one did. This form will have sun and warmth."

I knew this wasn't the full story. She would die every year and then be reborn, all for the same woman who had cast her out of her home and stolen Hades's attention. I caressed her soft, dark green leaves, and they stuck around my fingers, eagerly feeding from me, sucking the life I gave them. They grew long and thin, like her old limbs used to be.

"I will be kinder," I promised again.

I walked away, leaving her to grow on her own. She would spread, her body multiplying, and that would be her new strength. Each version of her was weak, easy to root out, but she would always spring back up again in a different place. She would grow to be everywhere in Greece, I decided. That was the kindness I could offer her while she still remained the weak, fragile creature I could control.

That wasn't the story I told, though. I whispered to some nymphs who were looking for Minthe that I had turned her into a plant in punishment. Their eyes had grown wide in fear by the end of the story I narrated. I stared down at them and folded my arms.

"This is what happens when anyone dares to insult my daughter," I declared. "This is what happens to anyone who tries to rival my daughter. Tell that to everyone in the world," I ordered them, and they went running away from me.

I heard the story grow as I walked around, spreading more seeds for the rumours. There were stories of my anger about the way I stole the naiad's beauty, stripped her of all she was. My dark epithets were used again, and the world spoke of my wrath. Some strands of the story even spoke of my daughter turning her and handing her to me. We were a duo of death, as we once had been of life. Eventually, as I walked among the various creatures, I saw their fear. They had thought that my darkness was over, that the harshness of winter would be the only remnant of the battle I had for my daughter.

"No more," I whispered again. I was the mother of the Queen of the dead. Death had become my nature, to suit hers. I didn't hesitate to add terrible details and laugh as if Minthe's fate was a joke to me. All to convince them that I was not to be ridiculed, and I wouldn't stand for anything negative being told about my child.

Once I was certain the warning had been passed to enough creatures, I decided it was time to return to Arcadia. However, at each place I stopped I heard more rumours and stories about me. It seemed that simply by letting one story come to life, more sprang out like wild flowers in a field. There was nothing that could stop them.

It was perhaps vanity, the reason I stayed and listened to each of them instead of returning to finish off my deal with Despoina. I wanted to learn what kind of Goddess they considered me to be. I wanted to learn how much they respected me. So much prayer came towards me. So many sacrifices and dedications.

The more I listened, the more I craved for the stories that worshipped me. I heard numerous tales of my love for my daughter, of how I nearly made Demophon immortal, and how my sacred hero and prophet, young Triptolemus, flew around the world spreading the stories of my faith and my power. How in most places he went, he was loved and welcomed as he narrated to them my story and taught them how to worship me, how to take care of the soil in my honour. How he planned to go beyond Greece, into Asia, to spread my power and stories, and I found myself smiling. I had given him the chariot and the serpents partly to spite his father's wife, but the boy turned out to be a good choice, loyal and happy to oblige, ready to dedicate his life to me.

It was perhaps this overindulgence of love that made me so aware of anything going wrong. I was flying around with my chariot, soaking myself in all the world had to offer me, and watching all the greens turn into reds, oranges and yellows. I missed Persephone dearly, but I also loved the sight and love I received, one that was incomparable to anything else. Nobody had ever loved me as the humans did during that period. My stories grew, as did my power alongside them.

Each morning I thought of Arcadia, how I needed to return and face the little mistress and her father, putting a limit on her power before anyone else noticed what she could do. I was terrified of what she might do to me if Zeus found her and brought her on his side. But each day I was reassured that my power was further growing. How could that terrible girl ever reach me now? I simply left them behind, certain that Anytos would keep her in check, as I had ordered them to not violate our deal. I had made no promises to them, only them to me.

"Queen Deo!" I heard all the soil scream. "Help, Queen Deo."

The plea broke my harmonious stroll over Greece.

I looked over Greece, trying to locate where the plea came from. The name was an old one for me, one that I rarely used nowadays. My search led me to Thessaly. This was the place I had first worked on after the Titanomachy. It was where I had built a safe haven for the nymphs I had met during the war, the ones who had spurred me to escape the fighting and led me to meet Ouranos for the first time.

Even though I was flying on top of my chariot, I felt the chop reach me. I was too close to ignore it. The axe dug into the bark of one of my pretty, favoured trees, and my insides clenched as I was directly struck. I bent in half onto my carriage and had to hold tight onto its handles to make sure I didn't fall off. My serpents hissed in concern as they felt my body losing balance and the chariot shook from the movement.

"Go," I ordered them. "To my Dryad garden."

They flapped their wings hard and flew faster than ever before. The closer we approached, the harsher I felt the axes

as they dug into my holy tree. The nymph in it was screaming for me and begging the human, Erisycthon, the prince
of the region and a descendant of Poseidon, to stop.

Another harsh chop made me vomit. Not food, like humans did, but poison and disease, falling from my mouth in
drips onto unsuspecting creatures below.

This tree he dared to chop was inscribed with wishes towards me, from the beginning of the Olympian rule. These
Dryads were some of my earliest followers. Tears gathered
in my eyes, and I let out a gasp as I brought their faces to
my mind and imagined my trees—elms, pears, apples—all
so beautiful and under threat, or already dead. Even during
the time I was fighting Zeus, these trees held enough
strength to not completely die. They were able to survive
my greatest sorrow, as constant wishes and sacrifices were
given to them, in honour of me.

We were close, but I was in too much pain to jump, and
the human king kept using his axe.

"Vile enemy of Demeter!" The attacked Dryad
screamed. "You will die for this. My Queen Deo will not let
this go unpunished."

The human didn't care for any of her words, which enraged me further.

We landed as close to the garden we could. The trees
were too thick for my chariot to land among them. I rolled
onto the ground. I don't know how my serpents freed themselves from their harness; I had never seen them do it on
their own, but somehow they managed it. They moved close
to me, linked their bodies with mine, and supported me as
we headed towards my garden.

The pain was felt all over the soil, the earth below shook
from it, and I was unable to withstand. My faith was being

attacked, my direct link to the power that I used to inspire that faith, a vicious circle which made me crumble.

"You will pay," my dryad whimpered, and I knew I was going to be too late. These were her last words. "I curse you."

She was dead as my poplar tree fell, the one with which her power and divinity was linked. One of the rare times that an immortal creature ceased to exist. The pain stopped as the chopping ended. I stood, untangling myself from my serpents, and ran towards my sacred garden. My skin prickled as I changed into a different humanoid form. I remembered the face clearly, even though I hadn't seen it since before I lost Kore. Her orange curls were hard to forget: they were Nikippe, my priestess in Thessaly's most dominating feature.

He lifted his axe, ready to strike down another one of my trees.

"Child," I called and walked amid the trees, catching his attention. "Do you not know whose trees these are?"

He looked at me and I realized he was not as young as I thought he would be. He didn't have the excuse of lack of wisdom, he was a middle-aged man. He should have known better. Despite that, I kept my disguise and waited for him to answer. If I revealed myself, he would fall on his knees and beg for forgiveness, claim he didn't know who they meant when they called me Queen Deo. Many had forgotten I once used that name.

"How did you get here, Nikippe?" he asked and turned to his servants with accusing eyes. "Who dared to call you?"

He had about twenty attendants, all small and fearful men who stood together away from him. Their axes were lowered, and I inferred from his reaction that they had resisted and objected to his plan.

I turned to the prince again. "The Great Demeter told me. She orders you to stop the axing. These trees are holy and precious to her, and you risk her anger if you chose to continue."

Erisycthon started laughing and lifted his axe high in one hand. "You stupid cunt," he said and pointed his axe towards me, or Nikippe as he saw me. "You stop your preaching and get out of my way. Unless you wish to be chopped alongside those trees. I am a descendant of the Great Poseidon, the mighty God of the sea. I do what I want in my father's kingdom."

My divinity grew cold, and I felt more like the monster I had been fighting against all my life than ever before. I felt like the furry, dark and vengeful creature I was in the cave. My lips thinned and I scowled towards that stupid, pathetic prince. Boastful like my little brother, unable to show respect or decency towards any other creature. The world was his playground and everyone his toys. He was only able to show obedience through fear.

"But we are not at sea," I said coldly and slowly let Nikippe's form melt off me. My skin cracked with divine light and power as the façade of human flesh vanished. My eyes glowed with my power and anger towards this man, this pathetic man, who thought he could disrespect me not once, but twice. Because any insult towards any of my priests or priestesses was an insult to me.

He was slow. He didn't immediately understand the mistake he had made. His axe was still held high as his attendants scattered and shrieked in fear.

Light emanated from every inch of me, and most of the humans hid their eyes to shield them. Apart from Erisycthon, who kept trying to look at me directly. His divine heritage allowed him a moment of seeing before the light hurt him so badly that he was forced to lower his gaze. He dropped the axe and covered his face with a loud scream.

"You will pay," I repeated my dead dryad's words. "My nymph cursed you, and I am here to enact her curse. Have you not heard of my anger? Have you not heard of my wrath and what I do to humans who disrespect me?" I asked as I approached him. He had fallen on his knees and covered his eyes. The closer I got, the more his skin, his entire being couldn't handle me.

"How should I punish you, little prince, King-to-be?" I toyed with him. "Should I turn you into a lizard? Or has that gotten old and repetitive for me? Maybe a pig to be hunted?" I asked him, but he didn't have a voice to answer me. "But these are common punishments for common crimes. What you did, oh great descendant of Poseidon, was high hubris. You chopped down my sacred tree, you killed one of my creatures, you disrespected my priestess and threatened to kill her, and attacked me. You deserve a grander punishment."

I placed my index fingertip on his forehead and let my power sip inside him. I found his stomach and passed down a madness to it, one that I had never passed to any other creature.

"I am Demeter, the Karpophoros, the fruit bringer and nourisher. I am Demeter, the Sito, she of the grain that brings food into the world, and I will punish you. You will eat, and eat, and eat. You will crave everything, even your servant's shit, and you will eat it, devour it, and it will never, ever, ever be enough. You will never stop feeling hungry."

I finished uttering my punishment, intensifying the madness inside the prince's stomach. I removed my hand and Erisycthon let out a loud cry, like a mindless beast, and rushed towards the closest tree. I watched him grab leaves and fruit, shoving them in his mouth. He hadn't even managed to chew them when he grabbed another handful.

"You should all go," I ordered his servants, and they ran away before I had even finished speaking. My eyes stayed on the hungry prince. Unable to grasp any more leaves and fruit from that tree, and far too hungry to make it to another one, he fell on his knees and started devouring the dying, orange grass and the cold ground.

His face was covered with dirt, and he was still unable to stop. I wondered if he would eat his way to the core of Gaia, if he would dig his way to the Underworld.

"Pathetic man," I muttered, and began walking away, leaving my curse to take its hold over him. The rest of the dryads in my garden watched in glee at the manifestation of my power. They bowed at me, kissed the hem of my dress, and thanked me for coming to their side, renewing their vows of loyalty.

I didn't look back, but words of what happened to him reached me. I was flying in my chariot all over Greece and heard another tale of my wrath.

WINTER

I didn't seek to find his ending, but words of what happened to him reached me. I learnt that once his family managed to get him home, he ate every supply they had for the winter. He killed and ate all the animals of his household, and then he began rummaging through other people's houses to find food. He stole from the sacrifices to the Gods, and I couldn't help but smile at that. He was gathering the hatred of more Gods, bringing ridicule onto Poseidon.

I watched as my sea of yellow, red and orange leaves drowned the world, and then in turn became brown and finally black as the leaves died and only the bare tree trunks were left standing. I saw Minthe spreading over Greece, even though her plant forms were barely able to hold onto life.

I missed Persephone during that long flight, lasting for many human weeks. I was counting the time, a notion foreign to immortals, but it had polluted my life because of Persephone's life in the Underworld. I reminisced about Kore as I always did when I thought of my daughter, unable to accept that they weren't two separate beings, even though I kept reminding myself that Kore was never coming back. I wondered if Persephone was dancing with Hades all day and night, if she was passing judgement over the human souls that entered the world of the dead. What kind of Queen was she? What kind of wife?

The lack of knowledge over such a large part of her life was hard to swallow, as was the realisation that my daughter had a life separate from me.

Eventually, I urged my serpents to take me to Arcadia, where I ought to have returned a long time ago and put to rest the issue between me and Anytos's daughter. My serpents landed in the middle square, opposite the temple. The humans let out a loud sound of fear and awe as they stared at my animals. The temple doors opened and Anytos walked out with his daughter behind him. Her eyes pierced me and my holy animals. I stood gazing at her, suddenly thinking that in that cave, when I had merged with my monster, where I had lost the last bit of my innocence, instead of evaporating, this old self of mine had transferred into her. Our similarities made me wish to both caress her face and squash it into extinction, forcing her to learn that life was a terrible fight for survival and dominance.

"Prepare a space for my serpents to rest," I ordered the closest humans as I removed the serpents' harnesses and started walking towards my two hosts. "I hope you haven't broken our deal," I said, instead of greeting them.

Despoina's eyes turned to a scowl. Her expression made her look more girlish, and although I knew Kore never wore such a face, she reminded me of the lost nature of my daughter. Her hair had grown longer, reaching her waist, and had become a darker brown.

"Of course not," Anytos answered on behalf of his daughter. He placed his arm over her shoulders and pulled her closer towards me. "Daughter has been making sure that everything is as you left it."

I examined the surrounding natural life. Although plants were indeed dying, they were in slightly better shape than other regions I had recently visited. The terrible girl was delaying the effects over the area, even though she didn't reverse them. I was willing to have an argument with her, but her hard gaze made me pause.

She wanted a fight, and her little acts of childish rebellion, which I used to imagine for Kore even though she never acted in disobedience, were a bait for me. Did she want to draw attention to steal my place in the Pantheon? Or did she want to show me that she felt no respect for me, the one who gave her life? The notion stung, even though I also held no love for the girl and no desire to get to know her. She was simply the disease, half of the parasite Poseidon passed on to me, and I could never forgive her that.

We stayed staring at each other, and I hated her appearance. Her wild eyes, her slightly frizzy hair, had an element of the hungry babe that used to clutch onto me and tried to suck life out of me. She was also the Daughter of the Sea Beast, clearly having inherited something of him too.

"I will go to my room," I said. "I expect both of you to be here when I come out again. Don't go running in the woods, little mistress."

I felt her anger. It made her divinity spike and Anytos's arms were immediately around her body, whispering soothing words as he held her back.

To my surprise, she was still there when I was ready to exit the room again. She held her father's arm tightly, but she had stayed still in Lykosoura. I sneaked upon them as Anytos brushed her hair, and the sight of their familial love and comfort made me uncomfortable all over again. I didn't know how to describe the emotion I felt for the way his hands played with strands of her hair, braiding them slowly. I didn't know why that sight made me feel like there was still a dark and terrible monster living inside me, that there was an element of darkness I hadn't fully accepted about myself. It made me feel both hot and cold and I didn't understand it.

I feared it as I used to before Kore's loss.

I let myself be known, hoping that my presence would put an end to their comfort, but it was to no avail. She turned towards me, and her face's calmness and contentment were worse than the sight of their love. She looked so safe sitting next to her father, as if there was nothing that could ever hurt her as long as she was in his arms. How could she feel that, when her adopted parent was a Titan of no significance? What gave her that feeling of safety, settled inside her so firmly that my presence and the anger she held towards me wasn't enough to banish it?

Anytos turned and smiled at me, also content and happy, as if there was nothing he wanted more than to braid Despoina's hair.

"Hello," he greeted as he finished the braiding. He pulled a ribbon from somewhere amid his clothes and tied the end of the braid.

"Ready," he said and kissed Despoina's forehead. She stood next to him for an extra moment but stood up and began to walk away. Anytos grabbed her arm and pulled her back. "Daughter, don't be rude. You need to greet our guest. It is one of the most important rules of being a host. Hospitality is a sacred duty, bestowed upon all creatures by mighty Zeus himself."

"Zeus cares about receiving the best of whatever anyone has to give, that's why he says hospitality is one his main concerns. Not because he cares how others are received," I said.

They didn't comment on my words, which wasn't surprising. If Zeus heard of them mentioning anything negative about him, he would strike them down before they had the chance to lift their head to see the thunderbolt heading for them. I crossed my arms and waited for the terrible girl to speak.

She moved her braid towards her one shoulder and wrapped its edge playfully amid her fingers.

"Hello," she managed to utter, and I felt the struggle each sound was to her.

"Do you hate me?" I asked, suddenly curious. "I know you don't like me, but do you hate me?"

Her eyes darted towards her father at my question, as if she needed his help to answer, to tell her how to feel. So young. The thought struck me as it always did. So young and so loving towards her parent. It was difficult to understand her. I had never been young like her; my youth was sucked away in the darkness of Father's stomach, and I held no trusting love towards any of my parents.

I tried to think of Kore. Had she ever looked at me like that? Her innocent face came to mind, but I couldn't find a memory that had a similar look. I was stronger than Kore, she ought to have looked up to me for guidance.

"Daughter could never hate the one who brought her to this world," he began on her behalf. "She just finds it difficult to meet new people, to trust them."

"Then you tell me that," I pushed Despoina. "Tell me with your own mouth and words, not through your father."

She panicked and looked at her father again. He had given her the answer, and she opened her mouth to speak, but no sound came out.

"Come on, little mistress of Arcadia. You were much bolder as a baby, I am sure you have some of that spine left in you."

The mention of her birth made her face turn cold and angry, rather than hateful as I expected.

"Daughter," Anytos began, but Despoina stamped her foot.

So young. Still a child.

"When I reached towards you, and you rejected me?" she asked. "When you threw me away the moment I was born, letting me bang against the cold floor of the cave? When I cried and you ignored me? Or when you let all your anger and hatred slip into me before I was even born? When did I have that spine you speak of?"

I remembered much of my birth and first moments into the world, but I didn't think lesser deities could retain those memories. Despoina's potential was obviously high to be able to remember so much.

"You showed that spine now," I said. "So, do you hate me?"

She pressed her lips together into a thin line of soft pink.

"You mean nothing to me," she spat. "You are just another Olympian, nothing else. To hate you, I would have to care about you."

"Daughter," Anytos said, raising his voice. Their eyes locked and before Despoina had a chance to speak, her father turned to face me. He stood in front of Despoina like a guard, as if his body could do anything to stop me. "She is still so young, Great Demeter. These emotions are part of youth. Please give her the time to grow and with age, wisdom will come and control her tongue."

I couldn't see Despoina behind him, but I imagined her biting her lip, forcing herself to obey her father and remain silent.

"With age, innocence will be lost," I finally said. "Wisdom is not always what comes with age. But I think your daughter might achieve it. I am not angry." Relief flooded his eyes. "She spoke the truth, which is her right. I did do those things to both her and Arion." I made a motion for him to stand aside. He struggled with the decision, afraid of what I might do, but he obeyed, because he knew that he had little power to stop whatever I wanted to happen.

The terrible girl's face became visible again. She pushed her shoulders back, trying so desperately and—I was astounded by the feeling—cutely to act older than she was.

"Do you know who your father is?" I asked her, even though I knew she did.

I had never spoken of what Poseidon did to me. Everyone I spoke to already knew what happened, but I wondered if she knew the full story. If there was to be any peace between us, then I had to make sure she knew who she was and carried that burden.

Otherwise…

I didn't want to think what that 'otherwise' meant. I was part of a family of creatures that overthrew their fathers, and the daughter of the Titan who had eaten his children to stop them from becoming enemies. I remembered my dark moments with Hestia, my fear that mouths and lips made monsters, and her soft words that it was how one used them. If I attacked Despoina, transformed her into a flower or changed her in some way that she lost her independence, wouldn't I be the same as Father?

A quick glance towards Anytos verified my suspicion that she had been shielded from that part of her story. His eyes begged me to keep her safe, to not tell her the truth, and I momentarily wished I could spare her that. Simultaneously, though, my wish to crush her innocence was overwhelming.

"Anytos is my Father," Despoina insisted.

"Yes, he is," I agreed, because it was the truth. There was no point denying what they were. "Who your birth father is? What's his name?"

"Poseidon," she said, in a low tone, as if she felt guilty for even mentioning it. Her hand went immediately around Anytos's and squeezed, an apology for having another father perhaps, one she couldn't get rid of.

I nodded. "My younger brother. Do you know how you came to this world? Why I gave birth in that cave instead of Olympus, aided by my sisters and nieces?"

She slowly shook her head. "Because you were searching for your daughter," she guessed.

"That is part of the truth," I said.

Anytos pleaded with his eyes not to say it, not to hurt his child all over with another harsh truth, but I couldn't grant that wish.

"My daughter was stolen from me, and I caused infertility in the soil, killing everything, and beginning the first period of starvation. My youngest brother, the King of Olympus and Kore's father, was angry with me. He withdrew his protection from me because I wasn't obedient. I was vulnerable then, more vulnerable than I have ever been, perhaps, and Poseidon, who had always held a sick infatuation with me since he was a babe, took that opportunity. He chased me. I tried to hide by transforming into a mare, but he turned into a stallion and raped me."

Her eyes narrowed in suspicion. She hadn't known, not everything at least, but she had suspected. I now confirmed what she had tried to ignore, what her mind was telling her.

"I hated the entire world when that happened. I was consumed by anger when I went to that cave. You and your brother were a parasite inside me, creatures that were forced upon my body, which I had no choice but to bear. Your existence was another injustice inflicted upon me. It was one after another. My childhood was taken by my father, my daughter stolen by Hades, my position compromised by Zeus, my body violated by Poseidon, Arion and you. The two of you took the last pieces of peace I had been left with, and I stayed in that cave where I became a monster. I merged with the darkest part of me, the harshest and cruellest part of me, which I had spent all my life trying to avoid. I was left with nothing but my anger, and there was no space for new children then," I said to her. "I don't know if there will ever be space for you and Arion. I can never be the mother who—"

"You are not my mother," Despoina snapped.

"Daughter." Anytos spoke in a warning tone.

I lifted my hand to silence him. "I am not your mother," I agreed. "I have never done anything as a mother to you. But this world is very unfair, little mistress, and you are not Artemis, who has Apollo and Zeus to protect her."

"I protect myself," Despoina said, reminding me so much of myself when I was as young as her, right at the cusp of womanhood.

"So did I," I said to her. "And still, this world broke me and changed me. I had to lose the best parts of me to take back what was mine. And even though I am reunited with my daughter, I will never get back the child that was stolen from me. Persephone might be happy with her position, happy with her husband, and the change that happened, but my Kore is gone. I never got her back. I am learning to accept that, but the pain isn't going to disappear."

Despoina opened her mouth to object, perhaps wanting to say she would be different than me.

"I have shown the world that I am not to be challenged. I failed Kore, but I promise you if you join with me, if your cult merges with mine, if faith to you means loyalty to me, what happened to my first child will not happen to you."

She opened her mouth to speak, but no words could come out.

"That is all I can do as the one who gave birth to you. I can never be the mother who nursed you, who cradled you as a baby. The Demeter who raised Kore would have been, but she is gone. All I can offer you is my protection, as long as you vow to never stand against me. That is the treaty, the deal we can make, Despoina."

She opened her mouth again and was ready to speak, but a sudden noise stopped her.

I turned around, and then looked back at her. Her youth, her innocence which was still present, despite the horrible truth she learnt. I wanted to end it and at the same time protect it. I wanted her to remain as she was, I decided then. I didn't want her to be changed by force. Innocence would have to be lost, but why would she lose it through extreme violence and pain like I did. It could be a gradual loss as she reached adulthood.

For that, I had to keep her separate from the wild force that was coming towards us, getting closer with each second.

"Inside the Temple, now!" I ordered them.

I felt him coming, his pulsing presence, like a tidal wave coming in and out of the shore. I turned to Anytos and Despoina. "Gather the humans in as well! Nobody should be outside."

Despoina felt the presence of the God of the Sea as he approached and was stunned. She seemed to have lost her ability to move, to focus on anything apart from the wave that was going to crush onto us at any second. I didn't know what she might have felt. Did she recognize herself in that pulse? Did she have a hidden part in her, her own kind of monster, she didn't want to give in to, like I did when I was her age?

"Go!" I ordered, and Anytos grabbed her in his embrace and moved her inside. I stood at the steps of the temple while Anytos ordered all the humans to run inside the temple, to stand behind me.

They managed to empty Lykosoura and close the doors of the half-built temple right as Poseidon walked into the now deserted city. He glanced around and his eyes landed on me. When our eyes met, he hesitated approaching me. I wondered what emotion halted his steps? Guilt? Love? Or whatever he called his emotions towards me? Perhaps even lust. His long black hair was wavy and salty. His skin was brown from the sun and little bits of seashells and sea weeds were all over his body and clothes. He had never looked more like a God of the sea as he did in that dishevelled state.

His hesitation ended as quickly as it appeared. He advanced towards me. A small part of me urged me to cower and run because one of the greatest monsters of my story was coming towards me, ready to attack me again, tear me to pieces like he had the very first time he had touched me. I folded my arms over my chest and waited for him to reach me at the steps of the Lykosoura temple. Running hadn't saved me before and I refused to let him scare me again. I had tried so hard and changed so much to become stronger. I didn't allow any weakness of myself.

"What did you do?" he demanded, and I lifted my eyebrow in question. "My grandson sold his daughter for food because of you."

I hadn't expected that, but I didn't answer. I crossed my arms and shrugged. "He insulted me," I simply said.

"He is my descendant," he growled. "You humiliated me!" His tone made him sound betrayed, as if I had broken a promise to him.

"Have better descendants then," I simply said. "None of mine have caused such hubris as your grandson."

"How could you do this to me?!" he insisted. My divinity clenched inside me as anger spiked inside me at his insinuation that I owed him kindness and love. "Take that curse back, end it. I don't care how, but make it stop. He has eaten all the animals of that land, all the offerings to the Gods, breaking his father's heart. My son and great granddaughter have begged me to interfere."

"And you did," I said. My anger slowly cooling as I silently enjoyed his anguish and the fact that he was forced to come to me for help. "Ask me nicely and maybe I will do it."

He stared at me, as if I was speaking words he didn't understand. "Nicely?"

I nodded.

"Help him," he said.

"Nicer," I insisted.

"Can you help him?" he tried again.

I shook my head. "Nicer."

"Can you help him, sister?"

I shook my head again. His fury knew no bounds at that moment. I saw his anger rise and fall, like the waves that made up his nature. He wanted to drown me, to soak me, to take me and still perhaps, somewhere deep inside him, he was still the boy God who had wanted to be my saviour and couldn't tolerate that he needed me to help him. How I wanted to face that little boy God again and end him then, before he became the sea beast I now gazed upon.

"Can you please help me?" he managed to say the words through gritted teeth, barely able to let the sounds out.

I smiled at him and placed my hand over his face. I saw his eyes calm, the sea storm end, and my smile grew colder. I let my harshest, cruellest sense of myself deep inside him. He had always wanted to connect with me, and I finally obliged, but I was no longer the bright creature he had once loved. Perhaps I had never been. I was a different kind of being, a Goddess of both life and death, and I had long ago stopped denying the coldness that ruled inside me.

He tried to pull away, but I held onto him, letting myself dive into him, showing him the storm of death that was my domain, the orange, red and yellow colours that turned to brown and then black. I made him feel how ready I was to end all life. I showed him the creature I was in the cave, and the way I squeezed the dolphin in my hand, making it squeal in agony but never letting it die.

I had always pitied him, and now he had made me hate him, as I hated Zeus.

"Never," I finally said and removed my hand from his face.

He stood still for a moment, and I saw him age then. Soft strands of grey appeared amid his black hair, removing him even more from the boy God I had felt some affection for all that time ago.

"What have you done to yourself?" he asked and took a step back from me.

I could say that he had done that to me. He had been the one to push me to that cave and force me to change, but I didn't. I didn't want to give him that power. I had been the one who changed myself. I had transformed myself, again and again, so I could win this battle and finally stand my ground. My soil.

"Anything necessary to win," I said.

His eyes turned to the temple behind me. I sensed Despoina crack the door open and peak at us, her birth parents. I didn't turn to see her. I knew that there was a curiosity for the creatures that had made her. She wanted to see us together, even though she knew that she wouldn't see in us a happy family she could belong to.

Poseidon's face twitched as he took in the resemblance, and I knew that he could want her. He could take her as a memento of who I once was. The thought repulsed me. If he took her, it would be like he raped me a second time.

I stepped to block his view of her.

"I told you that I could give you a stronger daughter, not a soft little flower, but a wild one, able to pierce the world."

"She is," I agreed. "But it wasn't you who gave her strength. Neither me. It was the one who raised her."

He tried to look at her again, but each time he stepped around, I moved to block his gaze.

"This is her temple, you cannot stop me taking charge of my daughter," he said.

"Our temple," Despoina called from the door. She moved outside and closed the door behind her. I heard Anytos urge her to come back inside, but she disobeyed him. "This temple is both mine and the Great Demeter's," she said. "For our joint faith. Our powers align."

What did she see in his face that scared her into submitting to me, the one who had fed her poison while she lived inside me? What future horror did she see if he approached her that she preferred me? It might have been that he called her his daughter, that he claimed ownership of her to evade me. Her loyalty to the ones who were kind and nurturing to her was her defining and most impressive feature.

I turned to look at her and smiled, proud of that terrible girl who had grown to be a strong creature. She sent her divinity towards me to support me, should I need her to do anything.

"Go and save your grandson," I told him when I turned back to him. "Kill him or take him to your waters so he can lay waste to your kingdom. I will never lift my curse. Go. Before he eats his family, his father, his daughter." A dark thought occurred to me, the fitting end to my curse. "Before he eats himself."

He lifted his finger towards me. He tried to look at Despoina again, but I was faster than him and moved to block his view. He wouldn't see her. He wouldn't take her. He wouldn't pollute her more than he already had.

"I will speak to Zeus about this," he warned me.

"Do it," I said. "I doubt he will want to intervene on your behalf. Not for the prince who disrespected him. Anger and pride will never give way to reason and empathy. You know that."

He wanted to hit me, to send his divinity towards me and force himself on me again, as punishment this time rather than to please himself, but I was faster. I made my monstrousness visible again and pushed him back. He would never touch me again unless he wanted to bring the world to complete and utter ruin. Unless he wanted to risk changing beyond recognition himself. Despoina sent her divinity to me, empowering me further. He sensed the growth of my strength, the power that the wild daughter he had once prophesied we would have offered me, as she stood behind me instead of him. He could have had her power. If he had cared enough to pick her up when she was born, he could have taken her into his waters, and she would have been a formidable ally. But he hadn't cared. I hadn't cared. Only Anytos did.

I watched him leave. Once he was outside of Arcadia, Despoina walked down the steps of the temple and softly wrapped her arms around one of mine.

"We have a deal," she whispered against my skin. Her divinity caressed mine and it was an intimate exchange of vows between us. There was no hidden motive from either of us. Within that soft caress, we said all we had to in order to begin our partnership on honest ground.

She let me go. She went back to her—our—temple and opened its doors, letting the Lykosoura humans walk out and hiding in her father's, her only parent's, hug, the place where she was safe from all the cruelties and injustices of the world. I watched them and realized then that it wasn't the strength he could give her; she had enough of that on her own. It was the caring. It was that she could always depend on his love, that all the goodness and beauty that Titan held, he would offer her without restraint or need of reward.

SPRING

I couldn't stand still. I felt like a rosebud ready to open for the world's beauty and light as I paced outside the cave entrance. My eyes kept darting towards the sky, waiting for Helios to rise. I stared at that pitch black space, feeling and seeing nothing. Life in the soil was ready to erupt alongside my own excitement for seeing my daughter. Everything was about to begin again. Everything would be better soon. I just needed to wait a few more minutes for Helios to come out and the new day to begin.

It took longer than any other day for him to fly his chariot, but eventually I felt the soft warmth of his glow and a foot walked out of the darkness. My daughter' foot.

She took another step, and she was half-in and half-out of Hades's world. Another step, and she was free from that darkness.

"Persephone!" I ran to her and hugged her tightly.

She hugged me back, and I could feel her power having grown again. She had changed, again. Very little, but as her mother I knew her better than anyone else. I held her face in my hands and looked at her from top to bottom. "You look so beautiful!"

She did look stunning! Her hair had grown longer and was still cold to touch, as if she was made of ice. Her face was paler and her dress more formal than the one I had last seen her wear. She smiled at me in her sweet way, the one that she had kept from when she was Kore.

"I missed you so much, sweet Mother," she whispered as I caressed her face. She wrapped her arm around mine and we began to walk away. "Are the winged serpents here? What happened while I was gone? What have you done all this time? Tell me everything!"

I laughed at her eagerness and held her tight, squeezing her hands.

"Calm down," I coaxed her. "We will get to speak about everything. The chariot and the serpents are close."

That first return was the most special for me, it was the one that proved that I could survive without her, even though her absence caused me pain. Persephone and I visited the Seirenes, her old handmaidens, who had become agents of death in their new forms, linking themselves anew to the Queen of the Underworld.

I showed her Minthe, and she stared at the small plant without a word.

We visited Herkyna and Trophonious, and they promised to spend time together in the Underworld. He promised to visit her palace and give her news of the world above. He promised to pass messages from me to her and her to me. Another link made between us, even when we were separated.

We briefly went to Olympus, where Persephone visited her father, and I spent some precious moments with Hestia before we left towards our final destination.

"Where are we going, Mother?" she asked me, curious, as we stepped onto the chariot to leave Olympus.

"To a new temple I have," I told her, and my serpents flew away from the mountaintop where our family ruled. I felt Zeus's gaze on us as we moved further away. His eyes would always be upon me, upon us. He understood from that visit onwards that both Persephone and I were not his to control, not his to do as he liked. However, I knew this didn't mean either of us was free of his oppression. I had gained a small freedom, a tiny bit of fear, and he was going to punish me for it any chance he got.

The serpents knew the way as we approached Arcadia and slowly descended to the clearing of the cave where I had spent some of my darkest moments.

Arion neighed when he saw the chariot coming and flew towards us.

"Hello," I greeted my beast son.

Persephone watched him with interest, admiring his beautiful skin and magnificent dark mane. "Who is this?"

"Arion," I said, once we landed. I moved closer to the horse and caressed his face, even though I wasn't ready to offer him more affection. At the very least though, I was ready to accept responsibility for his existence and find him a purpose to live. He had spent enough time in this clearing and cave, waiting for someone to visit him.

"Welcome," Despoina said as she exited the cave where she was born, making her own grand entrance. She had grown too since I last saw her, even though she was still so clearly a young creature, neither child nor adult yet.

Persephone stared, recognizing her resemblance to me. Despoina walked towards us, and her power was let out. Vivid, soft grass grew around her feet and wildflowers populated the clearing. She was the wild nature of Arcadia, the untameable power of the wild flower, the weed. She could be pressed down, but would always return to fight for the sun, light and warmth of the world.

"You must be Persephone," Despoina said. She turned to face me. "Great Demeter," she greeted. We were still strangers, even though we had allied our powers, and I still found myself thinking of her as that 'terrible girl', but my anger and bitterness towards her had softened. I still didn't love her. I didn't regret throwing her away nor mourn the loss of her childhood, but I respected her and accepted her similarity to me. She was my offspring, even though I didn't call her daughter, and she still hadn't trusted me enough to tell me her name.

"And who are you?" Persephone asked, even though the answer was clear.

Arion moved his head closer to his twin sister and she kissed his nose. It was my turn to speak, to introduce the siblings.

"Your sister, the Mistress of Arcadia, and Arion, your brother."

I don't know what Persephone thought of having to share the title of my daughter, but she didn't show any hostility. She stared at them, examining these new relatives she had no idea existed, presented to her as fully fledged creatures. She turned to me, unable to speak any words, and then back to Despoina.

"You look like Mother, so much." She lifted her hand and touched her sister's face. Despoina stood her ground, allowing her touch. Persephone let go of me and moved closer to her siblings, touching Arion's nose with her other hand. "I am Persephone."

ACKNOWLEDGEMENTS

Winter Harvest is a novel that I couldn't have written without the help and support of many other people, and I am grateful to each and every one of them! Firstly, I would like to thank Antonia Rachel Ward, my publisher and editor, both for believing in my story and for the time and effort she put towards making my book better. Her notes on my manuscript were one of the most valuable learning experiences for me as a writer.

To Katherine Bethel, my wonderful beta reader for this book, whose ideas and encouragement kept me going through the terrible editing process, thank you. To my sister, Alexandra, who was always happy and eager to ready my slightly altered synopsis and query letters, I am always grateful for all the time you gave my little book.

I doubt I would have been able to get my book published without Danai Christopoulou's kind help. Her support in preparing my query letter and chatting with me about publishing was always such a boost to my confidence and helped me make the right choices. I also would like to thank my friend and former teacher, Zoi Kelaiditou, who taught me ancient Greek for years and was pivotal in my exploration of Ancient Greece and provided me with my original bibliography about Demeter's mythology.

I would also really like to thank Eugenia Triantafyllou, Natalia Theodoridou, Kara Terzis, Sophia-Maria Nicolopoulos, Madalena Daleziou, Eva V Roslin and so many other writers on Twitter who have continuously supported my book! You know who you are, and you all hold such a special place in my heart! A special hug and wave of gratitude also goes to Jelena Dunato for her support!

Finally, the person I would like to thank the most is my husband and writing partner, Kavan, who spent years listening to me talk about this book. There have been so many dinners that I said the same things, explained—possibly using the same words—why I wanted to write this book and he listened and encouraged me every single time. I know that there would not have been even one paragraph of this book written without your support and love.

Ioanna Papadopoulou
July 2023

ABOUT THE AUTHOR

Ioanna Papadopoulou is a Greek by descent and Scottish by residence author. Other than writing, she is passionate about art history and museology. She has been published at *Hexagon Magazine*, *Idle Ink*, Piker Press and *The Future Fire*.

ALSO AVAILABLE FROM GHOST ORCHID PRESS

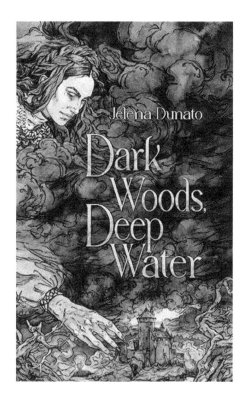